Gifts of Darkover

Darkover® Anthology 15

Edited by

Deborah J. Ross

The Marion Zimmer Bradley Literary Works Trust
PO Box 193473
San Francisco, CA 94119
www.mzbworks.com

CONTENTS

DARKOVER: AN EVOLVING WORLD

by Deborah J. Ross

Marion Zimmer Bradley's Darkover is one of the longest-running and best-loved series, one that straddles the border between science fiction and fantasy, and one that has touched the hearts and fired the imaginations of generations of fans. The earliest published stories date back over half a century (*The Planet Savers*, 1958; *The Sword of Aldones*, 1962) and the most recent, *The Children of Kings*, was released in 2013. Six decades is a long time for a series. Most have a "life span" of initial innovation and excitement, a maturity of delving deeper into established story lines and characters, and a decline in relevance and popularity as the original fan base ages or goes on to other series. Sometimes the author wraps up the story line, but at other times, the series simply dwindles until the publisher decides it is not longer financially feasible to continue.

Why has Darkover not only endured, but thrived? For one thing, with only a few exceptions, the Darkover series comprises stand-alone novels, often with different casts of characters. Bradley believed that each book needed to stand on its own, so that readers could pick up one at random and enjoy a complete story. She did not write them in chronological order and refused to provide a map, never allowing details of geography or history interfere with a good story. Thus, the Darkover series avoided becoming one long plot line, where it is impossible to begin reading in the middle.

More than that, one of Bradley's strengths was her sense of the political and social issues of the day. She never hesitated to tackle controversial themes. *The Shattered Chain* came out in 1976, just as the women's movement was gaining momentum; in *The Heritage of Hastur* (1972), she created a sympathetic and heroic gay protagonist; *The World Wreckers* (1971) looked at environmental issues and challenged conventional notions of gender identity.

The third and perhaps most important factor in Darkover's continued evolution was Bradley's inclusiveness of fans. Back when authors did not need to be as protective of copyright as they are today, Bradley welcomed fans to "play in her sandbox" and write stories or compose songs based on her novels. The Friends of Darkover, a fan group, held writing contests, and published a newsletter and fanzine. Eventually, DAW Books began publishing the Darkover anthologies and paying professional rates. Many writers began their careers with sales to these anthologies or found their early inspiration in the series.

Bradley did not set rigid limits on what the anthology contributors could write about or which characters or time periods they could use. (However, she insisted that Dorilys of *Stormqueen* could not be brought back to life, nor would there ever be a heat wave in the Hellers.) As a consequence, these authors, many still in their formative professional years, were relatively free to follow their own imaginations. Some stories fit well into the established canon, but others pushed the borders, with new characters and landscapes. Often these short stories filled in the gaps between the novels.

For various reasons, including the need to maintain legal control over the rights to Darkover, the anthology series came to a pause of several decades, as the old volumes went out of print and the authors created their own original worlds. Sometime after Bradley's death, her Literary Trust decided to reprint the old anthologies and to publish new ones as well. With *Music of Darkover* and *Stars of Darkover*, the series experienced a rebirth.

But something had changed in the intervening time. Instead of writing "fanfic" set in Bradley's Darkover, the authors had, with the astonishing alchemy of their individual visions, made Darkover their own. The world itself continued to evolve and grow. Mature writers tackled themes as challenging as those Bradley herself had addressed, only with modern concepts and language. Darkover itself had changed. It was no longer the creation of one person but of a community of talented writers.

I began collaborating with Bradley in the final year of her life, thinking we would write one or more novels together. We had worked out a general plot arc for three books when she died, and I went on to write them myself under the supervision of her Literary Trustee. Those three books, *The Fall of Neskaya, Zandru's Forge,* and *A Flame in Hali,* were followed by three more. At first, I strove to maintain Bradley's literary voice and creative vision. By the end of the sixth book (*The Children of Kings*), I realized how much of my own imagination colored the story. I found myself drawn away from the specific characters and situations that Marion had envisioned, and toward those I had invented.

This process parallels the development of Darkover in the hands of the anthology contributors. I believe it's a healthy thing to allow for the introduction of new characters, themes, and resonances while staying true to the *spirit* of the world, a wondrous place of telepaths and swordsmen, nonhumans and ancient mysteries, marked by the clash of cultures between a star-faring, technologically advanced civilization and one that has pursued psychic gifts and turned away from weapons of mass destruction. It's an engraved invitation to gritty, romantic, inclusive, poignant, uplifting action-adventure stories!

I welcome you to this, the second Darkover anthology I have had the privilege of editing. (The first was *Stars of Darkover*, co-edited by Elisabeth Waters and published by the MZB Literary Works Trust in 2014.) Some of these authors have appeared in previous Darkover anthologies, others are new, but all of them offer an extraordinary melding of their love for Marion's world and their own creative imaginations. Here you will find familiar places and cultures seen through a fresh new lens, given life through stories with unexpected twists that grapple with issues no less profound and unsettling than those that drew generations of fans to the world of the Bloody Sun. Some closely follow what has previously been written, others "fill in the gaps" in time and place, and yet others might be called "alternate Darkover"—true in spirit if not in canonical letter.

Darkover offers many gifts, many of them unexpected. Those who come here, ignorant of what they will find, discover treasures outside themselves and within themselves. The door to Darkover's magic swings both ways, however, and many a visitor leaves the people he encounters equally transformed. As an editor and as a reader, I find this give-and-take a most delightful pavane, for has it not been said that any time three Darkovans get together, they hold a dance?

Deborah J. Ross

LEARNING TO BREATHE SNOW

by Rosemary Edghill and Rebecca Fox

Many of the early Darkover novels opened with a character—often a misfit, an exile—arriving on the planet of the Bloody Sun. That character then has various adventures and is transformed by them. In the process, he or she not only receives unexpected, often surprising gifts, but bestows their own, as this tale by Rosemary Edghill and Rebecca Fox so beautifully demonstrates.

Rosemary Edghill describes herself as the Keeper of the Eddystone Light, corny as Kansas in August, normal as blueberry pie, and only a paper moon. She says she was found floating down the Amazon in a hatbox, and, because criminals are a cowardly and superstitious lot, she became a creature of the night (black, terrible). She began her professional career working as a time-traveling vampire killer and has never looked back. She's also a New York Times bestselling writer and hangs out on Facebook a lot.

Rebecca ("Becky") Fox started writing stories when she was seven years old and hasn't stopped since. She lives in Lexington, Kentucky with three parrots, a chestnut mare, and a Jack Russell terrier who is not-so-secretly an evil canine genius, but no flamingos, pink or otherwise. In her other life, she's a professional biologist with an interest in bird behavior, which may explain the absence of flamingos.

Cottman IV, on the far edge of the Terran Empire, was nothing but a frozen little ball of mud orbiting entirely too far away from a dim red star. The world was habitable in the sense that human beings could live here without dying, but the fact that anyone had settled here was a First Expansion mystery that the Crows hadn't yet been able to unravel. The planet's culture was still at the cow-and-plow stage, and not only were the Darkovans uninterested in technological improvement, they'd actively banned it.

In short, it was the last place in the Empire someone like Imria Hilte should ever have been sent.

She was hoping it was some kind of mistake, something that could be rectified as soon as she reached the Terran HQ. Her specialty was information systems—*advanced* information systems—and according to the briefing tapes she'd audited on her journey here, there wasn't a non-Terran computer system anywhere on the entire planet.

The short walk across the spaceport tarmac to the HQ building left her chilled to the bone. She'd been told Darkover was cold, and shopped accordingly, but they hadn't said it was *arctic*. And if her briefing was accurate, this was only autumn!

The Terran foothold on Darkover was still under construction (something the Darkovans clearly had little interest in completing). According to her briefing packet, the Terran delegation had relocated to the Trade City from Caer Donn a little over a decade before, but the courtyard (with the typical towering reproduction of Aisling Reinol's "Terra Bearing Enlightenment") was the only part of the future Terran HQ building that was finished: HQ was still located in the prefab structure meant only as a temporary stopgap. At least the building itself was warm, and the illumination was set to Terran normal. Imria wondered how long it had taken the original colonists to get used to living under that dim red sun. "Darkover" indeed!

"Cultural Reconciliation Officer Harris's office is this way," her escort said, gesturing for her to follow him.

At least the CRO's office didn't reflect the unloved air of the building itself. It was filled with artifacts from at least a dozen worlds, and the worn and ugly flooring was covered by a thick patterned rug that was clearly of local manufacture.

"I suppose this isn't anything like what you're used to,"

Varix Harris said, standing to greet Imria. He was casually dressed in a heavy knitted sweater of cream-colored wool and heavy trousers tucked into boots. "Welcome to Darkover, Analyst Hilte. We've learned a good deal since Jenny Lauren's day. I promise you'll get used to our eccentricities soon enough."

Jenny Lauren, Imria knew, was the first Cultural Reconciliation Officer for Cottman IV. It was odd she hadn't continued in the post.

"I'm not sure what I'm supposed to do here..." Imria said carefully.

Harris's face assumed a look of surprise. "You're a Crow, aren't you? A Cultural Reconciliation Officer, I mean."

"Of course," Imria answered. The Cultural Reconciliation Officers were half anthropologist, half spy: the department itself had been spun off from Imperial Intelligence when the First Expansion Colonies had been discovered and Mother Terra had realized they had to be understood before they could be assimilated.

Of course, some cultures didn't want to be understood. That was where people like Imria came in. "But, you see...my specialty is information systems analysis. And from what I hear, Cottman IV doesn't—"

"Doesn't even have universal literacy," Harris said cheerfully. He patted the folder in the center of his desk. "Your transfer orders are all present and correct, so it looks like you're going to be with us for a while. Don't worry. We'll figure out something to do with you. First, you have to learn to breathe snow."

"Come again?" Imria said. She kept her face impassive with an effort. It wouldn't do to alienate Officer Harris by showing how appalled she was.

Harris smiled. "Darkovan proverb: *'Once you learn to breathe snow, the rest is easy.'* I think it has something to do with figuring out how to make the best of things."

Imria didn't. But it looked like she was going to be stuck here long enough to figure the meaning out for herself.

She'd arrived at the end of the workday, and Harris was

sure she'd like to settle in before she got to work (though she'd have a week of Orientation to look forward to first, as well as a meet-and-greet with Temporary Coordinator Montray), so the same young man who had shown Imria to Harris's office showed her to her quarters. Other than being a little more worn, the little room was virtually indistinguishable from the room she'd occupied on Sapphire, on Argenta III, on any one of half a dozen other worlds in the Terran Empire. Gray walls. Hard little bed. Hard little chair. A small table. A workstation that allowed her to access the in-house data systems. (Such as they were.) Some of the people she'd worked with over the last few years had complained about how small these little cubicles were—never enough room, so they said.

It was a ridiculous complaint, Imria thought. She travelled light. She always had. *But why am I here?* "Why is anyone here?" she said, answering her own question aloud.

She knew the official answer—she was a Crow, here to gather information on the native culture to ease its entry into the Empire. She knew the unofficial answer—she was here because Imperial Intelligence had received information that the natives were planning an uprising against the Terrans. It was pointless (she knew that if the natives didn't). They could kill every Terran here, and all that would happen would be that the Empire would send more, possibly reclassify Cottman IV as a Hostile World. So Terran Intelligence wanted Imria to use her CRO cover to infiltrate the group and identify its ringleader.

It would be easy—if she was on Sapphire, on Argenta III, on Ficklewish. All of them were advanced and prosperous First Expansion worlds. All of them had planetary data systems. (All of them were vulnerable to Imria's particular skills.)

But this was Darkover. And Imria didn't have the first notion of how to find the woman she was looking for.

After two weeks on scenic Darkover, the only thing that

Imria knew for certain was that someone somewhere wanted to bury her career. (But not why. 'Why' would have been nice to know.)

Even her *official* job would practically require divine intervention to carry out in this medieval hellhole. Nobody at Central would care why she failed. All they'd see was *that* she'd failed. And the rising star of her career would become a fading ember. Fast.

But she tried. She read and collated (and organized: Harris's filing system was as medieval as this entire planet) a decade of reports from a bunch of wild-eyed CRO anthropologists and half a dozen semi-competent (and of course totally nonexistent) Terran spies. (If that was all the Empire wanted, they could have sent almost anyone else.) All she found out was that her counterinsurgent was using a work-name, and she only found that out when she came across the name "Sharra" on a list of native gods that the anthropologists (naturally) had no information about, because Darkover had an almost-strictly oral tradition, at least three native non-human species, and a population of humans so xenophobic that "don't talk to strangers" was practically a religious imperative. (Only nobody knew anything much about Darkovan religion, really. Of course.)

After a month on Cottman IV, she was desperate enough to admit what she'd known from Day One: if she wanted information about the Darkovans, she was going to have to go to the Darkovans to get it.

That, too, should have been easy: it wasn't as if Imria hadn't already been undercover on half a dozen other worlds, sometimes for months at a time. Hell, it should be *easier* to go native here—no database she needed to slip false records into, no ID documents to forge. No planetary secret service looking for people like Imria Hilte. By now, she even knew both the local languages. So she oiled her traps, and the tongues of her "fellow" CROs, and came up with an entire false history she could present if anyone asked, acquired herself a native costume, and took to the streets of Thendara Trade City.

But no matter where she went in the Upper City, no matter how many tiny alterations she made to her costume and her accessories, no matter how she worked at acquiring the mannerisms and idiom of the locals, *something* clearly marked her out as an outsider.

No one would speak to her.

"It doesn't matter what we do—it's like we have *'Terranan'* tattooed on our foreheads." Varix Harris said, hoisting his glass in an ironic salute.

Imperial work rules mandated three days of rest after every ten day work period. No matter where you were in the Empire, or what post you held, you could be sure of that much. Terran Headquarters kept Terran standard time, which meant that the four-hour-longer Darkovan day slowly wandered out of synch with HQ time (not that it was that easy to tell with Darkover's endless twilight), and their work schedule was recalibrated after each set of rest days. Most of the in-house staff preferred to spend their free days in the lounge, rather than wandering out into the city, though Imria wasn't the only exception.

"Maybe we do," Imria said lightly, pretending she didn't care one way or the other. Inwardly, she seethed. There had to be some secret to passing as Darkovan: something subtle, something seemingly inconsequential. (Something every other Terran agent had missed.) Whatever it was, Imria was pretty sure she wasn't going to find it wandering around Trade City. If she wanted to learn to be Darkovan, she was going to have to observe real Darkovans in their native habitat.

Which meant Old City. The *real* Thendara.

There was only a thin line on a map to mark the border between Trade City and the Old City of Thendara, but the moment Imria crossed that imaginary line she might as well have stepped into another world.

She'd thought she was ready. She'd spent hours wandering around Trade City. It had always seemed like stepping into some V-drama set in Terra's age of castles and cowboys. Now she realized that Trade City was bright and spacious and modern compared with Old City's dark warren of narrow twisting streets. In Trade City, the establishments and the streets were all labeled in Trade, icons, and at least one, possibly two, more languages (and sometimes, rarely, in badly-spelled and highly-confusing Terran Standard). Here there were no street signs at all, and it was hard to tell a residence from an inn or a shop— there were no signs, just unfamiliar symbols hanging over the door or sometimes painted on the wall. The smart thing—the *prudent* thing—would have been to turn back at once. It would be appallingly easy to lose herself here.

Well, Imria, she told herself, *if you're going to infiltrate Darkovan society, this is what you're going to have to deal with.* Having been sent on an impossible mission still rankled. If recklessness was her only hope of success, then reckless she would be. She squared her shoulders, wrapped her cloak more tightly around herself, and stepped forward.

At HQ, it was a couple of hours after the end of the work day. In Thendara, it was maybe an hour before sunset, and the streets were crowded. Personal weapons were banned in Trade City (those that were permitted outside HQ in the first place) but clearly they weren't banned here: nearly every man she saw was wearing a sword at his belt.

I didn't think it was so important to go armed, she thought, *but it's clear everyone does. Perhaps they won't notice that I'm not following the fashion.*

Her plan was to wander through Old City until she found an inn or a tavern where she could spend some time observing. Thendara had been a nexus of trade long before the Terrans arrived: Trade City predated their arrival by centuries, and Comyn Castle loomed over Old City like a predatory beast. As much as Darkover had a unified government, Comyn Castle was its symbol.

A petty, hidebound, superstitious, reactionary government, Imria thought stormily. *If I only had access to the Comyn Council, I bet I could identify "Sharra" within a week!*

A strong scent of horse led her to the right area—inns had stables—and she'd been so busy solving her navigational puzzle that it took her longer than it should have to realize she was being followed. Whoever he was, he was good. And not just good. *Trained.*

The question was, trained by whom?

Probably not by Terran Intelligence; Terra wouldn't insert two Intelligence agents without warning both of them. And CRO wouldn't follow her, even if there was someone in the department with the skills. When a large and rowdy group of young men passed between Imria and the man in the gray cloak, she took the opportunity to slip down a narrow alleyway. If she was very lucky, Gray Cloak would simply pass by without noticing her here in the shadows.

The alleyway was clearly in use as an open-air latrine—not surprising in an area filled with inns and taverns. What she hadn't realized was that it was also occupied. She swore softly under her breath and turned back toward the street. But before she could reach it, the opening was blocked by another man. As he walked toward her, he called out to her in a dialect of *cahuenga* so slurred she couldn't understand it.

(But she knew the tone.)

("Hey, baby, want to have a little fun?")

It wasn't as if she'd never been in this sort of situation before, but every other time she'd been armed—and not impeded by a heavy cloak and long skirts. Women had little status and even fewer rights on Darkover. Until just now, Imria hadn't stopped to think about precisely what that *meant,* beyond presenting a serious impediment to her mission. She took a hasty step back and glanced behind her. The men in the back of the alley were coming forward. Three of them. One was holding a lantern. He called out to her teasingly, and his friends laughed.

But before any of the drunkards could make a move,

16

another man appeared at the mouth of the alleyway. He raised a lantern high above his head, and Imria realized despairingly that it was the man who'd been following her. He called out to the others in the same incomprehensible dialect. The man blocking her escape flattened himself against the wall as he strode past. Before she had time to wonder whether this was a rescue or a prelude to something even worse, the stranger dragged her out into the street.

She was unable to break the grip he had on her arm as he hustled her up the street and into an inn with a well-lighted entrance. She barely had time to get her bearings as he hustled her across the common room. He didn't let go of her arm until they were seated facing each other in a booth in a far corner of the room. If she ran for it, he'd catch her before she reached Trade City, let alone HQ. *Look on the bright side. He's unlikely to murder you in a room full of witnesses.*

The inn was well filled with what looked like mix of prosperous merchants and high-ranking servants in livery. It was just the sort of place she would have chosen to polish her Darkovan disguise before moving on to the sort of place her quarry might inhabit. *Although I don't know. I don't know anything about them, including where they like to drink. Unless this fine gentleman here wants to tell me.*

She pushed back her hood and undid the clasp at her throat, then pulled off her gloves. At the sight of this tacit symbol of cooperation, the stranger stood to remove his own cloak and hang it on a peg just outside the booth. Now that she could get a good look at him, she realized he wasn't the young leg-breaker she'd been expecting. He was an older man: grey haired, brown eyed...

...and very amused by the situation.

Imria glared. She would have folded her arms across her chest if it weren't an utterly un-Darkovan gesture.

"If you don't mind me asking," he said in accentless Trade, "exactly what do you think you're doing?"

"Minding my own business," she snapped back (in *casta,* of course), doing her very best to present the image of a disgruntled native woman of middle rank who expected better manners from a man she'd just met. Darkovan manners were so damned nuanced; it was hard to tell if she'd was giving the right response. "As should you," she added.

The man opposite her raised an eyebrow and smirked. "Your accent's adequate," he said, still speaking Trade, "but as neither of us is Comyn, nor in service to a great lord, the mode is a bit elevated for an inn's common room. Let's save time. You're *Terranan,* and I can guess the reason for this masquerade. There's nothing *Terranan* like better than snooping."

It was interesting, she thought, that he used the Darkovan name for them, though she was starting to suspect he was about as Darkovan as she was. "And you are?" she asked, giving up and switching to Trade.

"Ercan Waltrud," he said. "At your service." He bowed minutely from the waist and grinned at her. "You must be new at the Hothouse. Very new—and very stupid."

"The Hothouse" was what the Darkovans called Terran HQ compound. It was an interesting double play on words—Varix had expounded on it one evening—both a commentary on the indoor temperature Terrans preferred, and a suggestion that Terrans were delicate creatures who couldn't survive on Darkover.

"Waltrud isn't a Darkovan name," Imria said in an accusatory undertone.

"Of course not," Ercan said with a laugh. "I'm Terran. It's not a crime."

She was saved from whatever blistering reply she would have made by the arrival of one of the inn's servants. The woman wore a gown of plain russet wool, a plaid shawl held closed by a carved bone pin, and a snood which kept her hair tidy and modestly covering the nape of her neck. Imria tried to see the difference between what she was wearing and what the servant wore, and knew she was failing. The woman set a tankard of mulled ale in front of Waltrud as a matter of course. He smiled at her, and she smiled back, but Imria noticed that neither of them was quite looking at the other. (CRO said the rules regarding eye contact varied by social class and relationships, but the Crows weren't clear on what those rules were.)

"Thank you, Dara," Ercan said in *cahuenga.* "The *domnina* will drink cider."

Before Imria could protest, Dara was gone.

"And it's no crime to go for a walk, either," Imria said, taking up the thread of the conversation again.

"I suppose it isn't," Waltrud agreed mildly. "Though no female of sense would go walking without an escort, particularly not at this hour."

"I've seen lots of women walking by themselves!" she protested. (*Not since you came down here,* an inner voice whispered.)

"Not dressed like that," Waltrud answered.

What's wrong with my clothes? They were bought right here in Thendara! Fortunately, before she could say that aloud, Dara returned with the tankard of cider and set it on the table. Waltrud pushed it toward Imria while she stared down at her outfit, perplexed.

"You're dressed as a respectable woman. But you're out without an escort, and you stride along as if you were more used to breeches than skirts. That makes you a puzzle. Those men I ran off thought you were for sale. And right now? Those four Renunciates in the corner are wondering if they need to come and see if you need help."

She looked in the direction he indicated. She'd taken the four at the table for men until he spoke. She wasn't familiar with the term he'd used—Renunciates—but if they were women dressing as men, she was looking at some of the nearly-mythical Free Amazons.

"Why would they think I need help?" she demanded, bewildered.

"Because you're staring at my face as if you're trying to run me off," he said gently.

She stared down at her hands, feeling the heat rise to her cheeks. All those weeks of work, the hypno-teach, the afternoons wandering in Trade City, and she still marked herself out as an outsider as clearly as if she'd stamped "spy" on her forehead!

"I suppose I should call it a night before something worse happens," she said bitterly.

Waltrud insisted on accompanying her back to Terran HQ, even though she assured him she knew the way back. It wouldn't do, he said, for a respectable woman like herself to go unescorted.

In all things, Ercan Waltrud was apparently a gentleman. A *Terran* gentleman living on Darkover, as a Darkovan, among Darkovans.

If he could do it, she could.

"I hope I will see you again, *Messire* Waltrude," she said, as they stopped at the edge of the Trade City.

He smiled. "I'm certain I can be helpful to you in... learning to breathe snow," he said with a smile. "I'd say you should come back to the Rabbit-horn and Barrel, but all things considered, it will be better if you leave a message for me at the Four Moons."

Since this benighted planet eschewed all forms of modern civilization, the only way to get a message to someone in Thendara—let alone elsewhere on the planet— was to take it yourself or pay someone else to. The Four Moons was a Trade City establishment where messages could be left until called for by their recipient—or delivered for a fee.

"And I shall," Imria said. There was no point in taking umbrage at his patronizing and condescending behavior. Not when she needed him.

Messire Ercan Waltrud, Terran expatriate, was pleasant company, and whatever time Imria could spare from her work at Terran HQ (because technically, officially, she was a Cultural Reconciliation analyst), she spent with him.

With his help, she corrected the thousand tiny flaws in her impersonation, from her body language (the way she moved, sat, walked, even acknowledged a casual greeting) to her spoken language (*casta* was for Comyn—more or less—*cahuenga* was the common tongue, and even there, there were a round dozen variations in mode and dialect.) She ceased to have the sense that every Darkovan who saw her, saw her first and foremost as a *Terranan* spy, and, best of all, she learned to see Darkover through Ercan Waltrud's eyes (she wondered why nobody else in CRO had ever used him as a resource). She came to understand that Thendara was as far from being the "real" Darkover as it was from being Terra (she wondered how the information about Sharra and the insurgency had reached Terran Intelligence if the movement wasn't Thendara-based).

She heard plenty of anti-*Terranan* sentiment in the hours she spent in Waltrud's company, but it consisted entirely of understandable grumbling. After more than a thousand years of isolation, it had to be discomfiting to discover that you were only a very small part of a much larger galaxy, and doubly disconcerting to discover that your nearest cousins, while technologically far ahead of you, were a bunch of ill-mannered boors. Still, if anyone was busy fomenting a revolution against the *Terranan*, Imria had yet to find evidence of it, let alone of this Sharra woman who was supposed to be leading the revolt.

And despite his open face and ready laugh and willingness to answer any question about Darkovan society Imria could possibly think of, one thing about Waltrud remained a mystery: his past. When she'd pushed, he said he was a former merchant spacer who'd decided that Thendara looked like as good a place as any to retire. "And I'm very much afraid that's all there is to the story," he said. "I'm not terribly interesting. Not like some."

She could hardly drag him into an interrogation room for questioning, so she let it go.

After all, it probably didn't matter.

Imria had been on Darkover almost three months when winter took her first steps into Thendara. Varix told her to learn to love it: snow fell for more than half the fifteen-month-long Darkovan year. "And that's just down here!" he said. "You should hear the stories the old-timers tell about Port Chicago."

Imria didn't share Varix's resigned good humor; halfway through another endless day spent spooling through meaningless reports, Imria caught herself watching the fat snowflakes as they drifted down slowly outside her window. She wondered how the Darkovans stood it without going mad. *Maybe you just have to be born to it,* she thought.

Waltrud wasn't. But he'd adapted. Right now he was probably comfortably ensconced at his usual table in the common room of the Rabbit-horn and Barrel, either reading or dicing with some of the other regulars. She felt a pang of longing that surprised her. *This is another job, nothing more. As soon as it's over, I'll be gone. No use getting attached.*

Terran Intelligence was generally not prone to jumping at shadows. Still, Imria had to wonder if it wasn't possible that her superiors had simply misread the situation here. *Or invented it.* It was hard, staring out at the snow, to push the often-recurring thought away again. *Invented it, and set me chasing a rabbit I'm never going to catch, in a pre-technological culture where I'll never have the tools to be sure.* Telling Center there was nothing to find would be the same as admitting failure.

And just as fatal to her career.

Or she could stay here, year after year, finding nothing. Which would have the same result. The carefully-worded preliminary report she'd sent off (that had emphasized the medieval level of development and therefore the *complete lack of Darkovan cybernetic databases)* had been the closest she could get to a complaint. It would take months to arrive, months to work its way through the review process, months for her to receive a response (if there was any response at all).

Meanwhile she could rot. Or freeze. Or both.

Imria was so lost in her own thoughts that the baby-faced clerk who helped Lieutenant Templeton in Customs—she thought the kid's name was Beale, but she'd never actually paid that much attention—had to clear his throat three times before she noticed he was standing in front of her desk.

"This came for you in the diplomatic pouch," he said, and proffered a sealed folder. The sleek SpaceForce courier ships were the only ones that landed at the port during the Darkovan winter, adding to everyone's sense of isolation. And they rarely brought personal mail.

Not that Imria Hilte ever got personal mail.

She stared at the packet for a moment before she realized what it must be. The day after she first met Waltrud and realized she might be able to use him, she'd filed a routine request to be sent a copy of his file. She'd forgotten all about it: after all, she hadn't bothered to mark the request urgent. There were limits to the sorts of trouble a retired spacer was likely to be mixed up on, and too many "urgent" queries from a field agent resulted in another black mark in the file. Field agents were supposed to be independent and self-sufficient.

Hefting the packet in her hand, she wondered if there had been some mistake. Even a merchant spacer who'd led a blameless life should have more in his file than this: personal history, licenses, ships and routes he'd worked, specializations...

Curious now, she broke the seals on the folder carefully with her fingernail, and pulled out the single sheet it contained. The two lines of type on that single sheet were enough to make her swear feelingly.

ALL RECORDS IMPERIAL CITIZEN ERCAN WALTRUD SEALED ORDER DIRECTOR OF IMPERIAL INTELLIGENCE. MAY NOT BE ACCESSED OR DISSEMINATED WITHOUT APPROPRIATE SECURITY CLEARANCE.

Appropriate security clearance? I'll show them appropriate security clearance! She shoved her chair back and got to her feet.

By the time she reached the Communications Room, Imria had managed to compose her expression into something that could pass for civility. The tech on duty looked sleepy and bored—there wasn't a lot of traffic in winter—but he looked up from whatever he was reading and smiled at her.

"Analyst Hilte," he said, after glancing as covertly as he could at her name badge. "What can I help you with today?"

"You can unlock the farcomm room for me, Mr. Foa," she said pleasantly, just as if this was the sort of thing she did every day.

Technician Foa looked from her to the door of the farcomm room and fiddled with his stylus. The farcomm allowed communication to take place nearly in real time—and was so expensive that the cost of a single five-minute conversation would buy you a majority share in one of the big merchant freighters. He was no doubt considering what his superior might do to him if he permitted unauthorized use of the farcomm.

"You know you need a special authorization code to use it, right?" he asked dubiously. "Otherwise, we'll both get in trouble."

"Don't worry," Imria said. "I'm only planning to make trouble for other people."

The farcomm room on Cottman IV was just like every other farcomm room in the galaxy: an airless, claustrophobic little space filled with blinking lights and the hum and chortle of machinery ticking away. For all that it had probably been a year since anyone had used it, the space was immaculately clean: farcomms were temperamental, and the technicians tended to them with the same sort of fussy meticulousness with which a gardener might nurture a prize orchid.

With a sigh, Imria sat down at the transmission console and began typing in the long strings of numbers that had defined her existence for the decade since she'd left the Academy: identification number, farcomm use authorization number, the code that gave her access to information classified above Top Secret.

The few minutes it took for the response to come back seemed like hours, and what Imria saw when the response from Terran Intelligence began to scroll across the screen did absolutely nothing to improve her temper.

She'd never been to Waltrud's lodgings. He'd said it would be "improper." His concern for her reputation had seemed quaintly chivalrous when he was squiring her about Old City. Now that she knew the truth, Imria had to wonder if Waltrud's real motive for keeping her away from his lodgings had less to do with propriety and a lot more to do with keeping her away from his secrets. Perhaps the reason she hadn't seen any evidence of the insurgents had been his doing; his records suggested that he was a very clever man.

Knowing (now) what (who) she was dealing with, she made her plans very carefully. Just because she'd never visited him at home didn't mean she didn't know where he lived. It was nearly midnight when she slipped out of the Terran compound and moved like a silent ghost through the falling snow. At this hour, the streets of Thendara were deserted, the torches quenched, the lanterns guttering. It didn't matter. All any observer would see was a Darkovan woman making her way home, and if they thought she was easy prey, she had a dagger that said she wasn't.

The cold that knifed through her heavy cloak and skirts, the ache of forcing her way through the drifting snow, did nothing to cool her temper. Every breath was a hiss of fury by the time she dragged open the nondescript door that led to Waltrud's lodgings above the Rabbit-horn and Barrel.

The stairs were covered with hoarfrost, but at least the door at the top of the stairs opened to her touch. She knew, from an offhand remark he'd made, that Waltrud's rooms overlooked the street. She pounded on his door as hard as she could with her gloved fist.

After a minute or two, Waltrud hauled it open. He'd obviously been sleeping (just as any sensible *Darkovan* would be at this hour); he was bleary eyed and wild-haired, dressed in nothing but a nightshirt and house boots—and holding a sword. Imria shoved past him without speaking.

"What are you doing here at this hour?" he said, turning to face her. Has something happened at Terran—?"

"You might say that." She cut him off angrily. "You *lied* to me! All this time you've lied!"

"What?" His face showed nothing but surprise and confusion.

"Do you really think I'm so stupid? You and your charmingly medieval concern for my female virtue! Your insistence that of course it was *no trouble at all* to show me around Thendara—and keep me away from anything you didn't want me to see, I have no doubt!"

His brow furrowed as he stared at her. "I'm honestly not sure—"

"You're not *honestly* anything!" she shouted, slamming her hands down on the table she'd put in between him and her. "You're Terran Intelligence!"

"I was," he said levelly. "And you still are," he said flatly. "I'd thought so."

Imria felt a cold lump in her chest as she realized she'd as good as told him that the moment she accused him. How the hell else would she know who he really was?

"And I don't think we have anything further to say to each other, Mr. Waltrud. Good night." Cheeks burning, she pulled her cloak around herself and turned toward the door.

Waltrud put a hand on her shoulder, stopping her. "You're not leaving until you tell me what's going on."

She frowned and tried unsuccessfully to shake his hand off. She closed her fingers around the knife at her waist, and hesitated. "So you can report back to Sharra? You've got to be working for her, because I know—"

Waltrud stared at her for a moment and began to laugh. Imria gazed at him blankly, her fury fading into puzzlement. Of all the possible reactions he might have had, she hadn't expected laughter. He laughed until there were tears running down his weathered cheeks and Imria stared at him, dumbfounded.

Finally he caught his breath enough to speak, though he was still shaking his head and chuckling. "Who exactly do you think Sharra is?" he asked, dabbing at his eyes with a big linen handkerchief.

Imria didn't answer. There was a certain sinking sensation any halfway decent field agent got when a mission had just gone completely to hell, and she knew her face mirrored it. *A primitive's goddess? A code name? The head of the Comyn Council? If only I knew...*

"Why don't we start with something a little bit easier?" Waltrud said, when she didn't answer. He still sounded amused.

"Like what?" she asked cautiously.

"Like the truth," he said, reaching up to take down his cloak and wrap it around his shoulders. "About me, I mean. Why don't you make yourself comfortable while I get dressed? Don't worry. I'm not going to murder you, even if you are a *Terranan* spy."

"I didn't find out the Empire meant to have Everdawn reclassified as a Hostile World until long after I was boots on the ground. I thought it was the usual thing: lamp lighting for the Crows."

After he'd come back from dressing (and put away his sword; what sort of civilized man carried a sword in the first place?) Waltrud had lit some lamps, stoked the fire in the stove, and made them both tea. The little apartment was cozy rather than cramped, the corner desk piled with Darkovan books and a reader of Terran manufacture. There was nothing at all remotely incriminating. Ercan Waltrud was apparently a man who took his masquerades seriously.

Just as you do.

Imria cradled the cup in her hands, focusing all her attention on it so she wouldn't have to look at his face as he spoke.

Waltrud had been born and raised on New Eden, one of the first Second Expansion colonies. He'd joined SpaceForce, got posted to Security, transferred to Terran Intelligence. His career path echoed her own.

Until Everdawn.

"Your records say you went MIA from Port Chicago," she said cautiously. If this was a debriefing, it was certainly the strangest one she'd ever conducted. "Commander Stone just assumed you'd frozen to death."

Waltrud sighed heavily. "Cottman IV was my next assignment after Everdawn. By then, what I'd...done...was starting to sink in. If I'd known sooner, maybe I could have changed things. I don't know. All I know is that one day I started walking and didn't turn back. I ended up here."

And the fact that he'd been living in Thendara a short walk from Terran HQ this entire time showed just how little attention the Terran Empire paid to Darkover.

So why send her here?

"What was so bad about Everdawn?" Imria asked. She knew the assignment of Hostile World status to a colony was a tragedy, but it wasn't a disaster. Reclassification happened when a planet had accidentally been colonized because the initial survey had missed something harmful to human life, or the culture of a Rediscovered colony had drifted so far from Terran norm that it could not possibly be allowed to continue. When she was still at the Academy, Imria had heard stories of human sacrifice and ritual cannibalism on some of those worlds. When such a situation was identified, SpaceForce and Terran Intelligence stepped in to set things right efficiently and humanely.

Waltrud gave her a sour look. "It sounds so clean, doesn't it? Evacuating the colonists to an established colony world where they can be reeducated, can take up their lives in safe and civilized surroundings. We put up warning beacons, maybe leave behind a science mission. Sounds nice, huh?"

"You're about to tell me it isn't," Imria said wryly, holding out her teacup for a refill. Instead, Waltrud got to his feet and took down a stoneware bottle from a shelf and uncorked it. He poured his cup full, and then held it out to her inquiringly. She caught the sharp scent of whiskey and raised her cup in answer.

"Who decides that a culture needs to be destroyed, that a planet is unfit to live on?" he asked. Maybe it was the flickering firelight, but the lines in his face looked deeper than usual. "What gives us the right? They don't ask for our help. They don't get a say in whether or not their home gets Reclassified."

"But—"

"In training I'd read about closing down a Hostile World," he said. "I imagine you have, too. Noble SpaceForce officers, grateful colonists, orderly lines. There are even V-dramas. Stories. 'I Survived Mandragora.' That sort of thing." He drained most of his cup and poured it full again. "It isn't like that."

As he spoke, Imria heard a story that bore no resemblance to the version she'd been taught at the Academy. Waltrud told of the armed roundup of an unwilling population. The use of lethal force. Thousands of people held in hastily-built stockades for days—*weeks*— with no food, no clean water, no medical attention. Men and women shot for trying to escape, for trying to reach a child on the other side of a fence.

"And when it's over, the population is pacified, the settlements are dismantled, and the survivors are packed into the transport ships like cargo. Which is what they are."

"But they're relocated," Imria whispered. "They're taken somewhere better."

Even as she said it, she wasn't sure she believed it.

"Oh yes," Waltrud said bleakly. "Relocated to serve as client-workers in some thriving Terran colony. They can buy their way to full citizenship, of course—only they have to work off the cost of their relocation first. Funny thing, though. Somehow they never quite manage it."

"All right," she said. "Maybe that happens in some places. *Maybe*. But it isn't going to happen here. Not after all this time."

He met her eyes. All she could do was look away. He poured them both another round. They drank in silence for some time before either of them spoke again.

"You said you'd been sent to look for Sharra," he finally said.

"I was told to locate the head of the isolationist movement that wanted to end all Terran involvement with Darkover. I was told its leader was a woman named Sharra."

It was the strangest thing, but for a moment she thought she saw something like *relief* flicker across Waltrud's weathered face. "There's no Sharra," he said. "There's no isolationist movement. But you were sent here to dig for one, and there's only one possible reason."

"Do enlighten me, Messire Waltrud," Imria said acidly.

"Reclassification," he said simply. "And believe this: the Darkovans don't want to leave, and Terra doesn't want to see what will happen if she tries to make them."

"I suppose the natives would drive SpaceForce off with swords and pitchforks," Imria mocked. "I'd like to see that."

"You wouldn't," Waltrud answered. "If the Comyn wanted the Terrans gone, we'd be gone." He gazed at her thoughtfully. "You know about the Compact, of course. Have you ever wondered why a society would forbid the possession and use of something it never had?"

"No, I've been too busy wondering who wants to destroy my career by sending me after something *you* say doesn't exist," she said tartly. "And how can I prove it?"

"By talking to people," he answered simply.

"My specialization is in cybernetic information systems, not people," Imria snapped.

"I can see you're ideally suited to Darkover," Waltrud answered ironically. "So what happens when you tell your Imperial masters you can't find Sharra?"

"I'm not in the habit of failing," Imria said.

"So you'll look until you find something. Whether it's real or not."

"I came here to find the *truth*," she corrected hotly. "If there's no Sharra, I'll prove that, too. While I'm sure it interferes with your wonderful narrative of conspiracy, I'm hardly an *agent provocateur*."

"Aren't you?" he asked. "Mother Terra can be a duplicitous mistress when politics and greed are involved."

Imria set down her cup. "I think it's time for me to go."

For the next two weeks, it snowed at least part of every day. Reason enough to pass on visiting any part of Thendara outside the Terran Compound. At least here the snow was cleared and the buildings were adequately heated, and besides, there was plenty for Imria to do. Files that needed cross-checking, databases to be gone through with a fine-toothed comb...

For nothing. Because there was nothing to find. Sharra didn't exist. And if she didn't, it would be difficult, if not impossible, to infiltrate her insurrectionist group. Imria was sure of that much. It was the only thing she was sure of.

In the hours she'd used to spend wandering Thendara, she did research. It was easy enough to bring up a list of the colony planets that had been reclassified as Hostile Worlds. The reasons given for Reclassification were as varied as the worlds themselves. Amaranthine warfare, regressive cults, dangerous fauna, poisonous flora, destructive storms. Fine. All good reasons to intervene. But run a cross-check of the catalog numbers of the stars of those colony worlds, and you pulled up a different set of names: all of worlds rich in resources the Terran Empire needed; all locations of extensive—*automated*—mining operations.

31

It wasn't as if any of the information was classified—just buried where no one would think of to look for it if they didn't already know what they were going to find. The only problem was that it didn't support Waltrud's lovely conspiracy theory. It undermined it. Imria looked down at the exhaustive geospatial survey of Darkover that dated back to the initial phase of Recontact. No heavy metals. Not much in the way of metals at all. Darkover's only abundant natural resource seemed to be snow.

'The quality of the information depends on the source' ran the old Terran Intelligence proverb. But unless she was going to impugn both the integrity and the sanity of all of SpaceForce, the information she had was good.

And worthless.

Maybe I should learn to breathe snow, like everyone is always telling me to. Then I'd be dead of frostbite and not have to worry about this.

She looked up when Beale poked his head around her cubicle partition and cleared his throat politely. "Ma'am," he said, looking uncomfortable. "There's a Darkovan man down at the gate asking for you. I tried to get him to come in out of the weather, but he won't. Want me to have him sent away?"

There was only one person in Thendara it could possibly be. With a sigh, Imria got to her feet. "No," she said. "Go back to work. I'll deal with it myself."

Waltrud looked a great deal warmer in stout boots and a heavy fur-lined cloak than she felt standing here in the best low-temp gear the Terran Empire could manufacture.

What's he doing here?

"If you came inside," Imria said, gesturing at the courtyard behind her, "you wouldn't have to stand out here in the snow." The duraplast in the central courtyard was infused with heating elements, so the courtyard remained snow-free regardless of the weather (which was more than could be said for the rest of Thendara).

"If I came in," Waltrud said with a sardonic smile, "I'd

have to look at that towering monstrosity you like to call a statue."

"It's Terra bringing the light of civilization to her lost colonies," Imria commented archly, glancing over her shoulder. "Aisling Reinol is a very famous sculptor."

"I know exactly what it's meant to be," he said. "It's still hideous."

"I'm sure you didn't come here just to criticize the Empire's taste in art," she said cautiously. They hadn't really parted on the best of terms. And if there'd been any truth in the story he told her, Terran HQ was the last place he should be willing to come.

He shook his head, smiling. "I came to invite you for a walk. You've been shut up with your hideous statue for the last two weeks. You can't do what you came here to do in there."

"I can't do it at all," she said heavily. "You already know that. Congratulations, Mr. Waltrud. You win. But I don't advise you to try the same story on the next impressionable young Intelligence agent who comes through here. It's got a hole in it I could throw a freighter through."

"Does it?" Waltrud said, giving her an appraising glance. "Go put on something warmer. I'll wait. You need some fresh air."

She wasn't sure why she accepted. One more chance to cross sabers with Ercan Waltrud? A chance to find out why he thought Terra was trolling for a pretext to Reclassify a planet with no valuable resources? Or just to find out why he didn't seem to be worried that she'd tell Imperial Intelligence that their wandering lamb was alive and well and living on Cottman IV?

She'd handled that badly. But she hated being lied to. Her forte was machines, not people. Machines didn't lie.

And people never told the truth.

Trade City was bustling despite the weather. The streets were full of porters carrying packages, women with their escorts, and small boys laughing and pelting one another with snowballs. Waltrud seemed more inclined to wander around the shops than have the conversation Imria was expecting. A public street was no place for it anyway. None of the Darkovans here gave Imria a second glance (just another woman out with her brother or her cousin or her husband). Even a month ago, that would have delighted her. Now all she felt was a vague sadness.

The light was fading, and it was still snowing gently. Lamps glowed behind windows and delicious smells wafted from the doorways of inns and taverns and cook shops. Imria's stomach rumbled as if to remind her she'd never eaten lunch. Waltrud regarded her consideringly and took her arm.

"Come on," he said. "There's a place I've been meaning to show you. The food's good. I think you'll like it."

What I'd like *is to have a straightforward conversation with you!* Imria thought. But she followed him without demur.

Their destination wasn't on any of the main streets, but down a narrow little alley (much like the one she'd been trapped in the night she met Ercan Waltrud). Under her cloak, her hand closed tightly over a tiny needle-gun (shouldn't have it outside HQ, but it was a lot more effective as a method of self defense than a dagger), because she might be willing to wander around the Trade City with Waltrud, but she wasn't gullible enough to go unarmed.

But nothing happened, and he opened the door to usher her into what was quite possibly the oddest place Imria had been on Darkover. The common room was packed with an astonishing assortment of people. Spacers in outdated civilian clothes, prosperous Darkovan merchants, Free Amazons, Terrans, even what looked like a couple of minor members of the Comyn attempting to dine incognito. The furniture was clearly Darkovan, but the menus were written in both Terran script and Darkovan symbols, and the mix of dishes on offer made her blink. She recognized dishes from a half-dozen worlds, and she saw the servers pouring both coffee and cider for the patrons. (It was too easy to imagine the people here being herded into stockades to await resettlement. What if the ships came in the dead of winter? What then?)

"You said I had a hole in my story," Waltrud said, after the serving girl had brought a pot of tea for the table.

"I've been doing some checking," she said. "Everdawn was rich in a scarce rare earth element used in the construction of ship engines. The colonists wouldn't permit mining. Bowling Green had extensive deposits of raw power crystals. Mischance had nearly pure veins of *unobtainium*. And so it goes. But Darkover doesn't have anything anybody could want. So your theory about the Empire's evil plots..." her voice trailed off.

Waltrud studied her for a long minute, and Imria had the strong sense of being judged very carefully. At last he spoke. "Fits the facts," he said, finishing her sentence. "Because unfortunately Darkover has something the Empire wants very much indeed."

"*Messire* Waltrud, I've been through every report, document, and addled fantasy logged by Terran HQ in the last twenty years. Darkover has—"

"*Laran,*" Waltrud said flatly.

She looked at him uncomprehendingly. It must be Darkovan, but it was a word she'd never heard.

"You can call it psionic science, if you'd rather," he offered, as if conferring a favor.

She scoffed. She couldn't help it. She'd heard the stories from the people who'd been here since Port Chicago, but religion and fairy tales weren't the same thing as facts. "I'm too old and too well-educated to believe in magic, *Messire* Waltrud."

"Not this kind of "magic", you aren't," he said, the lines in his face deepening.

"Call it magic, call it *laran,* it's nothing we haven't seen on a on a dozen worlds," she said, waving a hand dismissively. Telepathy was fairly common across the

Empire, but while the natives were generally pretty impressed with their own ability to read minds, it wasn't much use for anything substantial.

"Not like this," he said. "The Darkovans have been studying it and breeding for it since before the end of the First Expansion. But whether it's real or not doesn't matter. The Empire thinks it is, and the Darkovans aren't interested in sharing."

Imria stared at him, trying to school her expression and failing miserably. This was all starting to make a horrible kind of sense. *If they'd just told me from the beginning they wanted me to forge evidence for Reclassification, life would have been so much simpler,* she thought. Hadn't she based her entire career on doing what the Empire asked her to?

But if they'd done that, she would have asked: "Why?" And when they didn't tell her, she would have dug until she found the answers. And this time, the prize worth counterfeiting a case for Hostile World status wasn't metals or gems or rare earths. It was living people.

People who would become *property.*

She wouldn't do it. Anyone who'd seen her file would know that.

So instead of ordering, or even asking, they'd tricked her, backed her into a corner, made her so desperate to save her career and get the hell off this planet that they were sure she'd fabricate the evidence they wanted without asking any of the wrong questions.

"If the Empire thinks Darkover has some kind of well-developed psionics," she said in a low voice, "it hardly matters if there's an insurgency or not, does it? The Crows are already being pushed toward more invasive missions farther away from Thendara." She sighed heavily and poured a cup of tea for each of them. "From what I know, the Comyn are adversarial enough without finding out they're being spied on. If Terra wants a full-blown insurrection..."

You won't even need to make anything up, will you,

Agent Hilte?

The server came back and Waltrud ordered for both of them. Imria smiled and nodded, approving his choice. When the server had gone, Waltrud met her eyes and gestured around the room. "Look around, Imria. Tell me what you see."

What do you have and what do you need? The words from her training echoed in her mind for a brief moment and she shook her head. "I see something I thought was impossible," she said slowly. "Something that *shouldn't* be possible."

Two tables over, a Terran merchant stumbled through a joke in halting *cahuenga* and his dining companion, a Darkovan man-at-arms, laughed and applauded. A Terran woman approached the table of Free Amazons and was greeted with welcoming gestures. A small child sat on a bench between his parents—one Terran, one Darkovan.

"This is what the future could be," Waltrud said, smiling. "Not just in one cook shop, but everywhere. It's already starting. There's travel between Terra and Darkover. Acculturation. Cultural contamination, if you want to use the Intelligence term for it. In a generation or two, that Comyn Council of theirs will be a real government instead of a confederacy of tribal warlords. And that government will join the Terran Empire. As an equal partner."

"First, learn to breathe snow," Imria said wryly. *'Once you learn to breathe snow, the rest is easy.'*

Their meal came, and they ate in silence.

It was a lot to think about. A lot to integrate into a worldview that had been turned on its head. No large-scale political system was immune to corruption. That had been one of the first lessons she'd learned. But something might draw Terra's attention away from Darkover at any moment; the terrible future Waltrud prophesied might never come to pass. If it did, wasn't the good of the many more important than the happiness of the few?

How can I choose?

Waltrud didn't press her for an answer as they walked

back to the Spaceport gates. He made a face as the statue came into sight again. "I don't know how you can stand to stare at that thing all day," he said.

"My window faces the other way," she said dryly. "It's a nice sentiment, though. Whether it's the truth, or not."

"Something to aspire to," he agreed.

"I'll be leaving in a few weeks," Imria said, holding the bunch of snowlillies Waltrud had brought her. Their cautious truce had continued through the winter. He'd never pressed her for a final answer, and she'd never offered one.

"It's spring," Waltrud agreed, nodding toward the flowers in her hands. "You'll miss summer, though."

"It's time to go," she said. "Facts all found, report done. Don't you want to know what it's going to say?"

"I hope I already do," he answered, offering her his arm. They walked between walls of packed snow. In winter, Thendara was a walled city in more ways than one.

"The Darkovans are perfectly peaceful and the majority of them are completely indifferent to Terran contact. Sharra is a myth even the mountainfolk don't believe in any more. If they want a different answer, they're going to have to send a different agent."

Waltrud shook his head slowly. "It's a good answer. And I'd like to believe it's that simple. But your report is going to make a lot of stops on its way to the top. By the time it gets there, it will probably say exactly what they want it to say."

She favored him with her most innocent look, and reached to take his hand. "Oh, but you see, *Messire* Waltrud, I'm not going to transmit my report. I'm going to deliver it personally. And as you well know," she added with a brilliant smile, "computer systems are my specialty."

The ship that would carry Imria Hilte home to Mother Terra lifted off in predawn darkness. Two men watched as the ship, illuminated by spotlights bright enough to render darkness into daylight, lifted skyward to disappear behind the clouds.

In another lifetime, Terran Intelligence Agent Ercan Waltrud, too, had moved among the stars as easily as a man might travel between Castle Aldaran and Thendara.

Lord Felix Hastur of Elhalyn looked toward Ercan and raised a carefully-groomed eyebrow. Everything about the old spymaster spoke of a certain grave and fastidious care, from the hair he wore bound neatly at the nape of his neck to the brooch emblazoned with the device of a silver fir tree surmounted by a silver crown at the throat of his cloak. His golden eyes, however, danced with mischief as he regarded his old friend.

"She wasn't at all what I expected when you first told me about her," Felix said, drawing his cloak tighter around himself.

Ercan mirrored the gesture; the wind blowing across the landing field was bitter. "I remember," he said, smiling a little. "You didn't think she'd help us."

"You have to admit the notion was a bit farfetched," Felix said. "A *Terranan* spy forsaking her sworn oaths for the greater good."

"You know better than anyone that Darkover softens the hardest hearts," Ercan said off-handedly.

"And convinces a servant of the other side to join the just cause," Felix agreed with a smile.

"Aldones, Lord of Light, grant more will come to our need," Ercan said automatically. More who would take up the burden of doing what was right no matter the cost. A just and lasting peace with Terra was, as Felix often said, a possibility. But it was a fragile one. And right now it rested on Imria Hilte's slender shoulders.

"Do you think we'll ever know if she succeeds?" Ercan asked.

"If we learn to breathe snow," Felix answered quietly.

HEALING PAIN

by Jane M. H. Bigelow

Not every Terran who travels Darkover comes eagerly, and not every Darkovan wishes to remain. Sometimes it's necessary to leave in order to return, or in the case of this story's heroine, to learn how to blend the best knowledge of two cultures.

Jane M. H. Bigelow had her first professional publication in Free Amazons of Darkover. *She has always been interested in history and in fantasy; Darkover fit her interests so perfectly that she no longer remembers just when she started reading about it. She says it's wonderful to play in Marion's sandbox again. Jane has published a fantasy novel,* Talisman, *as well as short stories and short nonfiction on such topics as gardening in Ancient Egypt.*

She loves traveling to faraway places and cultures. The different ways that people interact are both fascinating and frustrating, and excellent food for thoughts of writing stories. Travel does conflict with her gardening and cats. Sometimes trips involve plants, such as the wild orchids of Crete. However, Shiraz and Thunderpurr do not travel.

Jane is a retired reference librarian, a job which encouraged her to go on being curious about everything and exposed her to a rich variety of people. She lives in Denver, CO with her husband and two spoiled cats. She adds, "my trained pink flamingos protect my garden from the urban raccoons."

Taniquel fidgeted her skirts into yet-better order as she stood waiting for her stepfather to finish reading her news. Had she made the print large enough? Not much afternoon light made its way past the closely-built town dwellings of other minor nobles, and the branched desk lamp added little. *He'll give himself another headache reading in that dim light.*

"*You're* giving me a headache, not the lamp," he said.

She was giving him a headache? She'd just won a full scholarship to one of the best medical schools in the Empire, and she was giving him a headache?

"Kinsman," she said, with the full formal intonation that acknowledged his rank, "I thought you might be glad for me." *And turn loose the dowry money I'll need to get there.* Oh, plague. Had he perceived that?

He forced a smile. "Tani."

Why does he smile like that, when we both know it's false?

The smile never wavered. "It's an honor in Terran eyes, I'm sure. But you have obligations here; your mother needs your help, especially now."

Oh, no. Is she pregnant again? At their age!

"No." He bit off the rest of his words, but she heard some of it anyway. *Our age? What a child! Off across the galaxy alone? I wouldn't send her across the city alone.*

Taniquel hated setting her psychic barriers tight; it felt like walking around with a stone wall inches from her face. It wasn't usually necessary, since her own telepathy was weak. She tightened now. *Should've known I'd need to.* Considering how much she and her stepfather argued, it was odd how easily they could hear each other's thoughts.

He continued, "Your betrothed won't be happy to see you run off to another planet. He greatly respects your knowledge of healing, you know."

No doubt he did. His estate in the Kilghard Hills lay a week away from outside help. A medically-trained wife would be very useful to Cathal. "I am not bound by promises made for me when my hair was still too short to braid." Of all the ridiculously old-fashioned things!

Her stepfather sighed. "Taniquel. May we not ask you to honor promises made in your name, and your interests, when you were too young to make promises? You're not being asked to wed some aged monster. Cathal is an attractive young man of good family."

Very good, in fact. Important in government and

commerce.

Dom Ann'dra's mouth twitched in a half-smile. "Yes. Would you rather we'd pledged you to the younger son of a younger son?"

If he was going to overhear her thoughts, then she might as well say them aloud. "I'd rather you hadn't pledged me to anyone."

Now he smiled openly. "Don't be foolish, daughter of my heart. Your mother and I will provide for you. You'll not be left to make your way alone, however slim our funds."

She should know better than to argue over the betrothal. Now she wished that she'd waited for her mother to return. Taniquel had thought that her stepfather would understand and help her to overcome her mother's fears. *Domna* Margali Syrtis had never so much as entered the Trade City herself, though many Comyn ladies enjoyed shopping for exotic goods there. *Dom* Ann'dra seemed comfortable visiting there on business and tolerant of the *Terranan.* Taniquel had hoped that tolerance would extend to her own wish to study with them.

Well, that was wrong. She mustn't say it, though. Howling, *"You don't understand!"* would make her sound twelve, not twenty-two.

"I honor our own sciences *and theirs.* If I can learn more of theirs and use each to give strength to the other's weak side, then think how many more people will benefit."

"They've talked about this for generations, Tani. How are you going to make it happen, when no one else has managed? I hate to say this, daughter, but the last time you tried, it didn't work well."

That was putting it as kindly as possible. It had seemed so obvious. She'd studied hard with one of the matrix mechanics who could do simple surgery, and equally hard with the Terran doctors who ran the med tech training.

In truth, Taniquel had studied medicine since she was twelve. Her mother had not *intended* to make her into a doctor. She had only wanted Taniquel taught not to cast the pain of her own stubbed toe or cut finger into anyone who laughed at her. Taniquel's teacher, the *leronis* Aliciane, sweetened lessons of self control with answers to Taniquel's medical questions, and so it had begun.

It should have been simple for her to block the pain of a man whose lungs made anesthesia terribly risky. The Terran surgeon and Taniquel had worked together before on other, less critical cases. He trusted her even while he doubted some of the Darkovan theories. Unlike several other surgeons, he accepted that a starstone was not just some piece of germ-carrying jewelry.

Only the brutally sudden onset of symptoms had made this open-abdomen surgery necessary. Yet it was precisely the sort of challenge that doctors often faced in villages here, with only basic tools. Taniquel couldn't help being glad of a chance to see the procedure.

Most of it had been simple. The patient breathed more easily than when he wasn't enduring surgery. The surgeon's deft movements were almost too fast to see as he excised and removed the swollen appendix. Taniquel watched, scarcely breathing.

But she had betrayed their trust and failed to keep the patient safe. Other paths of pain glowed within the lungs, etched by the flow they'd carried so long. As Taniquel watched the surgeon, fascinated by his skill, the patient's breathing faltered. Taniquel reached with her skills to steady it and the patient wakened, screaming.

Panic rose in her like frightened birds. She forced it down, heart racing as she set simple blocks of all sensation in place. Dr. Abrams had finished quickly. The patient dropped into sleep like a stone into a well. He lived; he recovered. She was glad of that, at least.

Taniquel still didn't know what went wrong. Something slipped. Afterward, not even the *leronis* Aliciane could tell Taniquel what had happened. Doctor Liu told Taniquel not to think about asking to do that again until she had more theory behind her.

Yes, it had nearly been a disaster. A screaming, struggling patient with his abdomen open! *But I didn't panic*, Taniquel thought.

She had been able to help salvage the situation. Well, if she could force herself to be calm then, she could surely do it now. "Which proves that I need to learn more. Stepfather, if I don't leave then I'll never get to try!"

He looked away. Taniquel bit her lip. She must show the good of it. "We worked together to fight the Trailmen's Fever twice. Even the old vaccine saved many."

He stood up so suddenly that his chair fell over with a loud thud. "Not your father." Anger shimmered around him. His barriers thinned before it; Taniquel could hear a jumble of longing, loss, and anger. *If I could... If I had half the gift this ungrateful girl has... Why didn't we take him earlier? Let strangers jab disease into us to fight disease? Take him to strangers for treatment? And now his daughter as good as charges me with blame in my sworn brother's death. Gods. If that betrothal fails... I'll lose this house! Send her to Uncle Damon for a month. A little time.*

Taniquel found she didn't quite have the nerve to protest that they'd delayed taking her father to the Terran clinic until too late. She remembered the grownups arguing, louder and louder, their voices full of fear. She had climbed up on his bed and held his hand with both of hers; he smiled. She'd thought that meant he'd be all right. Her presence did seem to ease him, and she herself was safe from the fever. Getting that vaccine must be the only time in her life that Margali Lanart Syrtis had defied her family. That, and when she let little Taniquel stay with her papa until morning. Taniquel remembered watching as he was carried into the temporary medical building.

She'd never seen him again, though she'd promised miracles of good behavior if they'd only let her go to him. She'd even promised not to say anything, just to be allowed to see him. They hadn't, of course, allowed so young a child into a medical building at the height of a crisis. Other people came out of that building later, but not her papa.

She had done ill in letting herself think of it. She looked across the desk, opening her mouth to apologize, and saw the shimmering anger disappear as her stepfather's barriers slammed shut.

Taniquel rose, shook her heavy tartan skirts into order, and left. As she cleared the door, she heard her stepfather call her name. She kept walking.

Slamming her door felt good. The room was crowded with both Terran and Darkovan clothes and projects, but it was hers. No man in the house, least of all her stepfather, would open that door without her permission.

There had been worry about the house itself in his jumble of angry thoughts. What other promises had he made? The house was her mother's, not his—but she'd sign anything her husband put in front of her.

Then Taniquel heard the soft click of a key turning in a lock. *Oh, no. No, he couldn't have.* She kicked a cushioned stool out of the way in her hurry to reach the door.

He had. She was locked in. *Locked in,* as if she were a naughty child. *Dom* Ann'dra held to the old-fashioned notion that parents had every right, and sometimes a duty, to confine misbehaving children. It was supposed to give the children time to think better of their errant ways. "Your mother will speak to you when she returns," said *Dom* Ann'dra from the other side of the door.

Oh, honestly. Taniquel had known how to get past that door lock since she was twelve. She'd always been careful to leave the door locked behind her with the key in it, as though she'd escaped some other way; evidently the ruse had worked. For a time her parents had worried that she had the rare ability to teleport. Fortunately, no one from their fire-plagued valley would ever lock someone in a room and not leave the key in place, not even here in Thendara.

She stood with her ear to the door, listening until his footsteps receded into silence. Good; he hadn't been there nearly long enough to set a binding on the lock.

Taniquel scrutinized the room. What did she have that was truly hers, that she could sell without reproach? She couldn't imagine that anyone would mind if she sold those two hideous lamps, but they'd be hard to carry. *Ah.* As a proper young woman of the Comyn, she'd embroidered nearly everything she wore. Folk art sold well in the shops near the spaceport; on one of her rare trips there she'd been surprised at what people would pay to have someone else do their stitchery. Never mind that "folk art" seemed to mean, "not real art." If the shopkeepers paid her enough for a ticket to the med school, they could call her work whatever they liked.

Hastily, she packed a travel satchel with clothing both Darkovan and *Terranan,* and every bit of finished embroidery in the room except the sheets. She laughed quietly at the image of smuggling sheets out of the house.

The key hung loose in the lock. Even her weak *laran* was enough to nudge the hanging key out and down.

Clink. Steadily, now. Yes. She could hear it scrape on the well-polished boards of the hallway. as she pulled it in under the door.

Taniquel grinned as she stooped down to pick up the key.

She was not exactly sneaking out of the house. She was simply leaving without speaking or letting anyone see her traveling satchel. Its sides bulged like a mare about to foal.

Taniquel fastened the brooch of her cloak and pulled the fog of the household thoughts around her own. The general hum of people thinking about dinner provided concealment.

Quietly now, she slipped past the side stairs that led to the children's rooms. Her mother was back from her errands; Taniquel heard her soft exclamations as the younger girls told her stories of their day's events. Aliciane had spilled juice on Elorie's favorite skirt, a major tragedy. Mother would be feeding baby Rafael at the same time. Finally, after all those girls, she'd given birth to a boy.

Taniquel half-ran into her mother's sewing room, travel satchel bumping against her right knee, and pinned a much-rewritten note to the pincushion. To leave without seeing her mother...was probably the only way to leave.

At this hour she'd get far more questions trying to slip out by the servants' stairs than by going out by the family's way. Her soft boots made little sound on the stone stairs.

Down the main staircase and out into the narrow courtyard, Taniquel strode away with unladylike speed. She slipped as she crossed onto the Trade City pavement from the cobbles that felt safer under her feet.

There was still time to go back home over those cobbles; she'd be only a little late for dinner. She could turn back. Taniquel straightened her shoulders. She'd decided to leave when she applied for the scholarship. She had hoped to have her parents' agreement.

Now she hoped that Emma Malone had really meant her casual offer of a place to sleep if Taniquel ever found herself stranded. Probably she did. Emma wasn't an official cultural liaison. She was just the person that most students, both *Terranan* and Darkovan, went to for help in solving cultural conflict. She would understand that such an offer might be taken seriously, wouldn't she?

Taniquel fingered the coin purse that hung at her belt. She seldom carried much money, since her bills would always be settled at home. Was there enough for a bed in a decent hostel? Probably. Alone. She shivered at the thought of walking into a hostel alone. Even the Renunciates went always in pairs.

No one would escort her across the galaxy. She'd just have to get used to it. Right now she'd better move on; people were starting to stare at the lone Darkovan woman standing where the street and the paved walking path met.

By the time she neared the block of apartments where Emma lived, Taniquel's stride had slowed to a trudge. The evening mist had thickened to cold rain.

Emma's building's security scan recognized Taniquel from the times she'd met Emma there for tutoring. Even the blindingly bright lobby was welcome shelter; it was warm. So was Emma's voice over the security link. "Sure, come on up. You have news?"

"Both bright and dark." The elevator no longer made Taniquel jump when it started up; she was glad not to have to walk up any more stairs.

Emma waited for her at the apartment's door. Her dark hair stood out around her face, freshly released from the clips that held it when she was at work. "Tani, sweetie! What's wrong?" She started to hug Taniquel, then pulled back remembering that Taniquel, even more than most Darkovan students, disliked being touched. "Welcome to my messy house!"

Taniquel hauled her traveling satchel across the threshold and touched Emma's hand lightly. "Thank you for your welcome," she said, and let Emma take her dripping cloak.

The small room, crowded with furniture and artwork, impressed Taniquel as interesting rather than messy. Through a half-open door, she could see one corner of a neatly-made bed and what must be some kind of clothes storage. The top drawer on the stack was missing one knob. The place was tiny, but close enough to the spaceport's medical center that only the worst storm would stop Emma from getting to her work as a medical technician.

"Emma—" Taniquel began.

"Taniquel—" They both laughed. "Please, sit down," Emma said, waving at the large, squashy divan that took up much of the room. "There'll be coffee in a minute."

Taniquel preferred *jaco* to Terran coffee; it was more flavorful and didn't do nasty things to her stomach. Still, coffee would be warm. A civilized, and unexpected, guest did not criticize. She sipped it and gave polite thanks.

Emma sat beside her on the couch and leaned forward. "Well?"

Taniquel grinned. "I got the scholarship."

Emma let out a whoop loud enough to make Taniquel jump. "Oh, that's fantastic. Oh, I can't help it—" and she hugged Taniquel, who to her own surprise, hugged back.

Then Emma frowned at her, head to one side. "Okay,

why has good news brought you here half-soaked and well past the curfew for good Darkovan girls?"

"*Dom* Ann'dra doesn't want me to go off-planet to study, and he holds my dowry money. I, ah, had to leave the house fast, so I didn't get a chance to talk to Mama. You know how she is about the wider world, anyway." She swallowed a mouthful of coffee. "Emma, can I stay here a few days?"

Emma touched her sleeve. "Of course. Stay as long as you like, or as long as you can stand sleeping on this couch. Are they still trying to marry you off to the chinless wonder?"

"No, really, he's handsome enough if you don't mind a beaky nose!" Taniquel protested. Cathal was also easy-going and without known bad habits. In Comyn society, one's bad habits generally did become known.

Taniquel opened her travel satchel. "Anyway, what do you think of these as a..." Taniquel fished for the Terran term, "Fund raiser?"

Emma leaned forward, grasped a piece done in colored wools and held it up to the light from her reading lamp. "No wonder you suture wounds so well."

Taniquel pulled the rest of the embroideries from her satchel and began smoothing and sorting the pile. "Do you think I can raise part of my fare from these, anyway?"

"Are you serious?"

Taniquel's chest felt tight. "No? I'd hoped..." What was she to do if she couldn't get enough money from selling them? Tickets to Terra cost almost half her dowry. Her few Darkovan coins didn't come close, and the difference was more than she could borrow even if Emma had it available.

Once she'd thought all Terrans were rich. They surely looked it, with their bright thin clothes and their machines for doing any boring or disagreeable work. She'd clearly been wrong. The maids at Syrtis House had better quarters than this tiny apartment, though they did have to share. Maybe the prices she'd seen in the shops were just asking prices. Maybe no one actually paid that much. And of course, they couldn't give her as much as they charged.

Emma touched her arm. "Relax."

Relax? Relax, when her hopes were thrown down again? When she might have to crawl back home?

"It's fine. What I meant was, these are enough to buy you a luxury cabin. This one alone," she held up the cushion cover done in wool, "will get you about a quarter of the ticket price. It'll be hard to sell, though, because it's worth so much."

She laughed at Taniquel's expression. "Oh, come on! How many hours did you put into it?"

"I've no idea. I don't just sit down and stitch away 'til it's done, for Evanda's sake! I stitch while I'm talking with visitors, or, or," she shrugged. "There's always something else going on."

"Well, if you did keep track—if you were trying to earn a living with it—you'd value your work higher. Even those little demonstration pieces would bring something. In fact, it's a good idea to have something more affordable to sell to people who can't afford a big piece."

Demonstration pieces? "Oh, the handkerchiefs!" Emma's blank look told her that word hadn't made it across the language barrier. She explained. "For when you cry, or when you sneeze."

"You mean after you've used it to wipe up body fluids you use it again?" Emma swallowed hard. "I'm sorry, Tani, it's just...."

"Well, we do wash them first." The expression on Emma's face said that didn't make much difference. "Very well. Demonstration pieces."

If she hadn't been in such a hurry, Taniquel would have enjoyed the experience of selling her work. Did these shopkeepers think that no Comyn lady had any idea of commerce? They hadn't apprenticed with her mother, then. Rank didn't necessarily bring money, but it always brought obligations.

The experience of finding the places to sell was less

enjoyable. As a child she hadn't wanted to go to Thendara's tourist district. As a med tech student, she'd seldom had the time. All boxy Terran intersections looked the same. After four days of trudging from shop to shop she finally sold a piece bigger than a handkerchief. She didn't get a great price—the shopkeeper could tell she was in a hurry—but good enough. She was so close now to having enough! She dropped the heavy coins into her purse with a grin.

Just outside the shop, she jolted to a stop. "*Reish,*" she muttered. She couldn't remember crossing these streets.

Time was short. She needed the price of a ticket within a week, and sooner would be better. She was embarrassed at having to ask directions. Some Terrans, especially men, were almost too helpful. It didn't take *laran* to understand their "helpfulness."

How would she manage in a strange Terran city? Wouldn't it be better to just stay home where she knew the parts of town that she really needed?

Taniquel shook her head hard. Where had those thoughts come from? It wasn't like her to whine. *You know how to diagnose,* she told herself. *Diagnose this problem.*

She dodged hastily over to a *jaco*-seller's stall and paid for a place to sit down by buying a cup. Had she lost her way in more than just city streets? She had won that scholarship. Doctor Liu had encouraged her to apply, even after her near disaster. Her Darkovan teachers had encouraged her, too. How could she even think of not going?

She might lose track of time and social obligations when she was studying, but now she was concentrating on the work at hand: selling enough embroideries to get that ticket. She was not lost! Someone had deliberately interfered with her mind.

Taniquel nearly choked on her mouthful of *jaco*. When she could breathe again, the answer lay clear before her. Either her mother or her father was trying to compel her mind. No one else would have both reason and ability to betray her thus.

No, that couldn't be it. Not Mama! Not even *Dom* Ann'dra. He was an honorable man, for all his faults. Yet what other answer was there? Who else would even know the childish fears she'd almost managed to forget? She set her cup down hard enough to draw a frown from the stall holder.

It was surprisingly simple to find two matrix mechanics, a brother and sister by their looks, in a shop in the borderland between the two cities. Darkovan tapestries divided its beige Terran interior. A woman with as much white as auburn in her hair led Taniquel into a small room well away from the door.

Taniquel rarely let anyone else handle the tiny starstone that hung at her neck. In truth, she seldom used it directly. When doing Terran healing, she needed both hands free. When doing Darkovan work, she was always with someone stronger. None of her brief uses of telepathy had been so pleasant as to make her wish to do more with it.

The tech was deft and gentle, though, touching the starstone only briefly before focusing on her own. Taniquel felt a brief tingling sensation as if someone had passed by, close enough to her arm to make the hairs stand up.

The mechanic shook her head as she drew the cloth back over her starstone. "*Domna*, I'm sorry. It's all too intertwined. Every mind has traces of other minds and wills; it doesn't necessarily mean—"

"Yes, I know about that." *And so does everyone over the age of about thirteen. Everyone with* laran *and a little training, anyway.*

The woman continued as if Taniquel hadn't spoken. "Strictly speaking, this isn't a compulsion, and I'm glad. That would be dangerous for both you and the person casting it."

Taniquel bit her lip. "Strictly speaking?"

"No one has actually placed any thought that wasn't yours before into your mind. There's nothing for me to undo."

"But if they push me to do things I wouldn't otherwise

do—"

"It still isn't a compulsion. This is a diversion, a much less serious charge. Even so, if you try confronting the sender, be sure to take help with you. Use the starstone, at the very least."

"I don't care about charging anyone with anything." Gods, no! Even a minor court case would keep her here for weeks, if not months. "I just want it stopped."

The mechanic frowned. "It is still an abuse of *donas* and ought to be reported."

"No! I haven't time for that!" Taniquel rose from her seat. "Thank you for your service, *Mestra*."

Taniquel found her way back to Emma's without difficulty. So far as she could tell, no one even tried to "divert" her. She allowed herself to hope that the matrix mechanic had scared off whoever it was.

She was still late enough to worry her hostess. Emma stared, eyes wide, mouth agape, after Taniquel had explained.

"This is one of the psi things you hinted about? Damn it, Taniquel, is this legal on Darkover? Can't you charge them with, with..."

"Abuse of *donas*?" Taniquel said. "Yes. And then I have to be here for the duration of my legal case, while my scholarship expires."

"Can't you fight it somehow? I mean, you psychic sorts used to be able to set cities on fire."

Taniquel groaned. She saw no point in telling Emma that some of the *vai leroni* probably still could set cities on fire.

"The best way to fight it is to avoid it, I think; I'll just have to pay more mind to what I'm doing." She pretended not to hear Emma's chuckle.

"I have almost enough money for my ticket. And, no—" she cut Emma off, "I do not want to borrow the difference from you. You've barely let me pay for my food here."

Emma shrugged. "So acknowledge me when you write

53

the great Terran-Darkovan medical concordance."
Taniquel laughed. "I'll do that."

The next day's sun hadn't yet reached its midpoint when Taniquel dropped the last of the needed coins into her money pouch. Her skirts flapped in the breeze of her half-sprint for the spaceport ticket office.

There wasn't even a line. Most people, it seemed, took care of this on computer. Well, most people weren't hauling a mixed lot of Darkovan coinage from half the Domain lands. The clerk courteously turned the screen so that she could see his computations. "You'll want to get used to going cashless," he said. "Most Terrans won't even know what to do with coin."

Taniquel agreed, thanked him, and tucked the precious tickets into a pocket in her blouse.

She could leave the day after tomorrow. That was perfect. She'd tell Emma first, then they'd see which med techs were free for a party. Not too much of a party, of course; she'd heard that hangovers and interstellar travel did not mix well. Maybe they could find that sweet fizzy drink instead.

And maybe she could somehow see her mother before she left. She'd never imagined that Mama would not answer any of the notes she sent.

She stopped where she stood. This was not where she had meant to be. This street formed part of the boundary between the Trade City and Thendara itself. How had she come so close to her home?

The mists now lay heavy in the city. Some of the garish Terran lights had come on, but their illumination didn't reach to where she stood.

It was impossible to focus here in the noisy public street. Yet it was only in places like this that the compulsion came upon her. She could feel it now, nipping at her feet like a herd dog. She couldn't tell whose dog it was.

Mother or stepfather? Taniquel had hoped so much that she need never know. Not Cathal, certainly. Her betrothed might not even know that she planned to leave Darkover. Certainly, she couldn't picture either of her parents telling him any but the most carefully edited version!

Mother? Taniquel's throat closed at the thought; tears welled up. *No tears, not here.*

No. Mother had the good and the bad of her old-fashioned codes of honor. She'd never use *laran* in this manner, even if she could, and the necessary rapport was absent between the two of them. Yet the misdirections had happened when Taniquel was thinking of her... no, they hadn't always. Any thought of *home* opened a door to—whom?

It had to be her stepfather. The man who claimed to love her as a daughter and could read her thoughts better than her own mother.

The wide Trade City streets thinned before her eyes. With her mind's eye she saw instead the winding streets of old Thendara. There was the wall that sheltered the shallow front courtyard of her home. Sunlight turned the upper-story windows rose; there was the sewing room where she'd sat with her mother. Above it ran the three windows of her own study room, chosen because it caught the first light. She'd had her choice of rooms, and hers was larger than Emma's whole apartment. Her home—

No. No, not my home. Not now, and probably never again. I have left my tower. Taniquel struggled to brush the illusion aside. She certainly didn't remember all the windows as being that clean!

Both real and visionary streets were full of people coming and going from the mid-day meal. The man nearest her had clearly just finished eating spicy sausage. That had to be real! She couldn't possibly fish her starstone out of its insulating bag, not with so many strangers so close around her.

The starstone lay under cloak, vest, and blouse. Yet without it, she had only her scant strength against a more experienced opponent. She would have to find a way. Or would she?

She could see one street clearly. Maybe if she just set forth along that one street, she could slip away from this illusion as quietly as she'd left the house five days ago. She'd be out of here in another two days; less than that, really. Surely there was no need to do battle like a *leronis* of legend.

The mists thickened into fog. The streets shimmered; the half-seen houses stood doubled in her sight.

She had to get out of here. Fog was illusion's friend. The sound of her own heart drowned out the clatter of the crowd. Up that street, there, she could see that far, and when she was out of this illusion she could find her way back.

Just up the street, one building sat a little farther from the street than its neighbors did. Taniquel huddled into the corner where two buildings met and grasped the bag that held her starstone. There; she clutched the starstone in her hand. The bag and its cord lay tangled in her cloak strings.

And then she was in truth outside what had been her home, with no memory of how she got there. The sunshine she'd seen in that too-pretty illusion was gone. Water dripped down the courtyard wall.

The gate stood open. She took two steps towards it and then stopped so suddenly that her damp skirts slapped loudly against her legs. She sent her thoughts in a silent shout, without stopping to make certain that only one mind would hear them.

No. I'm not coming back. Turn loose. This is abuse of donas. She hoped she managed to hide the thought that there was no way she could bring charges.

She felt a mental touch like a hand grabbing her shoulder. *Dom* Ann'dra had heard her. *There's no abuse. If you didn't want to come back to your home, I could never put the thought into your head.*

Then I reject the thought.

But this was her home. She could remember no other. How could she not think of coming back here someday?

Right now, she must. If she passed through that front

gate, the one they almost never closed or locked because a bright child of ten could get over it, then she would be within her family's domain. Her feet had stepped closer to it while she spoke telepathically with *Dom* Ann'dra. He had used her own anger to pull her closer.

She had one strong talent. She could trace and use the path of pain, there, lying small along her wrist, a narrow stream close to the surface, nothing too complicated. She didn't dare risk doing herself real damage. She wasn't even sure she could still send her pain elsewhere. She'd learned to refrain from that so long ago.

Carefully she wrapped her fingers around the starstone. Now, put a dam across the stream to block the pain that she was going to cause.

She had to look to be sure that her hand was still clenched around the starstone. It was.

Her stepfather's voice spoke now of love and duty. Where in Avarra's name was her mother? Why had her mother not answered any of her letters? Was she so angry as that? Was she ill?

I wondered if you'd ever ask that. She's well, but come in and find out for yourself. The mind-voice was so calm as to be off-hand. It gave no hint of shame or anger.

He really felt no shame. He had sown discord between mother and daughter. He had misused *laran* to deceive and compel. How had he come to this? He truly believed that he had done no wrong.

Because I haven't!

That hadn't changed, that sudden blaze of anger like wildfire in the hills. It would have terrified her once.

Not now. Under cover of his anger's distraction, she seized her wrist with the hand that could still feel and pinched the soft skin of the inside of it, digging her nails in. She could see the blood well up.

Looking with her inner sight, Taniquel could see the pain pooling behind the dam she'd set. She gathered it and flung it into the man who'd used her *laran* against her. *Let me go!*

Taniquel could hear the cry of pain ring out from the house with the ears of the body and the mind. Other shouts followed.

Confusion and fear flooded through her. This should have hurt him no more than a hard slap. She'd expected a shout of anger, not screams.

Mine, or his? This pain is more than I meant to cause! I wasn't even sure I could cast it. All I meant was to go free!

Oh, Evanda and Avarra. The gift was not given me for this. I did it and I must undo it.

Taniquel's legs shook as she stormed through the gate, into the house and up the stairs to the family rooms two at a time. Servants scattered to avoid her. Her half-sisters peered large-eyed around the skirts of their nurse.

Taniquel gasped for breath as she reached her stepfather's study. The old-fashioned lamp seemed to throw shadows, not light. Papers lay strewn across the worn carpet. On it, *Dom* Ann'dra lay curled on his side, one hand clutching the other to his chest. Her mother looked up from where she knelt by his side. *Have I killed him? I can't have killed him!*

No. He clutched his wrist and hissed with the pain, but he lived. Taniquel's breath sounded loud to her as she let it out.

Taniquel's mother spread her arms out to block her from coming near him. "No, you've done quite enough already! He's been heart-sick ever since you ran off to the Terrans and now you've made it worse. Why did you come back here at all? Stay away!"

Hearts did not stop beating out of sorrow. Taniquel had more than enough training to know that. *Why does mine feel as though it had?*

"I must undo what I've done."

Her mother shook her head without a word.

"I can help. Please let me help!"

Her mother glared at Taniquel with narrowed eyes. Then, with reluctance in every move, she shuffled aside without rising or letting go of her husband's shoulder.

Taniquel sat down with a thump. She had another chance to undo harm. *Softly now. Gently. The lines of pain run there, and there.* They tumbled over each other like a stream in spring flood. She reached out to calm the waves, but they continued to thrash.

Taniquel's temples throbbed as she strained to force the lines back into the calmness.

Was she pushing too hard? She pictured the lines as they normally would lie, faint and smooth.

The lines shivered and twisted. They still glowed dark red. Again, she pictured them calm; again, they remained tangled and angry.

It isn't working. Evanda help me, was I wrong when I said I could help?

Her stepfather curled tighter, holding his wrist to his belly. His heart was thundering.

He's not a young man.

Taniquel knew what she needed to do. She glanced at her unfeeling wrist. *I did quite a job on that, didn't I? This is going to be bad.* She threw all her strength into blocking Ann'dra's pain.

She swayed forward as feeling rushed back into her wrist and hand. *And he must have felt more than this, to cry out so.* She cradled her arm against her chest. The trick was to let the pain flow back into her own body without losing her focus.

Ah. That loss of focus had been the problem all along, hadn't it? That was how she'd failed during the operation, too fascinated by the surgeon's technique to maintain her control. That was how her stepfather had been able to misdirect her. *Dom* Ann'dra groaned, and Taniquel snapped her mind back to the task at hand.

"Oh. Oh, that's better," he muttered as he uncurled.

The lines of pain were lines of sense now, the body's awareness of itself flowing calmly in the narrow channels. He raised himself on one elbow and Mother helped him to sit up.

Taniquel tried to speak, failed, and cleared her dry

throat. "I'm sorry," she croaked.

Ann'dra's lips tightened. Then, "And I. Taniquel... We needed this so much. We still need it." He levered himself up off the floor. "Don't you see? I am not used to justifying myself to my family, but if I must—Taniquel, if I explain how hard it's going to be for us if your betrothal fails, how much the connection will help, then will you reconsider?"

Taniquel rose. She was not going to say this sprawled on the floor like a child. "No. It's too late for that. I leave the day after tomorrow. Doctors do often make quite a lot of money, you know. If you can just be patient, I'll be able to help..." Her voice trailed off. His face told her without the need of words or *laran* what he thought of that idea.

The silence grew between them like a stream freezing from both sides inward. Finally, still silently, *Dom* Ann'dra looked away. He didn't look back to her.

Mother climbed to her feet. She shook out her skirts and dusted off all three of them as if that could set her world back in order. She cleaned and bandaged Taniquel's wrist without comment.

The younger girls were allowed in to see for themselves that Papa was well again. "Though what I'm going to tell Elorie about this I don't quite know," Mother whispered to Taniquel. "She's old enough to ask questions."

"And the others aren't?" Taniquel hadn't paid them much mind, she realized. Oh, they shared a fire and meals; she knew that Elorie loved chervine stew but Aliciane burst into tears at the idea of killing and eating something so pretty. She'd no idea what any of them were really like. The baby would meet her as a stranger.

Mother shook her head. "Not every child is as full of questions as you were, Evanda be thanked! Well, you've turned things upside down for this; I suppose you'd better have it. No, Ann'dra, done is done."

Taniquel gasped. *She speaks to him like that in front of me? In front of the children?*

Margali Syrtis, demure and dutiful, snorted. There was no other word for it. "I heard some of that argument. One can only hope no one else did. Taniquel, I trust you'll consent to learn more from the *leroni* when you return?"

"That would be wise."

Taniquel had packed in a blind hurry, but when she looked at her room again there was nothing she wanted badly enough to pay for the extra freight. In spite of the late hour, she didn't wish to sleep there again.

Only her mother came with her to the outer door. "Write to me," she said. "I'll get your letters now."

On the steps to the courtyard, Taniquel hesitated. She had to know one more thing. "You've forgiven him already, haven't you? How can you?"

"He did believe that he was protecting us all."

Hah.

"And, *chiya*, are you arguing against forgiveness?"

Taniquel felt a shamefaced grin spread across her face. "Ah, no. No, I won't do that."

She kept most of the day's events to herself when she got back to Emma's. They said their farewells at the apartment.

"You're going to be insanely busy, I know, but promise me you'll let me know you're still alive now and then," Emma said. Taniquel promised.

At the edge of the plaza outside the spaceport, Taniquel stopped to look back at Thendara. The shadows were still long; their deep red outlined both Terran and Darkovan buildings. She'd have to get used to the glaring white-gold light of Terra.

Taniquel Syrtis embraced her mother once more, and each of her half-sisters. Then, with the shadows shortening around her, she turned and walked through the doors of the spaceport without looking back.

BLOOD-KIN

by Diana L. Paxson

One of the pleasures of editing an anthology series is witnessing the further development of characters from one story to another in the hands of a skilled storyteller. "Blood-Kin" by Diana L. Paxson includes characters that first appeared in "The Motherquest" (Free Amazons of Darkover) and "A Season of Butterflies" (Renunciates of Darkover), as well as those introduced in "Evanda's Mirror" in Stars of Darkover. It takes the themes of healing and healers, Terran and Darkovan, in a different and complementary direction from the previous story, with equally satisfying results.

Diana L. Paxson is the author of twenty-nine novels, including the books that continue Marion Zimmer Bradley's Avalon series. She has also written eighty-six short stories, including appearances in most of Marion's Darkover anthologies. She is currently working on a novel about the first century German seeress Veleda.

The air shook as the passenger liner broke atmosphere. A fiery glow intensified the red of the sunset clouds, flaring for a moment against the smooth surfaces of the tower that housed Terran HQ. A moment later came the extended reverberation that always reminded me of the great waterfall near the Caves of Corresanti. After a two year trip off-world to visit her son, Caitrin n'ha Laurian was coming home.

As her oath-daughter I had a right to welcome her, and so had Stelle, her freemate for almost thirty years. I name myself Kiera n'ha Leona, but to my birth mother I was only the child who should have been a boy. Caitrin, the

Renunciate who gave my father a son, was the one who loved me. But as we made our way past the tawdry taverns and shops beyond the Terran walls I heard the rumble of an angry crowd, and began to wonder if bringing Cassi and Adriana, who were *my* lovers, had been wise.

Beyond the housetops yellow floodlights glared from the outer wall protecting the terminal. I had travelled with my father to planets with yellow suns, but against a Darkovan sunset those lights looked wrong. Was it my nerves or was the breeze actually warm? That would have been unusual for late summer in Thendara, but with plague in the city, very little was natural here right now.

"Kiera, don't stand there staring—" Cassi turned. "The ship is already here!"

I gave her a quick smile, checked to make sure that Adriana and Stelle were still with us, and started walking once more, slowing my longer steps so they could keep up. Cassi had a solid strength beneath her curves and Adriana could run like a chervine, but Stelle was not as young as she used to be.

If my oath-mother didn't approve of my choices, was I still a Renunciate? And if I did not belong to the *Comhi-Letzii*, what was I? Suddenly I felt as if I were walking on melting ice. I had tried to be the daughter that Caitrin needed. Sometimes I wondered if I fell in love with Cassi because Caitrin set me such a good example with Stelle. But then again, there was Adriana...I cast a glance behind me and once more felt that stab of wonder at her grace.

I blinked at the glare as we turned the corner into the great square in front of the terminal, flanked by the garish, neon-fronted Sky Harbor hotel. It was full of folk from Thendara's poorer quarter, focused on the man who stood on the steps of the monument in the center of the square. I shuddered, sensing an anger that fed on itself, avid for prey.

"Yellow suns! Yellow faces! Yellow demons who bring death!" he cried.

I flinched, belatedly remembering to bring up my

mental barriers as a new wave of hatred surged in reply. I had not been good enough for the Circle at Neskaya, but trying to train Adriana had forced me to practice what skills I had. They were stronger now just because she was near.

In the stark light the leader was easy to see. I'd heard about him—a man called Dermot Sandoval, the loudest of the rabble-rousers who was giving voice to the city's fear as the sickness they called the Yellow Plague took hold. It was worse than Trailmen's fever, which had swept the planet several times before, because it was something new from off-world, something the people did not understand.

"Death to the aliens! Pull the Terran abomination down!"

Stelle pushed past me, her white healer's coif standing out against the dark woolens most folk wore. Whether from respect or because of her focused assurance, no one got in her way, and the rest of us had no choice but to follow. When someone turned the jaundiced yellow of the plague, there was little enough that anyone could do, but at least the healers tried. Stelle herself had trained with the Terran medical service during one of the periodic attempts to improve Terran/Darkovan relations, but lately she had been leaving that out of her biography.

I took Cassi's hand to hurry after, and gave Adriana an encouraging grin.

Her pale eyes widened as they met mine. *Caitrin won't like me—how could she?* she sent silently, *I should not have come.*

"Maybe not," I said aloud, "but not because of Caitrin. Look around you!"

With a squeak and rumble the steel gates were opening. As a line of Terran guards filed out, weapons ready, Sandoval fell silent, glowering. We followed Stelle forward, and a few others who had come to meet new arrivals fell in behind us.

The Departures section of the waiting room was full of Terran families who were being evacuated. Word was that the Empire was reducing its presence to a minimum, but whether that was in response to Darkovan pressure or out of concern for the safety of its citizens, I didn't know. Those waiting in Arrivals consisted of us, a half-dozen Darkovan families, and several Terran officials who looked as if they would rather have been on the departing side.

A disembodied voice squawked something in Terran Standard. A door slid aside and passengers began to debark, stumbling as they adjusted to the slight difference in Darkover's gravity. There were not many—a few techs who looked around suspiciously until they were collected by the waiting officials, three whose uniforms bore medical insignia who were greeted by someone from HQ, three Darkovan men who were swept into the embrace of chattering families, and then a long-striding fortyish woman dressed in a blue jumpsuit who paused, looking around her expectantly. There were no more.

"But where is Caitrin?" Cassi broke the silence.

"There—" Stelle said suddenly. She stifled a laugh and began to wave.

"But—she looks like a *Terran*—" said Adriana. "In those clothes. And her skin is the color of gold…"

The woman saw us, grinned, and suddenly she was Caitrin, my oath-mother, once more, but a Caitrin whose skin had been tanned by suns far brighter than Darkover's ruddy star.

By the time we collected Caitrin's baggage the strangeness was wearing off, and the latest news about my half-brother Donal Ridenow had been shared.

"How glad I am to be home!" Caitrin exclaimed. "The gravity feels right, and it's so good to hear Cahuenga again! And food—the first thing I want is a big bowl of tripe stew!"

"No—" Stelle shook her head. "The *first* thing, *breda*, is get you back into Darkovan clothes. I know you took one festival outfit with you for celebrations. Let's find the women's retiring room so that you can change."

"But why?" asked Caitrin. "Is there trouble with the Terrans again?"

"You might say that," I answered grimly. As we escorted Caitrin into the ladies' room Stelle began to explain.

"The Terrans' machines take our livelihood!"

As we emerged from the terminal, Sandoval's voice rang out beyond the outer wall. Darkness had fallen and a little rain was filtering down, but the area outside was as bright as a Terran day. Caitrin, dressed now in skirts and Stelle's shawl, took a deep breath, but I pushed her along. Black-clad Terran guards opened the gate, and we started through the tunnel that led through the thick wall to the outside. Another gate stood open at the other end, but guards were waiting to close it as soon as we passed. When we reached the opening, I stepped forward. Dermot Sandoval was still standing on the monument, and the crowd, far from dispersing, seemed to have grown.

"They seduce our youth to foreign ways! And now they kill our children with their foul plague!" Sandoval cried, grey beard tossing. One might have passed him in the street without a glance, but with hundreds of eyes upon him he *glowed.*

"Terrans go!" came the reply.

"He's feeding off their energy!" Stelle exclaimed. "Look at him!"

"Terrans go!" the shout came again, and from some, "Terrans die!"

"Do you think he knows?" asked Cassi.

"He knows it feels good," Stelle said bitterly. "There's nothing so satisfying to the twisted soul as a chance to wallow in righteous zeal!"

One of the Terran guards cleared his throat and gestured toward the ramp that led down to the square.

Cassi tossed her head. "Well, we don't need to feed his fire. Let's go home."

But we had left it too long. As we came out into the light Sandoval's wild gaze caught the motion. "There's one of them!" he bellowed. "A yellow woman! Face as yellow as her hair! Disguised as one of us so she can spread the plague!" He pointed and the crowd surged toward us.

"Halt!" I felt as if I were pulling up power from my boot soles as I stepped between the other women and the mob, hand on the hilt of the knife that was not quite a sword. The leaders hesitated. "'Tis a respectable woman of this city, coming home to her kin. We stand surety that she will do no harm."

Adriana always wore skirts, and except for the lock she had shorn when she came to the Guild-house, her black hair was long, but my breeches and knee-length tunic marked me as a Renunciate. Angered at the necessity, I turned so that the light would shine on my ginger hair, reached for Adriana's hand and held it high so they could see the six fingers there. "Avarra strike me if I do not speak true!"

"Free Amazon bitches," came a snarl, but from others, "Comyn...You lend us grace..."

"Go now," I kept my voice low. "Stelle, get them away. We'll be safe enough when you are gone."

Adriana's presence was amplifying my undependable *laran*, and I blessed the Ardais gift she bore. "Let me draw on your strength, love, and we'll show the *reish* that two can play this game."

I felt Adriana plant her feet, and then a flow of power like a blast of Heller wind. Adriana was still learning to use her *laran*, but as she settled into her true identity she had been gaining access to the abilities she had suppressed before. *This* she could do!

"And what have the Comyn done to help us? What has Hastur done, safe in his tower?" Sandoval began.

Raise a sphere that will negate his energy—I sent as the mob began to murmur again.

Not a mirror?

The hatred will escalate if we throw it back at them. Retreat into a well of darkness; become invisible.... For a moment I closed my eyes, filling my mind with shadow, then directed my thought toward the crowd.

67

There is nothing here.... Nothing to fight.... They are gone....

Straining with all my senses, I held the double image of the alley behind us and the darkness that obscured it, and drew Adriana backward until real shadows replaced the illusion of darkness that we had cast. I took a deep breath and opened my eyes. A babble of confusion broke out behind us as we ran.

"But I still don't understand why we couldn't go straight to the Guild-house!" Caitrin sat down on the bench by our hearth and looked around her.

I lit a candle, and winced as the warm light flickered on a stain on the wall where the roof leaked and the worn, uneven floorboards that the rugs Cassi braided from rags could not disguise. For the past half-year this had been home to her and to Adriana and me, but I had to admit that compared to the Thendara Guild-house, a rambling, stoutly built structure whose every board and stone echoed with Renunciate history, it was a poor place indeed. In the Guild-house, there was always somewhere else, and some*one* else, to go to when one of your sisters annoyed you. Love was not always enough. Crammed together, I sometimes found Adriana's uncertainties and Cassi's insistence on order exasperating, and I am sure that they were annoyed by the Comyn assumptions I was still trying to shed.

"When you get to Thendara House everyone will be talking at once," Cassi exclaimed. "The homecoming feast is already on the stove. You know how it will be!"

"You are really living here?" Her gaze went from the hearth to the worktable to the bed. Clothing hung from pegs on the wall. That was all the room held beside the two benches and a chair.

"Please..." I found my voice. "Give us a candle-mark to explain."

Caitrin looked at her freemate. "Stelle?"

"You might as well hear their side first. The Goddess

knows you'll get everyone else's opinions when we get home."

Caitrin's glance moved from me to Cassi, and from her to Adriana.

"It should be me who does the telling," she said softly, the Hellers accent intensified by stress. "'Tis because of me that the two of you are denied the companionship of your sisters and the comfort of your home." She turned to Caitrin. "I was born with a man's body. The Goddess has changed me, but the women at Thendara House cannot forget."

Caitrin's eyes widened. Then she looked at Adriana's six-fingered hands and nodded. "*Chieri?*"

Adriana's pale skin flushed. "So the stories of my family say."

"What she does not say is that Kiera and I love her—" Cassi burst in. "The Goddess has bound the three of us together."

"That's what we wanted to say," I said stiffly, afraid to meet her eyes. *Forgive me!* I bit back the words.

"The law does not require all Renunciates to live at the Guild House," added Cassi. "We have done nothing wrong! But some of our sisters fear that we weaken their position. That's why we can't live there anymore."

"This is hardly the welcome I expected...." Caitrin rubbed her eyes. When she looked at me all I could read was confusion. "My daughter, I have to honor your choices, but right now I cannot understand them. For me it's the middle of the sleep cycle, and all I can really think about is bed. Stelle, take me home—"

After Stelle and Caitrin left there didn't seem to be much to say. We crawled into our own bed, but for me, sleep would not come. I sat gazing at the fading coals, listening to Adriana's regular breathing and Cassi's gentle snore, at once glad and resentful they could sleep so peacefully.

But why not? If they were concerned about Caitrin's reaction to our situation, it was more for my sake than their own. Adriana had no reason to love the *Comhi-*

Letzhii, and I thought that Cassi could have been set down in a nest of Trailmen and found contentment there. I was the one who depended on the Renunciates for a place and purpose to replace the heritage I had denied.

What was my oath-mother doing now? What were they telling her, and did she believe them? Regrets circled like banshees—I should have married the man my brother picked for me, or stayed, even as a drudge, at Neskaya. Instead, I had sworn to defend myself, support myself, to depend neither on clan nor kin. I was bound to my oath-mother and sisters. If Caitrin demanded that I return to the Guild-house, how would I choose?

Unable to sit still, I began to move through the forms of the weapon dance. As my muscles warmed my tension eased. Awareness extended to the two women who slept in the big bed; from there to the men who were drinking in the nearby inn. But the ale brought them no joy. Farther still I sensed grief, pain... Death stalked the streets of Thendara, and compared to the fear that gripped the city, what did Caitrin's opinion of me matter, after all? I brought my attention back to my movements, focusing mind and body, seeking harmony.

Whatever happened, I would need to be strong.

On the third day after Caitrin's return, Stelle appeared at our door.

Cassi, who could practice her trade as a glove-maker at home, was working. Adriana had already left for the inn on the corner, where she washed bottles and scrubbed floors with an effectiveness one would not have expected from her slim frame. I was chafing at an enforced leisure. My experience off-planet and familiarity with the class of people who hired guides or female guards had made it natural for me to do expedition organizing with Caitrin, but no one was going anywhere now.

As Stelle came in, Cassi looked up from the scraps of leather spread across the table and smiled sweetly.

"Good morning, Stelle, how nice to see you—will you

have some tea?"

I pulled out a chair and with a snort the older woman sat down.

"Caitrin sends her greetings, if that's what you wanted to know," she replied.

Is that all? I wanted to cry out in protest. Was there no word for me?

"I have to visit a woman with a difficult pregnancy on Tanner Street," Stelle continued, "but they say there's been looting there. I've been advised not to go alone."

"I'll come—" I reached for the belt that held my long knife. Maybe as we walked she would tell me more.

Cassi lifted a hand as if to hold me, then let it fall. "Be careful...."

I nodded. If the Terrans had a way to fight the evil spirits that brought plague they weren't sharing. But at least I could fight the evil that fear bred in men.

As we started down the road I could feel a difference even from two days ago. The acrid stink of smoldering thatch hung in the air. Rumor had it that the City Guard was trying to burn out the infection by torching buildings where people had died. A brown pall lay over the city. Perhaps that was why it felt so warm.

At the entrance to Tanner Street we saw a wagon drawn up in front of one of the houses. Terran guards faced down the crowd that was gathering as men in bizarre suits of some Terran synthetic brought out a stretcher with a foil swathed form. One of the guards sprayed a circle of yellow paint on the door.

As they pulled away, two women ran out, hair streaming and clothing torn in grief, screaming the dead man's name. As if that had been a signal, the crowd erupted.

"Cannibals!" "Witches!" came the cry. "How many of *you* have died?"

I pushed Stelle behind me as clods and cobblestones flew through the air. The Terran guards turned, weapons lifting, but they did not fire, and in another moment they were gone.

"It's been like that all over Thendara," said Stelle. "The Terrans say that the sick and the dead can infect the living, but the people know only that their loved ones are being taken away. It is hard to mourn properly at a mass grave."

"Are the Terranan telling the truth?"

Stelle shrugged. "I think that *they* believe it, or they would not swathe themselves in such garments when it is so warm."

"Do *you* have such garb?" When she shook her head, I added, "If one of your patients gets the plague, what will you do?"

She stopped, and I saw her face gone grim. "I will fulfill my oath..." she said softly.

For a moment I thought she meant her oath to the Renunciates, and my heart eased. Then I remembered that she was also a priestess of Avarra.

The maid who ushered us into one of the better houses was small and neat, her mistress a very young woman who was bearing her first child. Her husband, a grain merchant, had lost his first wife in childbed, and was taking no chances. His generous payments had been very welcome at the Guild-house, but I knew that Stelle would have come even of the woman had been poor.

I thought the girl's worst problem was boredom. Throughout the examination she kept up a stream of chatter, and when the tally of her own discomforts ran low she switched to the neighborhood.

"And what about this dreadful illness? Mira tells me that Master Sebastian down at the corner has died! A terrible thing, surely. They say it is a Terran disease, set loose to weaken us so the Empire can seize control. They say the Terranan have sent a witch to spread it, a yellow woman disguised as a Free Amazon—" Her babble faltered as her gaze fell upon my breeches and short hair.

"I didn't mean—" she started, and then, almost gleefully, "Oh, I hope she won't try to pass herself off as one of you!"

She meant Caitrin! Indignant explanations trembled on my lips. Stelle gripped my wrist, and I swallowed them as I realized what would happen if I dared to say a word. Against hate and hysteria truth and reason were no defense. Dermot Sandoval's bile had been bad enough when aimed at the Terrans. I felt sick, imagining it turned on me. I knew how to face physical danger, but I could not fight this enemy.

Stelle turned back to the pregnant girl. "Do not disturb yourself," she said steadily. "I know who my sisters are."

By the time we left Stelle's patient, the Terrans had quarantined the entire quarter, but their maps showed only the surface of what was a very old town. There was hardly a home here where Stelle had not treated someone, and even in their fear people were willing to help us. It did not take long to find a house whose cellar included a tunnel that brought us out near Comyn Castle.

The Great North Road that bisected the city had more traffic than I would have expected at this hour. Single figures hurried past with burdens; whole families trudged along with hand-carts piled high. Fleeing the city, I thought, and though the air was still unseasonably warm, I felt a chill. New posters had appeared on the walls, telling people to stay home, to boil their water, to wash frequently. Many of them had been defaced already by blood-red slogans telling the Terrans to go home.

"I apologize for taking you into danger," Stelle said after a little while. "I did not know that the disease had progressed so far."

"*You* did not hesitate to go—" I replied, slowing my stride.

"I have sworn different oaths," she said, "and..."

"And?" I moved between her and the road as two couriers splashed by.

"When I trained with the Terrans they gave us injections to protect against many ills. Some of them made me very sick indeed. I don't know if this plague was among them. Darkover was on its own long enough to change us. Not all the Terran medicines will work on us, but it is possible that

I am immune."

"Is that why the Terrans aren't afraid of the plague?" I exclaimed. "If they have a cure they should be cooking up their potions and distributing them wholesale!

"Oh, they fear it—you saw the protective gear they wore. These diseases change swiftly, and their medicines might not work against the strain we have here. But their greatest fear is that one of their cures might instead do harm. They are bound by regulations, and they test and test, for years sometimes, before they will use something new."

We don't have years... I thought, watching the refugees stream past.

I averted my face as the pale walls of Comyn Castle loomed up before us, though any lords still resident there had more compelling concerns than the dereliction of one Ridenow female. My brother had stopped asking me to give up this Renunciate nonsense and marry, and it had been over a year since the last appeal to at least bear a child who might carry *laran*. If my gifts had been strong they would never have let me out of the Tower. It was just as well they did not know how my connection with Adriana had strengthened the little *laran* I had.

"You don't have to escort me all the way home—" said Stelle as we continued up the hill.

"Yes I do," I said grimly. "Even the Terrans can't quarantine rumor. That piece of gossip about the Free Amazon plague bringer could be all over the city by now. I will see you safe to the Guild-house door. Tell them to bar it behind you when you get inside."

"Avarra preserve us," muttered Stelle.

I nodded. The wings of the dark goddess were spreading wide, but I did not know whether She came to shelter or to slay.

"If you keep sharpening that knife you'll take the edge right off—" Cassi's voice was even, but I heard the frustration there. The situation in the city was getting worse, and there was nothing we could do. My fingers clenched on the hilt, then I sighed and picked up the oiled cloth to wipe the blade.

The door slammed open. I was on my feet, knife held to guard, before I realized it was Adriana.

"A mob—" She caught her breath. "A mob is forming to attack the Guild-house! A man came to the inn to recruit more!"

"We must warn them!' Cassi's chair tipped over as she stood, reaching for the biggest of her knives. By the time I got my belt buckled, the other two had kilted up their skirts. No need for cloaks today. We ran.

Mhari, on light duty since the birth of her child, had the door.

"Where's Caitrin?" I gripped her shoulder. "I need to see—"

"Trying to get back into condition—in the Armory—" she replied, and then, "What's *she* doing here?"

At least, I thought as I pushed past her, Mhari reacted to Adriana as a woman now.

"Call Mother Doria," cried Cassi, wrestling the bar back into the rests that held it across the door, "Go!"

As I dashed through the kitchen and across the garden to the Armory a babble of women's voices rose behind me. I found my oath-mother, stripped to shirt and breeches, struggling to swing the stone weights and looking every one of her fifty years.

"Caitrin, get dressed!" I panted. "Sandoval's whipping up a crowd to get the Yellow Woman, and they mustn't find you here!"

"What in Avarra's name are you talking about?" she exclaimed, but she put the weights down.

"They saw you with us at the spaceport, remember? They know you're a Free Amazon!" I grabbed her and pulled her, still protesting, up the stairs to the dormitory. We met Cassi and Adriana in the hall.

"Get her in skirts, and one of Stelle's coifs to cover her hair! And flour on her face—she's still too brown! I've got to talk to Mother Doria—" Leaving my oath-mother in

Cassi's competent hands I dashed back down the stairs.

I could hear Mother Doria's voice as I reached the front hall.

"There is no need for panic. Why do you think we insist that all of you learn to handle weapons? We have fought off attackers before...."

"Not this many," I exclaimed. "That door you keep as a trophy in your office was hacked down by one angry husband and his sworn men. Dermot Sandoval has half the city behind him."

Janetta brandished a long-handled axe like one of Avarra's furies. "We won't give up Caitrin—"

"We won't have to. Cassi and Adriana will take her away!" I replied.

"Lord Hastur—" Mother Doria began, but I cut her off—

"Hastur can do nothing. They will be too many for the City Guard. There will be one moment, before the wretches nerve themselves up to attack, when they might listen. Tell them you'll admit a small party to search the Guild-house."

"Men in the Guild-house? Give up the rights we have fought for so long?"

"They're not men, they're a mob," I answered.

I had heard stories from my cousins who served in the Guard. When the violence reached a certain point, even the Comyn could only flee to their country estates or wait it out behind barricaded doors. Cleindori Aillard and Cassi Lanart-Ridenow, my own kin, had been murdered by a much smaller mob of traditionalists who feared their attempt to use matrix technology outside a Tower.

I felt a familiar presence, and turned to see Cassi, dark curls bouncing, gripping one of the halberds from the Armory. Plump and fierce, she looked like a rabbit-horn defending her kits.

"Caitrin and Stelle are safely away."

I had wanted my oath-mother to see more of my new lover, but Cassi was supposed to go with them.

Cassi grinned. "Two healers and their servant will go faster. Adriana has lived rough and knows a lot of back ways. She'll get them there. I'll stand with you."

"Will they be safe?"

"Where have they gone?"

"The best person to keep a secret is the one to whom it has not been told—" Mother Doria said repressively.

All heads turned as little Cora, who had been stationed at an upper window, came clattering down the stairs. "They're coming!" she gasped.

"Then we must greet them." When Mother Doria rose from the bench it was if a mountain had moved. "Kiera, Janetta, Lassandra, stand with me. You others will wait here. If talking fails, sell your lives as best you can," she said grimly. "But if we succeed, set your weapons aside and let their leaders in."

Hatred pulsed like a blow from the crowd that was gathering in the square before the Guild-house. This was more than fear of the plague. To bring such a crowd, Sandoval must have played on every festering resentment men held against the women who dared to deny their authority.

As I brought up my own barriers I saw Lassandra flinch and realized she must have more sensitivity than she knew. I wondered how many of my sisters were here because some trace of *laran* had made the conditions in which most women lived just that much harder to bear. Some Renunciates had children, but whether one kept the child or gave it up, it was hard, and most of us were unwilling to face the pain. It occurred to me that if this was so, Darkover was preventing some of the people who made us unique from passing their gifts on.

Then Dermot Sandoval's fanatic features emerged from the blur of faces and I snapped back to full awareness, trying to project calm as I had done when I faced the mob before. But then, Adriana had been by my side.

"Send out the Yellow Woman and we will let you live!" Spittle sprayed as Sandoval screamed. "Resist, and you will die!"

"Give us Caitrin n'ha Laurian," said a man in a

merchant's dark cloak. "We know that she came in on a Terran ship two weeks ago. She is listed as resident in Thendara House."

"She is not here—" Mother Doria used the voice that had cut through more than one cat-fight in the Guild-house.

"You lie!" "Break down the door!" came the shouts. I loosened my long knife in the sheath. It was likely to be needed soon.

"By law no man may enter except by our leave," said Mother Doria, "but choose a dozen, and they may come in and look wherever they please."

"Two dozen—" said the man behind Sandoval. "The records say that there are eighteen of you living here."

"Burn the bitches out and make sure!" came the cries, but some of the men were looking interested. The gods only knew what fantasies they harbored about what went on inside.

"How do we know you won't murder us as soon as we come in?" called someone as Sandoval began to choose. There was a feverish glitter in his eyes.

"How do we know you won't do the same?" Janetta glared.

"Both sides must give their weapons to one man to guard. I will stay here as your hostage. I swear in Avarra's name that from us there will be no treachery."

"We will come!" spat Sandoval, "and we will destroy the evil!

"Lassandra, take them in—" said Mother Doria.

We stepped aside as the men moved past, ignoring the muttered insults and leers, then moved back into position flanking Mother Doria. Hatred had a stench of its own, I realized, or perhaps that was disease. It seemed to me that the faces of more than one had a yellow cast.

The wait seemed endless. As the insults and catcalls fell to an uneasy murmur we stood, our faces showing no more emotion than a ceremonial guard. Deprived of their leader, the crowd was losing focus. When someone collapsed, those near him began to edge away. By the time the search party returned, the crowd held barely half of those who had been there before. Sandoval's disappointed expression proclaimed his failure before he even said a word.

I let out my breath in a long sigh. My sisters here were safe. It was time to go home.

"No, I am not shocked by you—" Caitrin poured tea and offered it to Adriana, who did not so much sit as perch on the bench beside me like a wild bird who at a word might fly away. Caitrin had been full of praise for Adriana's service as an escort, including fending off a drunk who had lurched out of a doorway and vomited as he fell into her arms.

She went on. "I was bred up as a *cristoforo*, and as you know their views on sex are somewhat... limited, but I learned long ago to accept that the package love comes in is not what matters. Some of the Terrans are as rigid as the *cristoforos* about these things, but on Vainwal they have clinics where people change bodies like costumes. I don't know about their souls."

I took another sip of my own tea as I felt Adriana's body ease. She had always had a woman's soul. She sighed and rubbed her forehead. I suspected that she felt that the cabin, which had been a snug nest for three, was not really big enough for five. I was beginning to look forward to the day when she and Stelle could move back to Thendara House.

I turned to Stelle. "Are the Terrans' measures having any effect on the plague?"

She frowned. "The spread of the disease seems to be slowing, though I don't know what is happening in the areas under quarantine."

"In the tavern, they said that Dermot Sandoval, Zandru take him, has died," Cassi put in.

"Perhaps Zandru did," said Adriana. She shifted position uncomfortably and I moved again to give her more room.

"Some folk say 'twas the witches in the Guild-house gave it to him," Cassi went on, "but some of the men in the crowd looked sick. I'm thinking he brought it with him, the banshee-spawn!"

"One good result—if they know they can catch it from each other they won't be forming any more mobs..." Caitrin said dryly.

"Excuse me!" the bench lurched as Adriana got to her feet and hurried from the room. After a moment I followed her.

I found her on the back porch, vomiting over the rail, and held her, fear curdling in my own belly, until she straightened and wiped her mouth with the end of her shawl.

"I don't know what..." she said, shuddering.

"Darling, look at me—" I turned her face toward the light. In the house it had not been noticeable, but here I could see that the whites of her eyes already had a distinctly yellow tinge.

Ah...Goddess...no!

I thought I had made no sound, but suddenly Cassi was there, holding us both. After a moment Adriana began to push us away, moaning that it hurt. Joint aches, I thought, remembering what I had heard about the plague. I smoothed the sweat-soaked dark strands back from her brow.

"We'll put you to bed, *bredhiya*," I murmured, and then, "Cassi, get Stelle!"

For two days and nights we nursed Adriana as if we were fighting a war, with Stelle as our general. Another thing, I thought, to blame on men, since it was most likely the fellow she had thought drunk who gave her the disease. We made a pallet for her by the fire and plied her with endless cups of sweet, salty tea. But I could see that she suffered, and each day she seemed to lose ground.

On the third night I woke from an uncomfortable doze in the chair to the sound of singing.

Tell me o' Towers lookin' over the land,
Speak o' Thendara, so great an' so grand,

Eh, but 'tis better to walk the lang day,
To wander the hills o' the Hellers....

It was Caitrin who had the midnight shift today. She was singing an old song from the Hellers that she had learned while guiding explorers through those hills. My brother Donal used to sing it with her when he was a little boy. Her face was tender. *She has accepted Adriana as she did Cassi....* I thought in wonder. We had won that, at least, whatever else might befall.

An' 'tis westering home, wi' a song in the air,
Light in the eye, an' a goodby to care,
Laughter an' love, an' a welcoming there,
In the land o' my heart, my own one....

Then I stiffened, for a second, higher voice had joined my foster-mother's croon. Adriana was singing too, her voice little more than a breath, but there.

Where are the folk like the folk o' the west?
Canty, and couthy, and kindly, the best.
There I would take thee and there we would rest,
wi' my ain folk in the Hellers....

Stelle rolled out of the bed and stumbled to the bedside to feel Adriana's forehead.

"The fever has broken!" She lifted Adriana to give her some more tea. A smile like the rising sun illuminated Caitrin's face.

From that moment, Adriana began to get better. It was Caitrin who was the next to fall ill. Looking at her gaunt face I wondered how anyone could have confused the tan with which she had returned from Terra with the yellow of the plague. I tried to hold on to hope. Adriana had survived. But she was young, and Caitrin a woman of fifty. Almost as bad as the thought of losing her was the possibility that she had learned to love Adriana only to die.

It was early one morning, as I turned over the nursing to Stelle, that something the older woman had once said occurred to me.

"Didn't you tell me that when you were training with the Terrans, they injected you with protective medicines? How are such medicines made?"

"There are two kinds," said Stelle. "The Terrans have some that will cause a person's body to make what they call antibodies, so if it ever encounters the illness it will be immune. But such things take a long time to develop and test, and I think this plague is something new, which I suppose is why they have not tried to give us any."

"If our people would even consent to take them," said Adriana, sitting up in bed, "and not stone the nurses as witches. That's likely what would happen in the Hellers, to be sure."

"You said there's another kind—" I turned back to Stelle.

"What they call *passive* protection, made from the blood of someone who has survived the disease. The antibodies don't last, but they can protect for awhile, and help someone who is already sick to fight the disease." She frowned, remembering. Her training had been many years ago.

"Then some of my blood might help Caitrin, and protect all of you—" said Adriana.

"Not all blood is the same. Injecting it can kill if it is not the right kind. Most of our ancestors came from old Terra's Celtic lands. Over sixty percent of us have Type O positive blood, but without the Terran devices that let us see the cells, if someone didn't match we wouldn't know."

"With a matrix," I said, "we could see...." I drew out the silk bag that hung beneath my shirt. I had not used my starstone since I left the Tower, but I had enough *laran* to feel uneasy without it.

Stelle looked up, eyes suddenly intent, gaze going from Caitrin to Adriana and then back to me. "She's not getting better. Put some water on to boil and bring my bag. It will do no harm to try."

Stelle's bag proved to contain a number of things I had never seen before. When everything had been boiled, she jabbed Caitrin, then used a thin glass tube to transfer a drop to a porcelain plate.

Let me be whatever you need me to be... in Avarra's name. I could hear Adriana's thought as the blood welled beneath Stelle's blade. Slowly the two drops joined.

"Look now—" Stelle said to me.

"What should I see?"

"The blood cells will look like discs. If they stack up like coins on a moneylender's counter we're in trouble. But if they keep rolling around...." She managed a smile.

Nodding, I slid the blue crystal from its bag, I felt the lurch and drop of shifting awareness as I looked into pale light flickering there. I tried to look at the blood through the matrix, but could make no sense of what I saw. Then I felt strong hands grip my shoulders. *Adriana...* At her touch, my barriers went down entirely, and vision exploded in blue flame. When it steadied the world had become a thing of planes and lattices, with the starstone the most complex of all.

"What do you see?" The voice came from leagues away. I focused on the plate.

"Moving..." I whispered. "They're moving around...."

"They're not clumping?"

"No.... some close together, but not sticking at all...."

"Well...the Terrans say, 'Do no harm,' but I think we have to try."

"*Kiera, come back!*" Adriana did not speak aloud. I felt her touch on the crystal, and a fragment of awareness noted that she was the only one who could have safely taken it from my hand.

When I could focus again, Stelle was injecting a syringe full of Adriana's blood into the vein at the bend in Caitrin's arm. *Now,* I thought, *Adriana is Caitrin's daughter too.*

By the following morning, Caitrin looked better.

"Now, for the rest of you—" said Stelle. "Immunization

can help someone recover, but it would be better never to get the disease at all."

With practice, the process got easier. Stelle's brows went up when she realized that Adriana's blood worked for everyone. But she was part *chieri*, after all.

"What is a knife-oath to this?" Adriana grinned. She was still thin, but her face shone. "Now we are all truly kin."

As I laid my hand to the knocker on the Guild-house door, for a moment I was back in the day when Dermot Sandoval had gathered his fanatics to bring us down. But behind me stood my sisters, not a mob.

This morning Lassandra, her eyes already going yellow, had knocked at our door. There was plague in the Guild-house. Mhari had already died, and now Mother Doria was ill. They had asked for Stelle, but they were going to get us all.

I looked at Adriana. "Are you sure you want to do this? Will you give blood to women who rejected you?"

"To give a gift takes two," came her reply. "If they will receive, I am offering."

Caitrin snorted. "As the catman said to the banshee when they found themselves on the same ice floe, there's no peacemaker like necessity."

Then the door opened. Cora's eyes widened as she let us in, but she had little energy left for either hostility or wonder.

"Come this way—"

Mother Doria was sitting up in bed with a wax tablet on her lap, continuing to work by sheer will. But she had lost weight. Her face was yellowing, and drops of perspiration stood out on her brow.

"What are you all doing in here?" she growled. "Stelle is oath-bound to take her chances, but the rest of you should stay away."

"They will come to no harm—" said Stelle with a triumphant grin. She took Adriana's arm and drew her forward. "You had Terran medical training when you were young, so you will understand what I say. This girl has survived the plague, and her blood now holds antibodies that can protect others. She is a Universal Donor. We can use her blood to vaccinate you."

For the first time since I had known her, I saw Mother Doria amazed. Her gaze moved from Stelle to Adriana and back again.

"What if it kills her?" Cora exclaimed.

"We've all had it done—" I replied, and Stelle added, "It helped Caitrin, who was already ill..."

"It is important, I see," said Mother Doria, "that the gift should come from her. Stelle, you always did know how to make your patient choke down a bitter pill...." I remembered the Guild-mother's love of saying two things with one word and wondered if there had been another meaning here.

"But I can recognize the need for change when it stares me in the face, and I will lead the way." Mother Doria went on. She smiled at Adriana. "If you can help me, child, do so with my good will."

Stelle had already taken out the clean syringe. I watched in fascination as the life-giving liquid, ruby-red, filled the shaft. Then she changed needles and injected Adriana's blood into the old woman's arm.

For two days we waited, prisoners as Mother Doria grew a little worse, and saviors when she began to get better. After that, the rest of us were kept busy nursing the sick while Adriana gave her blood to protect the women of Thendara House against the Yellow Plague.

This morning I woke to the sound of sleet against the window-panes, and blessed the cold. The number of new cases of plague is going down. People still get sick, but in those households where the Renunciates trained by Stelle have volunteered to help with the nursing, more survive. It is doing wonders for our reputation.

For now this is all we can do. To reveal our secret would provoke a riot, so we dare not tell them why we do not fear.

The whole of Thendara House could not give enough blood to immunize them all, but the Terrans are using Adriana's antibodies to make a vaccine that will work for everyone

She and Cassi and I are still in the cabin. Mother Doria has invited us all to move back into the Guild-house, and the other women agreed, but we are not ready to leave the home we have made. Still, the midwives in the Neskaya Guild House were trained in Terran techniques long ago, and they are surprisingly open to change. If Adriana decides to take the Renunciate oath, we might go there for her house-bound year.

For now, it is enough to watch the changing colors as the rising sun scatters ruby drops across the window-pane.

THE TOWER

by Jeremy Erman

Jeremy Erman offers a more poignant reason to leave, deeper than the wish to escape or the dream of weaving together the best of both worlds: the yearning to preserve what is so rapidly being lost as the colonists of the "Lost Ship" struggle to adapt to life on Darkover. I was particularly delighted to receive a story set in those early years, a time period rich in possibilities but not often explored.

Jeremy's fiction has appeared in Daily Science Fiction *and his nonfiction at* Black Gate. *He has a degree in Music Composition from the University of the Pacific and works as a pianist and music director for schools and theaters in the San Francisco Bay Area.*

The winter I turned ten brought storms so fierce we were forced to stay indoors for weeks. Many people sickened and died, including my grandma, and we had to hurry outside during a lull in the storms to bury her, then hurry back inside when the storms returned. I didn't cry, for I wanted to be a strong girl, strong like Grandma, but I spent many evenings alone after that, sitting by the fire remembering how Grandma used to sit beside me and tell me stories in her dry, husky voice, stories of the distant world she had come from and could never return to.

Spring was almost as violent as winter, but finally eased into a summer warmer than any I'd known. After so much time indoors I was eager to be outside, so I went to my father as he oversaw the reroofing of the meeting house one afternoon and begged him to let me go walking in the forest.

He frowned. "By yourself? I'm not sure—"

"Grandma showed me all the paths," I said quickly. "I promised her I would go and plant flowers in her memory."

This wasn't true. Grandma had died before she could show me all the paths, but since she was gone, the only way I could keep her promise was to explore the paths myself.

Father looked at me, my eyes wide and sincere. "Well, you're clearly not going to be of much use here," he said. "Go if you must, but be careful. This warmth may bring the Ghost Wind, and that could cause more trouble than the storms if you're not ready for it."

I grimaced. The Ghost Wind had not blown in so long that I doubted it ever would again. My father frowned at my impatience, then laughed.

"Go!" he said. "Enjoy yourself! I'll tell your mother."

The forest was bright and green and damp-smelling, but I couldn't get the darkness of winter and spring out of my mind. It wasn't fair that Grandma had died and left me, breaking her promises. I was angry at her for leaving me, and angry at myself for moping indoors so long. I came to the end of the paths I knew and began to run, letting my muscles stretch after months of inactivity, taking in deep lungfuls of fresh air, faster and faster until the speed of my legs matched the speed of my thoughts.

Exhilarated, I came to a stop and realized I didn't know how I'd gotten where I was. I couldn't even tell if I was on a human path or an animal track. But the air was so warm, the birds so cheerful, that I barely worried. Surely I would find my way back.

I walked in what I thought was the right direction. The trees grew denser and nothing looked familiar. After an hour or so I walked out of the trees into a bright field. Low cliffs, outskirts of the higher mountains, rimmed the far side. Greenery tufted some of the rocks, but a low, bald bluff caught my attention. Something gleamed atop it like a spear of light. At first I thought it was just sunlight on rock, then realized it was more. A tower, like in fireside stories? A sheer, branchless tree? But it gleamed like metal.

Closer, I saw that it *was* metal, a latticework wider at the base than at the top. It was hard to tell how tall it was, but it looked taller than any building in the settlement, especially raised on the bluff as it was.

I came closer and saw a small wood house corniced with stone nestled under the cliff. It was definitely not my imagination.

I could not hold still. No one, as far as I knew, lived this close to the mountains. Who had made it? Were there other people on the planet we didn't know about? Was it the strange people the adults spoke of in whispers, the *chieri* with their powers of the mind? But the house looked human, not alien. Up close, I saw a fenced garden next to it and a path leading up the mountain.

I heard a shout from inside the house. A man came out, human but astonishingly old, older even than Grandma had been. He had a bushy gray beard and eyes that moved in a perpetual squint, as if he had spent too long staring into the giant red sun.

"Go away!" he growled. "Leave me alone!"

I gaped, unable to think of a response. Despite hunched shoulders and a limp, his arms looked thick and powerful, and I shrank instinctively from him.

"Didn't you hear me?" he demanded. "Go away!"

I found my voice. "No one's supposed to be out here," I said. "Who are you?"

His lips twisted as if the question were too private to answer, but then he said, "Lewis. Who are you?"

"Callie MacAran," I said. "I'm Mhari and Bertram's daughter."

His eyes narrowed as if he recognized the names, but all he said was, "How many are with you?"

"Six," I said, not wanting him to know I was alone. "I came ahead of the others."

He peered at me, then the forest behind me. "You're lying," he said. "You're alone. What are you doing out here? Why did they send you?"

"No one sent me," I said. "I didn't know you were here."

He growled softly like a frustrated animal. "Well, you might as well come inside," he muttered. "Let's get out of this damn bloody sun."

It was the strangest house I had ever been in. Scraps of metal and tools were scattered everywhere, on tables and floor, and a large piece of paper was pinned to the far wall, covered with extraordinarily straight lines and scribbled text. After a moment I realized it was a picture of the tower on the cliff.

Lewis brought two cups of water from an adjoining room. "Don't touch anything!" he said sharply.

I pointed at the picture. "That's the tower above your house," I said. "What is it?"

"None of your business!" he snapped, and I gasped and dropped the cup, spilling water on the floor. He made an angry noise, then sagged like a fallen leaf.

"I'm sorry," he said. "I've barely talked to anyone in years, and you're only a child." He pulled out a straight-backed wooden chair and gestured for me to take another.

"I got tired of living in the settlements, you see. We were all supposed to go along with the colonization, pretend that this was what we wanted, as if we'd never known anything else, as if we couldn't *want* anything else. But I felt like I was losing myself. I tried to fit in, do my part—I built things, fathered children, but no one would let me be who I was."

I'd never heard anyone talk like this. I barely had time to understand what he was saying before he plunged on.

"Do you know what it feels like to have everything you've ever learned become useless, to be told you must forget it because it doesn't apply?" He paused only a moment before continuing.

"No, of course you don't. You were born here. You're part of this planet. But I..." He clenched his teeth and turned away.

I wanted to make him feel better, so I said, "My grandma came on the ship. She used to tell me stories about it, and the world she came from."

Lewis calmed down. "Your grandmother. Of course she would."

"You knew her?" I asked.

"Of course. Everyone knew your grandmother. How is she?"

I was startled. For a moment I couldn't breathe, and then, to my dismay, the tears I had held back all winter and spring came pouring out. Lewis's eyes widened and he rose awkwardly to his feet.

"Callie!" he exclaimed, reaching for me. "What's wrong? What—?"

I sniffed heavily and glared at Lewis. "She died in the middle of winter," I said.

Lewis bowed his head. "I'm sorry," he said. "I didn't know...what happened?"

"She was ill," I said. "She coughed a lot."

"An infection," Lewis said. "God. On Earth a woman her age would never..." He sat down. My tears slowed and I wiped my eyes. Lewis exhaled, a tense hiss.

"So she's gone, and her memories with her. Memories are all we have left. The records were destroyed, all the files. They said we didn't need them." Sudden energy roused him from his seat. "But I remember! I have no computer, no recordings, but I know who I am and what I learned. I'm Lewis Saunders, a starship engineer, and no one can take that from me!" Bristling with energy, his gaze strayed to the picture on the wall.

"But what does the tower do?" I asked. "Does it help you remember?"

He stared at me suspiciously, a teacher not certain his pupil could be trusted. "It will let us talk to the stars," he said curtly. "Come. I'll show you."

We went up the path beside the house. The tower was not as precise as it had looked from a distance, or as the lines on Lewis's picture: metal pieces of all shapes and sizes had been attached to form a roughly rectangular latticework that rose higher than the buildings of the settlement, ending in straight, vertical pieces atop the rest of the tower. Lewis climbed the first few rungs with surprising ease.

"The ship is gone, but there are other ships out there. If one comes near, my antenna will pick up its signal, and I can send a message back. The ship will land and take us home!"

I shivered in astonishment. Was it possible? Was there a way back to the world Grandma had spoken of? I was excited and disturbed. But if it was possible, wouldn't the settlers have done so after they crashed? Yet Lewis spoke with absolute conviction, babbling on as if I wasn't there.

"—kept going back for more metal; it took years to build, mostly in the summer..."

I asked, "It can really send a message to a ship? To another world?"

"When I get the radio to work, yes. But the signal will be weak. That's why I need the antenna to be as tall as possible. I'll get it all to work, someday, and we'll go back to the stars!"

He stepped up another rung, staring skyward with feverish intensity. My unease grew. As much as I wanted to see the world Grandma had described, I wasn't sure I trusted Lewis. I slowly backed away, but suddenly he was on the ground beside me and grabbed my arm.

"Let me go! I have to go home!" I cried.

"No. Not until I'm sure you won't betray me. The others think I've been dead for ten years; I won't let you tell them about me."

"I won't tell, I won't tell!" I cried. "Just let me go!"

"Quiet!" he snapped unhappily, and his grip tightened. "Don't scream. They'll take apart my tower, don't you understand? All metal is to be used for colonization; Earth technology is to be abandoned; do you even know what an antenna is? A radio?"

I tightened my lips against the pain before answering. "No, but I'm sure Grandma did. She wouldn't like the way you're treating me."

He eased his grip and lowered my arm, but didn't let go

entirely. "Let's go inside," he muttered. "I don't like being outside when the sun sets."

Inside, he bolted the door before releasing me. I rubbed my arm and glanced sidelong at the door, but didn't see how I could open it without being caught.

"I don't want to keep you here, but I don't know what else to do," he said. "Why did you have to find me? I suppose they'll come looking for you if you're not back tonight."

"Probably," I said.

He frowned and rubbed his beard. "Maybe the Ghost Wind will blow and they'll be too distracted to search. I remember what it does all too well."

At the mention of the Ghost Wind I felt a hot rush of fear. "It will blow here, too. So close to the mountains...we'll be helpless against it!"

"No," Lewis said, "The Ghost Wind doesn't blow here; the cliffs redirect the wind and pollen north and east, toward the settlements. That's one of the reasons I settled here."

A haven safe from the Ghost Wind, at the edge of the mountains themselves. It seemed a fantastical notion, as fantastical as the idea of a tower that could contact the stars.

"So I guess we'll be together a while," Lewis said, not sounding pleased. "I'll get some food."

The food was terrible: scraggly vegetables, under-ripe fruit, and some kind of smoked meat. Whatever knowledge Lewis had from the ship, it didn't include cooking. I hoped this wasn't the kind of food Grandma had eaten as a child.

Lewis unstoppered a clay jar and poured himself a drink, then another. After a few cups he relaxed, the angry lines of his face softening and even his squint easing.

"It's not just technology we've lost," he said abruptly, the roughness gone from his voice. "Poetry, art...there's so much we haven't written down, but I remember...*I remember...*"

Although I hadn't had any of his drink, there was

something contagious about his mood. Despite the unsatisfying meal, I felt a pleasant glow, and my thoughts drifted lazily, as if there was nothing urgent about the situation.

"No one wants to remember!" Lewis raged, his voice slurring. He knocked over his cup, which clattered loudly on the table. Swaying, he lurched to the front window and unshuttered it, letting in a gust of fresh air. The ground outside was shadowed by the cliff, and the sky above the forest had the deep, red-tinged glow of late afternoon.

"Why forget everything?" he pleaded. "So much beauty...maybe our technology won't work, but what about poetry, art...? Why can't we keep those?"

He stared out the window, so still I wondered if he had fallen asleep on his feet. Then, quietly, he began to speak with a strange, lilting rhythm I had never heard before:

"But, soft! what light through yonder window breaks?
It is the east, and Juliet is the sun.
Arise, fair sun, and kill the envious moon,
Who is already sick and pale with grief,
That thou her maid art far more fair than she."

Lewis rounded on me, his jaw quivering. "Do you recognize that? Do you know what it means?"

I could only shake my head. The words were beautiful, but made no more sense than a dream.

"It is one of the greatest declarations of love ever written," he said. "Juliet was so beautiful, even in the moonlight, that all Romeo could compare her to was the rising sun itself. It speaks to that which is most beautiful, most important to us, but here the colonizers would have us throw it out, declare it as useless as our Earth technology."

"But I don't understand," I said, trying to remember the words. "Why compare someone to the rising sun—it's so big and red! Did Juliet look like that? And why would a moon be envious? The moons are much prettier than the sun!"

With a cry of frustration Lewis stumbled toward me and grabbed my chin with one hand. His grip was strong; his whole body trembled and his face contorted with emotions that seemed ready to overpower him. My heart pounded and I wanted to run but my limbs were frozen, held in place by a power I couldn't control. The colors in the room were brighter than before, almost dancing in their intensity, and there was a sweetness in the air that both calmed and excited me.

Lewis froze as well, and then his eyes widened in understanding. We stared at each other, hearts pounding, fear rising.

Then Lewis dropped his hand and stumbled back, catching himself on the table. "No!" he said hoarsely. "Not here!" He staggered to the door and unbolted it. "Go!"

Startled out of my daze, I stammered, "But, if I'm outside—"

"I don't want to hurt you if the madness comes. You must go! I'm sorry! But I implore you, don't tell the others I'm here!"

I met his eyes, recognizing the anguish there. Then I was out the door, across the field and into the forest. The light was dim under the trees, a murky red like blood mixed with dirt. The air was warm and sweeter than before, bringing back buried memories of huddling in Grandma's arms while wind and pollen raged outside. Through the panicked pounding of my heart, I wondered if there was any truth to Lewis's claim—would the full fury of the Ghost Wind avoid this area, blowing further north, or would it catch me unprotected as my father had feared?

I fought rising panic. I couldn't be more than a few miles from the settlement. But if I went in the wrong direction I might never find my way out of the forest—it was immense, and the next closest settlement was over a day away.

I fell to my knees on the hard, needle-covered ground, fighting to catch my breath. I didn't remember this place. The trees didn't look familiar, nor the fallen log on the slope above. I was well and truly lost.

But what did that matter? I had a sudden urge to jump to my feet and run, run in any direction I wanted, as long as the weather held, as long as I could...

No, I thought, that's not right. I need to go home. I can't get lost again!

I have to go home!

I breathed deeply to slow my racing heart. The air was sweet with pollen and leaves and sap, blowing gently against my cheeks. I felt stones digging into my legs and heard something rustle in the trees above, small and harmless. None of it threatened me; even the pollen, which had seemed so terrifying earlier, was only one element of a much greater whole, a living, breathing world I had lived in all my life. Why should I be afraid of it?

I breathed in deeper and deeper, taking in everything: the smells of the forest, the wind on my cheeks, the pollen floating down from the mountains. It swirled through me, ancient and wild, opening my mind to a vastness I had never experienced before.

And then there was a new sensation, throbbing through me with a gentle yet insistent current like a stream pulling me forward. I stood. Everything looked the same, yet somehow different. *That way is north,* I thought, *so I must go this way—east, towards the settlement.*

The urge to run was gone. I was certain of the way, the certainty shining in my mind as clearly as the difference between right and left. I *knew* the direction to go, and didn't question the knowing.

Warmth filled me even as the air cooled. A light rain began to fall, dampening the sweetness in the air. Focused on the glowing sense of direction in my mind, barely aware of my surroundings, I was mildly surprised when I came around the bole of a giant tree and found myself face to face with two people I knew.

"Callie!" Mariella McAllister exclaimed. She was a rugged, pleasant-looking woman in her mid-fifties, normally full of smiles, but now showing concern. "Thank

God we found you. Are you all right? The Ghost Wind was blowing!"

"I'm fine," I said. "I went further than I should, and got lost, and—" I clamped my lips shut. I had promised not to say anything.

Mariella's companion, Elsa, frowned, "A lot of bother you've caused us," she grumbled. She was a small, dour woman my parents' age who always seemed suspicious of children, but I was so relieved to have found people I knew that I didn't mind her grumpiness.

"I'm sorry," I said. "I was mad that Grandma wasn't here to show me the forest like she promised, and went farther than I should have."

Mariella's tension softened. "We're glad you're safe," she said. "Your parents will be very relieved."

I followed them down the path, but my thoughts went back to Lewis. Was he all right? What had happened to him, enduring the Ghost Wind for the first time in years?

I felt a strange twinge in my mind, as if the thought had tapped into something deeper. Uncomfortable, I ignored it and moved on.

He had asked me not to tell others, but hadn't said *I* couldn't come again. Wouldn't he want to know I was safe? I sensed that underneath his bluster he was very lonely.

"Why are you dawdling and looking behind you?" Elsa said irritably. "Did you drop something?"

I forced myself to look forward. Tomorrow, if the weather held, I would go see if he was all right, perhaps in the morning before everyone was up...

Back where? came a thought from deep inside. *Do you even know the way?*

Right now, my mind expanded by the Ghost Wind, the path I had taken from Lewis's house to this place was as clear as the lines on his picture. I could go back without hesitation. But the awareness was fading. Would it still be there tomorrow?

"Callie!" Mariella said, interrupting my thoughts. "Why are you standing so still? Are you all right?"

I hesitated. I had promised! But if my silence meant I could never go back, would that be worse than breaking my promise? Was it right to leave Lewis alone?

What would Grandma have thought of that?

The words came out before I realized what I was saying. "I need to go back," I said.

Elsa frowned. "Back where?"

"I can't tell you," I said.

"What?"

"I promised."

"What are you babbling about?" Elsa demanded.

I bit my lip. "I met someone and I want to make sure he's all right."

Mariella took a step toward me. "Callie, did someone hurt you...?"

"No!" I said, "but you can't come. He doesn't want to see anyone else."

Elsa stared at me as if I'd gone mad, but Mariella said gently, "Callie, we can't let you run off into the forest alone. Not after this afternoon."

"But I *promised*."

Mariella knelt in front of me. "Callie, if someone's in trouble you should tell us. We can help."

I sighed. "I was going to go back tomorrow, but I'm not sure I'll be able to find the way then. But I can go back now." I chewed my lip uncomfortably. "You can follow me."

"Where?" Elsa demanded. "Who is this person?"

Mariella said, "Why don't we let her take us there and then find out?" Elsa shook her head but said nothing.

The house was completely shadowed now, but the antenna stood out starkly on the outspurt of rock above, glittering in the rain. The two women stopped when they saw it. Elsa looked bewildered, but Mariella looked shocked beyond words, as if seeing something impossible.

"What is that?" Elsa said. "It looks like a building of metal!"

"He calls it an antenna," I said.

98

"An *antenna*." The strange word fell easily from Mariella's lips, and I remembered that, although she was much younger than Lewis, she had also come on the starship. "Callie, who lives here?"

I took a deep breath. "His name is Lewis Saunders and he came on the starship and wants to go home. He thinks he can contact another ship with his antenna."

Elsa gaped at me. "Madness! So much metal..."

"I think he stole the metal," I said reluctantly. "He's been working on it for years."

"Lewis Saunders," Mariella said slowly. "All right, Callie. Go ahead and see if he's all right."

The door was closed and locked, the windows shuttered and dark. I listened a moment, then called out, "Lewis, are you there? It's Callie. I wanted to make sure you're all right."

No reply. There was no smoke from the chimney, no sign of life, no sound other than the soft patter of rain. I glanced back, and the two women joined me.

Mariella said, "Lewis, are you in there? It's Mariella McAllister. You probably don't remember me, but I took care of your daughter after she broke her leg, and I was on the ship with you, thirty-eight years ago. I'm a friend of Callie's. I want to talk to you."

Silence. Mariella said, "There's no need to hide. We're friends."

Still nothing. Elsa, her lips pinched in frustration, burst out, "Open the door, damnit!"

There was a growl from inside. "Go away!"

Mariella frowned. "Lewis, if Callie found you, others can, too. They won't leave your antenna alone. The metal is too important to the colony."

Silence again.

"Very well," Mariella said, "but others will find you, and they'll have no reason to be kind."

The door opened. Hunched, scowling, Lewis said, "I asked you to leave, Mariella. I'm glad Callie is safe, but I have no interest in further conversation."

"That's not your decision to make, Mr. Saunders," Elsa said, pushing her way past us. "Like it or not, your actions fall under the jurisdiction of the colony council, and you must abide their rules like everyone else. Hoarding metal for personal use is a strict violation of those rules."

Mariella frowned at the interruption, but said, "Elsa's correct. You're still a member of this colony and must obey the rules like everyone else."

"I'll never be a member of this colony!" Lewis shouted, "and if you touch my antenna, or anything else that's mine, I'll...I'll send you packing to the underworld!"

Elsa snorted, but Lewis grabbed a bar of metal from a table and swung it at us.

"Get out of my house!" he raged. "I'm not one of you! I don't belong on this planet. I'll never be part of it!"

"There's no need for this," Mariella said. "Lewis, listen to me!"

Lewis ignored her and advanced on us, swinging the bar, but the weight seemed more than he expected, and the movement nearly pulled him to the floor. He righted himself and tried again, but he moved unsteadily and stumbled, nearly falling.

"Be careful!" I cried. "Lewis, you said you wouldn't hurt me!"

He backed up, looking warily from side to side, then dropped the metal bar when he reached the table and scrabbled behind himself until he found a knife. He held it out defiantly.

"Why did you have to come here?" he said, anguished. "I just wanted to be left alone!"

"This planet is harsh enough as it is," Mariella pleaded. "None of us can survive alone."

"I can try," he said, the knife shaking in his grip. "I can bloody well try to live like a man from Earth if I want to."

"No," I said, "you can't."

His face twisted with emotion as it had when I left him earlier. "What do you mean?" he said. "So you take their side now? I thought you understood me!"

The violence in the room seemed to be holding its breath, waiting to hear what I had to say.

"Grandma said the knowledge we had didn't work here, that we had to find new ways of doing things to survive," I said.

"No," Lewis said, "I don't accept that. If I build the antenna high enough, get the radio working, I'm bound to contact a ship. The colonists are just superstitious because they want to stay here."

"No," I said. "You proved them right. The only reason you were able to live out here for so long and have the strength to build your antenna was because the Ghost Wind gave it to you."

The knife dropped from Lewis's fingers. "No!" he shouted.

"The Ghost Wind drives us mad, shows us things that aren't there, but it also opens our minds, isn't that what you say?" I said, turning to Mariella. "It opens our minds to things we couldn't do before we came to this planet, to things we didn't know we could do, the things the *chieri* can do." I faced Lewis again. "You wanted the strength to build a tower to call the starships, and when the Ghost Wind blew, it opened your mind to that strength and made it real, just like it helped me find the way home when I was lost today."

"No," Lewis shouted. "No! Today was an aberration. The Ghost Wind has never blown here before. I have nothing to do with the Ghost Wind and its perversions!"

"You're using it," I said. "It's affected you just like it's affected the rest of us, it just doesn't blow here as strongly as it does elsewhere. Look how weak you are now that it's gone."

He stared at me, his mouth open and his hands trembling. "I thought...I thought..."

"You're part of this world, just like the rest of us."

Lewis sagged against the table, then crumpled to the floor with a small moan.

"I just wanted to go home," he said.

Elsa looked away. Mariella sighed and went up to Lewis.

"What are we going to do with you? You know there won't be any starships in our lifetimes."

"I had to try," he muttered. "I had to try." His face was pale. Frowning, Mariella felt his pulse.

"You're very weak. You've exerted yourself far too much. You need to lie down. Do you have anything to rest your head on?"

"What do you care?" Lewis said. "No one cared before, just told me to do as they say and forget everything I know."

"Well, if you'd been sensible and not wanted to build useless things—" Elsa began.

"That's not fair," I said. "He was just trying to be himself."

"Callie," Mariella said gently, "you shouldn't encourage him."

"Why not?" I said. "Maybe the antenna was foolish, but you shouldn't be mad at him for remembering who he is. Maybe you needed to forget a lot after the crash, to survive, but aren't we past that now?"

"What would you have us do?" Elsa said. "Let every mad fool who won't forget Earth build whatever he wants? You said yourself that won't work."

"No," I said. "But you can't stop people from remembering. The memories are part of us. Grandma told me stories about where she came from even though she knew she couldn't go back. She couldn't bear that they be forgotten entirely."

Mariella sighed. "Will you come back to the settlement with us?" she asked Lewis. "I'm sure your children will be glad to see you. And you have grandchildren you've never met."

"I don't know," Lewis muttered. "Maybe. They were put off by my strange ways. I don't know if they'll want to see me."

"I'll see you," I said. "You can tell me your stories. I know they're only stories, that we can't go back, but I'd like to hear them."

Lewis took a deep breath. He put his hands on the ground and struggled to rise.

"You shouldn't move," Mariella said. "You're still weak."

"I'm not infirm," Lewis said irritably. "Let me stand."

We helped him to his feet but he shook off our hands and shuffled over to the wall. He stared at the picture of his tower for a long moment, then tore it down and came back to us.

He held it out to me. "Take it," he said.

I hesitated, surprised. "But it means so much to you. You should give it to your family. Your children and grandchildren will want to see it when you tell them where you've been."

"No," Lewis said. "They won't understand. Keep it. Give it to *your* grandchildren someday. Tell them my stories, and your grandmother's."

I took the paper, with its carefully-drawn picture and scribbled words, and looked up solemnly at Lewis.

"I will," I said, and the corners of Lewis's mouth crept up tentatively in the first smile I had seen from him.

STONEFELL GIFT

by Marella Sands

"Gift" can mean both something freely transferred and accepted, whether between people or worlds, or the Darkovan psychic talents known as laran. *In this powerful story, Marella Sands explores such a Gift and its terrible consequences.*

After being raised in St. Louis by a family of African pygmy hedgehogs, Marella Sands went off to school to study anthropology and earned two degrees in the subject, even though neither institution she attended makes accommodations for insectivore-Americans. She sold two books to Tor that were set in 4th century Mesoamerica, and most recently has published a paranormal fantasy/romance, Pandora's Mirror, *from Word Posse. When she is not writing or doing volunteer work such as sitting on the Board of Directors of a cemetery, Marella teaches at Webster University, where her classes have discussed issues such as cannibalism, the origins of vampires, and the bloodthirsty creatures like the Kinderfresser who have, over time, morphed into today's jolly Santa Claus. Marella has encouraged her classes to eat her—assuming she is already dead—should she and the students ever find themselves in dire straits.*

Three riders on chervines came over the saddle pass, their mounts picking their way carefully through the mid-summer snow and the rocks. Allista could hardly contain her curiosity; she couldn't remember the last time riders came over the pass to the mountain valley where Stonefell Keep nestled against the craggy knees of the Far Hellers. Their nearest neighbors did not keep chervines—the animals did not survive the winters here—so these people must be from farther away. Even, possibly, the lowlands; to Allista, a half-mythical place no one she knew had ever actually seen.

"They're lucky they got here today. I think we'll have a storm by tomorrow," said her brother Ailos. His bright silvery hair glimmered in the crimson light of the noonday sun.

Allista studied the sky but predicting the weather was not her gift. Ailos was the best the family had at weathercasting, but even he wasn't always right. Ailos, like many in the family, was much stronger at pushing plants to mature early, a decided advantage in this valley where summers were ridiculously short and winters foul. The family would have starved long ago if they'd had to depend on the plants to ripen naturally.

"We should inform Mother Rakhalla," said Allista. She pulled her coat tighter around her shoulders. It had fallen open, and the early afternoon breeze which slid down the slopes into the courtyard carried a scent of frost.

Allista caught a glimpse of one of the mothers in the window of the room on top of the tower. Loose, waist-length silver hair identified the figure as Mother Ranila. Allista suppressed a small shudder; although the rest of the family adored the upper room in the summer where daylight lingered a few extra minutes before the sun disappeared behind the screen of mountain peaks, Allista did not go up there. She had tripped down the stairs once as a small child and since then, had avoided the tower altogether. Sometimes, she rued the small bits of daylight she missed, but not enough to brave the stairs.

"Mother Ranila will already have seen them," said Ailos calmly; he, too, had noticed the figure in the window. Ailos never got upset about anything, or excited, either. His absolutely calm temperament was a blessing and a rarity in a family given to nearly uncontrollable fits of temper. Short winter days in Stonefell Keep were routinely filled with loud arguments when entertainments were sparse and the cold brutal even in the intimate family quarters, no matter how many fires were lit.

Every winter Grandsire Corinn claimed was even worse

than the one before, and that *this* time no one would survive, but every year they did. Barely. This year, the food had nearly run out by spring, and rations had been instituted, but the return of longer daylight hours and the efforts of Ailos and the others had brought new fruit and grain to the dinner table before they truly began to suffer.

One day soon, Allista hoped to help them in their labors. In the family, it was the girls who had the strongest powers, but also who died most often of threshold sickness. If she could just achieve puberty, Allista should become—if Mother Rakhalla were right—the strongest in the keep. She would be able to help the family survive. Provided she survived first.

Excitement at the thought of maturity was therefore tinged with apprehension, if not outright panic, for it would not be long now. She had grown taller over the winter, despite the poor fare, and the new way Ailos and her other brothers looked at her was more than enough proof that womanhood would not be long in coming. By next year, Allista would be a full-fledged adult member of the community. Or she would be dead, her bones picked clean by the *kyorebni* on the peaks behind the keep.

But as of today, she was still underage, a child to be indulged, and Ailos was always willing to spoil her.

"Let's meet them at the gate," said Allista, even though she knew it was proper for an adult to greet the visitors first. She counted on Ailos not to gainsay her.

He surprised her by hesitating. "We don't know who they are," he said. "Perhaps they aren't friendly. You should remain in the Keep and let Rafael or Rumal meet them. Or even Corinn or Callum."

A flare of anger rose up in her, and she frowned. But the thought that Ailos considered her a woman in need of his protection was pleasing, even if it were, in this particular instance, annoying, and that made it easier to put her anger aside. After a few moments, she sighed and nodded.

Ailos had seen her face, though, and relented with a worried smile. Allista had once heard him and Mother

Ranila whispering their fears of Allista's coming threshold sickness, and the uncontrollable rages that sometimes came with it. Ailos had almost died of threshold sickness himself, and had even attacked Grandsire Callum in a fit of illness; it made him especially fearful for her, Allista knew.

"Why don't we go down and wait for someone to come to greet the visitors, and we can be right behind them? No one could object to that," he said, clearly willing to indulge a childish fancy from a sister he could very well lose any day now.

Allista shoved her own fears aside, grinned, and grabbed his hand. "Of course, no one would mind. And we should greet our guests like proper hosts."

The two of them headed down the staircase toward the main courtyard, Ailos uncharacteristically taking the lead, another sign he felt Allista was more woman than child. Children could be allowed to run unimpeded or unremarked-upon, but women were to be protected, even from dashing headlong down flights of stairs in excitement.

Mother Rakhalla and Father Rafael were already in the courtyard. Rakhalla's hands rested on her huge belly. This was to be her last pregnancy, as she had already given the family two living children. The five miscarriages after her last successful pregnancy had been mourned, but now the family would finally have that last child, the third, that every woman of the family wanted so desperately to produce.

Next summer, that could be me, thought Allista with a heartfelt thump of panic-tinged joy. She just had to survive, and mates and motherhood could be hers. Would be hers.

The three chervines walked tiredly into the courtyard, heads hanging. The steep climb to the keep and the altitude were always hard on visitors, even their beasts. The riders themselves were bent over in weariness as much as their mounts, and they had not even had to carry anyone on their backs!

When the hoods of the visitors were thrown back, Allista was momentarily shocked enough to gasp. These people were so odd! Eyes of blue and hazel, black hair and brown, faces rounded, bodies plump. The people of Stonefell were, to a person, tall, thin, and angular with silver hair and near-white eyes. Allista had heard stories of people who looked different, but hadn't really given the matter much thought. Everyone she knew looked just like her.

It was clear the visitors were a bit bewildered as well. Father Rafael stepped forward and smiled benignly. "Welcome to Stonefell Keep. I am Rafael, and this is Rakhalla. You are welcome to the blessings of hearth and home and the fires which will be kindled to warm you while you remain with us." Indeed, the visitors looked chilled to the bone, even on a warm midsummer day such as this.

"Thank you for your hospitality, *vai dom*," said a dark-haired man whose hair was cut very short. The men of Stonefell wore their hair long, for warmth on their necks, but this man showed bare skin from chin to collarbone. No wonder he was cold. "I am Harlan MacAvoy, envoy of *Dom* Aldaran. My companions are Doric Eskeray and Kaitura Mellian-Eskaray."

Allista frowned at the odd greeting. What did *vai dom* mean? And what odd accents these people had, not to mention their alien names. She could hardly credit them with coming from the same world as she.

Mother Rakhalla seemed to be wondering the same thing, but she did not let much of her consternation reach her face. Allista could only see it because she knew Mother so well. "Your speech is strange, Harlan MacAvoy," she said evenly. "We who live at Stonefell are not much acquainted with the ways of the rest of the world; you must excuse our manners if we seem too rustic or do not have the latest news."

All three of the visitors sketched a bow, but again, it was the dark-haired man who spoke for them. "Your hospitality is much appreciated, and I am sure we can find no fault in your welcome. The cause of our errand will require some time to relate, and should be given to the entire family, and it is indeed about news of the world."

"Of course we could not expect you to reveal the reason for your errand here in the courtyard!" Rakhalla gave a small laugh, the one that made all the men in the family smile at her in adoration, but Harlan seemed oblivious. "Allista, please show our guests to the rooms in the gatehouse." She extended a hand to show the visitors which building she meant. "These are the warmest rooms we have and gather the first rays of daylight when the sun tops the eastern peaks. I hope they meet with your approval."

The visitors made sounds of appreciation and thanks, and Mother Rakhalla turned awkwardly and walked back into the family compound.

Ailos looked down at Allista but she shook her head. "She needs you more."

Ailos hesitated, but even he could see how wearying this pregnancy was on Mother. He nodded and retreated into the compound. As Mother rounded the corner, Ailos caught up with her and took her arm in his. Father Rafael, meanwhile, kept his eye on the visitors and nodded to Allista, "See them to the gatehouse, *chiya.*"

Allista turned back to her charges and smiled warmly. They smiled, but their eyes seemed haunted by something. "Are you quite well?" asked Allista as she led them across the courtyard. "I suppose that's rude, but I know you are not used to our weather."

Kaitura, the lone woman, whose hair was like darkest bronze touched with frost, shook her head as she scanned the courtyard. "No, we are quite well. It's just that, well. We knew conditions here at Stonefell were remote and primitive, but, really, we had no idea. How are *you*, child? This must be a lonely place in which to grow up."

That made Allista laugh. "Lonely? But my family is here. All my brothers and sisters, and mothers and fathers, and grandsires and granddams."

"All of your *mothers and fathers*?" asked Kaitura with a swift intake of breath.

But her companion Doric interrupted her. "This is quite interesting, actually, because we have never been to

Stonefell before, and its ways are strange to us." He gave Harlan a strange look Allista could not interpret. "But we should rest for a while, and then tell our news to everyone at once."

Allista was disappointed not to learn more of the strangers, but at least she could find out why they were here over dinner. She stopped at the gatehouse and opened the door. "Here are rooms where you may stay. I will see you at dinner."

The three entered the gatehouse and closed the door behind them without further comment.

Allista would have thought everyone would want to see the strangers, but dinner was a sparsely-attended affair. Mothers Rakhalla and Ranila, Fathers Rafael and Rumal, and Grandsire Corinn, had come to take their regular seats, but Ailos was the only sibling in attendance. When Allista gestured toward their empty seats, he shrugged. "They weren't interested."

The food was already on the table, and while it was not as rich a banquet as could be served in a few weeks at the full harvest, Allista thought proudly that the family had nothing to be ashamed of, considering how little they had much of the year. The visitors made no mention of the food, and ate sparingly.

"Are you quite well?" asked Ranila of Harlan, who sat on her right, a place of honor. "Or is our food so different from your regular fare?"

A tight smile crossed Harlan's face and he bowed in his seat. "Indeed, I am quite well, *domna*. The altitude is affecting all of us, I think. I am sure we will regain our appetites shortly. For now, it is difficult enough to breathe, let alone eat."

Doric put down his knife and said, "I, for one, do not mind admitting I am unfamiliar with this vegetable, and that red fruit there. I assume they are native to the area?"

"Yes, they are local foods," said Ailos in his unruffled manner. "I didn't know they were unknown in the lowlands, though. Perhaps we could find a way to send some with you, as a gift." He did not mention that every fruit borne away from this place would be a piece of fruit the family would be deprived of this winter, but duty to guests was important.

Who cared about fruit, though, when news was to be had! "Please, friends, what is it you wish to tell us?" Allista blurted out. That earned her a reproving "*Allista!*" from Father Rafael, but still, all the adults looked at the strangers in expectation, now that the subject had been broached.

Mother Rakhalla tried to make the request more courteous. "Please excuse Allista. The young are so impatient. But I'm sure we would all like to hear your news. And, of course, in return, you may let your own mothers and fathers know of our eternal good will and friendship with the Domains here in Stonefell Keep."

Again, the intake of breath from Kaitura, but Doric and Harlan kept their composures. Still, Allista felt they, too, were shocked, though she could think of no reason why.

"Actually, this is part of the news we bring," said Harlan. "But perhaps you could explain a few things to me first of your own customs, so that I might know how best to present our news to you."

Allista shared a look with Ailos, who shook his head. "We do not know what you do not know of us, and so cannot answer so broad a question."

"Then answer this," said Kaitura before Doric or Harlan could speak again. "What do you mean, *all of your mothers and fathers*? Are you truly living in the old style?"

"We live as we always have," said Rakhalla. "Every generation here mates within itself. We distinguish the generations with the initial letters of our names. Everyone in my childrens' generation has a name which begins with A. Besides Allista and Ailos here, we also have Alisande, Ayella, Averon, Ardos, Aberlain, and Alcor. This child," here she patted her belly, and Fathers Rafael and Rumal smiled at her, "will be the last of that generation. I will name her Avila."

"But everyone lives like that," protested Allista. "Your news is much more interesting than such ordinary things, surely!"

The three visitors again exchanged strange looks. "No," said Harlan softly. "You are among the last who are keeping to the old ways. Your remoteness means you have not heard of the changes that have been taking place elsewhere for several generations now."

"Even if our neighbors have changed their ways, there is no reason we need to," said Rafael, a thread of anger in his voice. Of all the fathers, Rafael had the worst temper and the strongest talent. If the visitors made him angry, he would be difficult to live with while they were here, and possibly for weeks thereafter. Allista bit her lower lip and waited to see if he would control himself. Usually, he could. Usually.

"No, I suppose you do not need to, but there are reasons to make some changes," said Harlan. He placed his hands on the table in front of him and leaned forward, his body language stiff and formal, though he kept his voice calm. "The inbreeding practiced at Stonefell Keep—and elsewhere—has led to the concentration of a great many lethal genes. More and more children die before they are born, or from threshold sickness, and too many women die a-bearing. The lords of the Domains have instituted new customs to try to weed out the lethal genes and breed in the useful ones, ones that will save our children and our women." He closed his eyes a moment, pain crossing his face.

Allista's heart went out to him. Three of her mothers had died trying to birth her generation, and all her granddams but one rested in Avarra's arms. The men died on the slopes in accidents, but it was the women who had the more dangerous road and suffered the most grievously.

"You know a way to keep more women alive?" asked Mother Rakhalla.

"Yes," said Kaitura. She held up a wrist, and showed off

a copper bracelet. What struck Allista about Kaitura's hand, though, was its deformity. She had only five fingers on each hand, unlike the Stonefell folk, who always had six. A quick glance showed that Doric and Harlan were similarly short of the right number of digits. "Doric and I are married *di catenas*." Seeing the blank looks of the family, she glanced at Doric, who held up his own bracelet-encircled wrist. Kaitura continued, "That means one man mated to one woman. The bracelets are a symbol of this. By breeding only within marriage, we can keep track of what genes are present in a bloodline. Within only a few generations, we hope to avoid breeding the most lethal of the genes into future generations. By breeding your daughters to young men of other lines, you can save their lives, because sometimes too much inbreeding causes not only miscarriages, but the deaths of the breeding mothers as well. Outcrossing can do away with the greater portion of that threat. A greater portion, but not all, because your pedigree is unknown to us, and Avarra does not grant guarantees."

"For this program to work, though, we *must* know the pedigree of everyone involved," said Doric. "Then genes can be traced through the lines and only the most efficacious combinations allowed." He glanced at Kaitura. "The Eskarays are gifted with a small amount of telekinesis, but when we breed too closely with other Eskarays, the children die of threshold sickness every time. When we outcross with others, though, the children survive. Thus my marriage to Kaitura."

"What of your heart?" asked Mother Rakhalla. "Women of our family may only lie with their own generation, it is true, but within that limit, they may share the bed of whomever they like. If you are tied to one man for life, do you at least get to choose the man?"

Kaitura straightened in her chair. "It is the duty of every daughter of the Comyn to wed where she is bid."

"Fortunately, my face was not unappealing to her," said Doric. He smiled at Kaitura, but smile he received in return was tight-lipped and formal.

Allista's heart pounded in rebellion. What nonsense was this, that a woman should be so restricted?

Father Rumal snorted. "This is some ridiculous lowland idea. One breeds chervines to a pedigree, not people. We are a family. We are one, and we will not be changing our ways any time soon."

Mother Rakhalla looked troubled. "Still, if it would keep Allista safe, keep her from dying in the birthing bed, wouldn't it be worth it?"

"Would you see her *married*," Father Rumal spit out the word Kaitura had used as if it were a curse, "Separated from family, alone among strangers? Sharing the bed of someone we do not know? Bearing children to another family? Never to call Stonefell Keep home again?" He turned to Kaitura. "Or am I remiss? Is it the men who marry who leave their families, or, as I suspect, is it only the women who do so?"

Kaitura wilted slightly. "Usually, it is the women who leave their families. It's not always that way, but it would be difficult to convince most men to come to Stonefell Keep when Allista, or one of her sisters, could come to them instead." Her voice was heavy and she did not look at Doric. Allista could guess that no young lordling would want to come to Stonefell Keep when it did not have wealth or influence, or anything beyond a green valley and poor rations in winter to recommend it. No lowlander would want to stay here through the dark of the year, when it was clear that even the warmest days of midsummer were too cold for them.

Father Rumal nodded and slapped a lean six-fingered hand on the table, his anger, too, reddening his face. "You see, they would take Allista from us, and all the children—Alisande and Ayella. And, someday, Avila, too," he added, glancing at Rakhalla's swollen belly. "We are only strong because we are one. Our visitors would change that for the wishes of this *Dom* Aldaran, who seems to think he lords over us."

"We should at least consider their words," said Ranila.

"We shall do no such thing!" Father Rumal stood so quickly, his chair overturned behind him. His hands shook with rage, and Allista cringed in her seat, any hunger forgotten in the desire to avoid the consequences of Father Rumal's fury.

"We have the family," said Father Rumal. "We are strong. They want to weaken us, to take Stonefell Keep from us." He turned stiffly to the guests. "I will not violate the laws of hospitality, but I will not be so duplicitous as to wish you stay longer than absolutely necessary. Good evening to you. We will not meet again."

Rumal swept out of the room, furs trailing the floor. Mothers Rakhalla and Ranila looked abashed and followed quickly while Grandsire Corinn merely ate his food without comment.

It was up to Father Rafael to break the silence. His anger was more controlled, but Allista could sense that Rafael's control was nearing its breaking point. Fear faded as her own anger began to surge within her, as well. A trickle of power flicked along the back of her mind and began to build, promising power and fury, but also savage destruction. Allista feared it, but its warmth beckoned her to let go of self-control. The temptation was strong, so strong.

"If you find there is anything else you require, please let us know." Upon those words, Rafael, too, stood and left the room, though with more decorum than his siblings and mates.

Allista sat, fighting the ire sparked by the news the outsiders brought. Leave Stonefell? Bed someone besides one of her brothers? She had always known Ailos and her other brothers would be her mates, the fathers of her children, should Avarra bless her with any that survived to be born. Leaving Stonefell Keep forever to live with another family and bear children to some stranger she had never before met—that was madness. Could it really be that the rest of the Domains were changing over to this custom?

Allista balled her fists, tempted to scream or yell at the visitors, anger warring with confusion and fear. Ailos shot her a look tinged with terror for her safety, and grabbed one of her hands. She concentrated on the warmth of his skin, the strong support of his shoulders brushing against hers. Family was everything. She could never be made to leave. She would never accept a life other than the one she had always been promised.

Harlan stood and bowed to her and Ailos. He also bowed to Corinn, though Grandsire was now asleep at the table. "We will withdraw to our rooms and see you in the morning. Good night."

Ailos stood as well and bid the strangers good night, though he kept his tight grip on Allista's hand. It was all Allista could do to stare at their guests' retreating backs and wish bitterly they had never come.

The next morning dawned frosty but fine. A few snowflakes could be seen wafting around the nearby peaks, but the storm Ailos had predicted did not come. Allista did not even bother to tease him as she normally would have. She had other concerns.

"Would you really send me away?" she asked Ailos, voicing her thoughts without preamble. "If the mothers and fathers decided to change our ways, would you see me go away forever?"

Ailos' silver-white eyes darkened and he caught her in a fierce hug. "No, never, *chiya*. You belong to me and to all of us. I would sooner be parted with my right arm than with one of my sisters and mates."

Allista leaned against him, welcoming the embrace. Her family was all she had known, all she knew to be loyal to. This keep was her home. She had been beyond its gates only briefly, on summer afternoons, to clamber on the nearby slopes and hunt for pretty rocks or other childish treasures like a *kyorebni* feather or some long-forgotten toy left out to brave the elements by one of her brothers or even, perhaps, one of her fathers during his own childhood.

She had not done that in seasons now, Mother Rakhalla unwilling to risk the family's youngest daughter to childish misadventure. And, truth be told, Allista did not miss it that much. Her life was bounded by the walls of the keep, and that was enough for her.

A small figure exited the gatehouse. Kaitura. Allista watched the woman as she walked hesitatingly around the courtyard. Every so often she stopped and closed her eyes and appeared to be deep in concentration. At other times, she peered wide-eyed and haltingly in every corner as if expecting to find something foul and dangerous.

"If she wants to spy on us, the courtyard hardly seems the place to learn anything by stealth," laughed Ailos. "Well, I believe I heard Alisande calling me. No doubt that the first few moons of pregnancy are the worst for everyone, but at least I only have to fetch things and listen to her complaints. She must bear the greater burden, as well as the rebellious stomach."

"Wish her a good day for me," said Allista. They had all been thrilled with Alisande quickened, and she had already pronounced she would name her daughter Tirza, thus constraining her sisters to choosing names for their children beginning with T. Allista wished Alisande had picked L because she wanted to name a daughter Layla. She and Alisande had argued about it, but in the end, it would be as Alisande wished. She who bore the first of the new generation had the right of it.

Allista watched Kaitura for a few more minutes, but did not have the heart to continue spying on the woman. Instead, she left the shadows and walked across the courtyard, her furred jacket tumbling from her shoulders like a mountain waterfall. She thought about leaving it behind—the weather was so fine today—but the threat of snow still hung in the air, even if the storm had not come.

Kaitura straightened when she saw Allista approaching and bowed slightly. "Good morning."

"Good morning," said Allista. "Did you sleep well?"

"Yes, thank you," said the other woman, but her

thoughts betrayed her. *The bed was hard, the fireplace cold. I will never be warm in this place!*

Allista suppressed a surge of elation that her gift was beginning to show itself. Her family had little telepathy, but the development of that small gift always presaged the greater gifts to come. Yet, more than that, if the minds of the strangers became open to her, she could find out anything she needed to know.

"It is not so easy, to read minds," said Kaitura. When Allista startled, the brown-haired woman smiled sadly and said, "Telepathy works both ways, child. Your thoughts are open to me as mine are to you. I can see clearly enough you have no intention of leaving Stonefell—no, not even to play on the rocky slopes just beyond the gate!"

Allista reddened in humiliation. "I didn't mean to be rude."

"No, you only meant to wonder how strong you would have to be to force telepathic communion on me," said Kaitura without heat, but Allista sensed a sharp blooming of the woman's interest in her. Kaitura continued. "All telepaths wonder it at some point, when their abilities first show themselves. But come, take a walk with me, and tell me more of Stonefell. I would see it through your eyes."

That would at least be a welcome change in topic. Allista led Kaitura up the stairs to the top of the keep's outer wall. The other woman was winded by the time they reached the parapets.

"By Evanda and Avarra, I have never felt so weary," said Kaitura almost inaudibly.

"But the view is perfect today, so you will be well rewarded," said Allista. "Look!"

Indeed, the small verdant valley that Stonefell Keep overlooked was a brilliant emerald in the midst of the snow-laden Hellers. No one was about yet in the fields, but that was to be expected. Once set in motion, the accelerated growth due to the gifts of the family could be maintained with minimal interference.

"If I may ask," said Allista, curious about the other

118

woman for her oddness, her strange customs, and her rounded alien features, "why did you agree to be bound to Doric? You do not seem to like him very much, from what I can see."

"He's a good man," said Kaitura, which didn't answer the question at all. "But I have a question of my own—how does the valley stay so green this far up in the mountains? Is this the result of the family's *laran*?"

"Our what?"

"Your gifts."

"Oh. Yes, most of us have the gift of making things mature out of season. A plant can go from seed to fruit in only a few weeks—a few days even, depending on the plant and the talent of the family member. Ailos is very skilled."

"I can see that," but Kaitura's voice was hollow and she sounded frightened, which made Allista wonder how terrifying a green valley could possibly be. Lowlanders were strange. "But what about you? Do you know what your gift is?"

"A few of us—always the girls—are good at *seeing*. I don't know how else to describe it."

"I don't know of a gift by that name. Describe it to me."

Allista didn't like the tone of command in the other's voice, but she had no reason not to answer. "It means we can see what we wish, at least for a short time. If granddam wanted to tell you a story, she would create the characters in front of you for a few minutes, until the story was finished. It is not a very practical gift, but it can make winter afternoons pass more quickly."

"That sounds like a very odd form of telepathy—being able to insert one's thoughts into another's mind as pictures rather than words. I can see how that would be welcome in the winter. The cold and dark must be extreme. Life is very precarious here."

"We manage. We survive."

"But don't you want to do more than survive? There is an entire world out there, with people, and schools, and matrix technology, and other gifts, and the Towers."

"The what?" Little of what Kaitura said made sense. Allista felt dizzy, as if the gulf between her and Kaitura were too deep to be crossed without falling.

"Never mind. But I assure you, there are wonders out there in the world. My favorite is the Lake of Hali, which is filled with clouds. The sound of them against the shore is...I cannot describe it."

But Allista could hear the sound well enough in the other's mind, the slow rolling of the not-clouds against the banks. *Home*, thought the other woman with pangs of longing. *When will I see it again?*

Allista laughed. "You are homesick, but you mock me for not wanting to leave Stonefell? You'd go home if you could."

"If I could," Kaitura said sadly.

"Then don't think you can convince me to leave."

Kaitura glanced around her. "I'm not sure I can, in good conscience, consent to stop trying to convince you. But we shall see. Thank you for showing me the valley. I must attend to my companions now." Kaitura fled down the stairs and across the courtyard, the intensity of her thoughts now chaotic and almost too strong for Allista to be near.

Allista rubbed her temples and fought the anger that threatened to blossom in her mind as a headache settled in behind her eyes. These lowlanders and their strange ways, which they thought were so much better than Allista's own! She would go down and tell them they had to leave, no matter the duty to guests. She went down the stairs and walked straight up to the gatehouse. Voices came from within and she paused to listen before barging in.

"...I'm not sure what it is," Kaitura was saying softly to her companions. "But something is not right here. A strong spell is woven among the stones, even in the very air. It is strongest around the girl."

"She's clearly almost a woman," said Harlan. "She's on the brink of threshold sickness, that much is clear. But she seems innocent of much knowledge of *laran*."

"I don't think any of them have any idea of what their *laran* really means. They live with it, and often die of it, and that is the end of the matter as far as the family is concerned."

"*The family.* I admit, every time I hear one of them say that, it makes me shiver. It is not natural, how they live here."

Not natural? Allista's anger surged upward and her headache grew worse. The throbbing in her head was becoming unbearable. If only Ailos were here to comfort her.

"Our families lived by such customs not so many generations ago, so don't get self-righteous," said Doric. "It will be difficult to convince them to change. *Dom* Aldaran will not be happy to hear of their refusal. His *laranzu* is just itching to start a pedigree chart for Stonefell."

"And Allista is of an age to be wed to his youngest son," said Kaitura bitterly. "Oh, don't protest, Doric. I'm fully aware we're here to look for a likely bride for Valentin."

"Well, and why not?" asked Doric, exasperated, it would seem, at his partner's reluctance. "Breeding Aldaran to Stonefell—can you imagine what might happen in only one or two generations? We know nothing of this gift; what if it could be used in combination with a diluted version of the Aldaran gift? What if you had one child who could predict the weather, and another who could make things ripen out of season? *What if those gifts could be held by the same person?* Imagine someone who could know when winter will strike and make sure the crops get in before the first frost? And what else could you do—bring a beast to term overnight and breed it two or three times a year? Foresee the danger of a pregnancy ending in miscarriage, and then use this gift to make the unborn child old enough to survive outside the womb before it has a chance to kill itself, and its mother? Think of it! The Lords of the Domains are, if you are not, and Allista will be sought after by everyone, and not just younger sons. Not to mention there's the passel of sisters we have heard tell of, but have not yet seen. Everyone will want to breed one of them into their line."

"We don't know that she has that form of *laran*, and you are dreaming if you think someone could have both this gift and the Aldaran gift and remain sane," Kaitura protested, but weakly. Allista felt sorry for her—were the women of the lowlands so dependent on their men that they could not even argue with them without submitting? No Stonefell woman would behave so!

"In any case," said Harlan, adding his voice to Doric's, "we do not need to imagine the possibilities when we can see in the valley the practical nature of this gift, whether bred to Aldaran or not. All the daughters of Stonefell must carry the genes, whether they are expressed in every individual or not. Many in the Domains will pay anything for a chance at breeding the Stonefell gift into their line."

"It's too bad you don't have the Aldaran gift," said Doric, "so you cannot tell us what course would lead to the best outcome."

"Most with the gift couldn't tell you, either," said Kaitura. "Some of them are so confused by the multiple threads they see that they cannot make any decisions at all. Do not wish for that *laran* in your line, Doric."

"That's not important," said Harlan impatiently. "I'm more worried about the strange spell over this place. I feel it pressing on me, but I cannot sense the true nature of it. I feel sometimes as if I am seeing double, awake and yet sleeping at the same time. I can't explain it, but it frightens me."

"You are the best telepath among us, Kaitura," said Doric. "What can you sense?"

"Nothing much. I'll have to try harder. So stop distracting me with gossip about bloodlines and which Stonefell child to breed to which Domain lord's heir. And don't even try to hide the thought that you'd like Allista for yourself, Harlan. Your thoughts are plain on your face!"

He grunted. "My family needs to outcross as much as anyone's. There's no reason she couldn't be for me."

"Except you are three times her age and have buried two wives already."

"They were too closely related, you know that."

Allista shrank back against the wall, now almost at the mercy of the pain in her head and the confusion in her heart. The family had welcomed these strangers into their keep, and what did they get in return? Plots that would destroy her family, foul plans to marry her brothers and sisters out among the Domains. It wouldn't be just her who would have to change her life forever, but Ailos, and Ayerra, and Aberlain, who was so tender-hearted, he cried for every bird discovered frozen to death in the courtyard in the harshest weeks of winter. He had always been slow— slow to walk, slow to learn speech, slow to puzzle out the rules of the games of his older brothers and sisters. But he was sweet and loving and so, so kind. Mother Rakhalla doubted he would mature to father a child, but Father Rafael thought it was possible. But even if he did not, he was family. Slow-witted as he might be, Aberlain should be a cherished pet among his sisters, and not given to a stranger for *breeding*. For a pedigree! Even if the woman were to come here to Stonefell, it was unacceptable.

Allista could stand it no more; the red rage built in her chest threatened to overwhelm her, but it was tinged now with exhilaration. She had power, and she could use it to defend herself. Her family. These guests should be ashamed to plots. Yes, ashamed—and punished!

Allista flung the gatehouse door open, uncaring that the world had taken on strange red and orange hues that danced in her vision, that violet spikes radiated outward from the shadows in the room. "How dare you!" she shouted, tears running down her wind-chilled cheeks. "How dare you talk about us as if we were chervines you could take to market! You are terrible guests and I wish you'd never come here!"

Kaitura blanched. "Allista, *chiya*, I am sorry you overheard that. We mean only the best, I swear."

"I care nothing for your swearing!"

"Calm down, child," said Harlan in exasperation. He stepped forward as if to grab her by the arm. Instinctively, Allista reacted. Power threaded through every pore, every cell of Allista's frame, forcing itself outward, into the world, in a whirlwind of snow and frost and deepest darkness. She pushed Harlan's body and mind, his very being, through the years of lifetime, the weight of decades falling upon him, compressed into minutes rather than years. Harlan screamed and fell to the floor, clutching his hands to his head, blood spewing from his nose, his ears, even his eyes.

Even in the midst of her exultation, Allista froze, terrified by the sight of so much blood. Blood everywhere...she had never seen so much blood. Or had she? Her thoughts whirled in sickness and confusion and she could not remember. There was *something* she should remember, something about blood, but her rage careered throughout her mind too strongly, and too chaotically, for her to recall it.

"Allista, stop it! Stop it this instant—you'll kill him!" shouted Kaitura, her voice high with panic. She turned to Doric. "Threshold sickness—she'll kill us all!"

Doric had already reached under his shirt and brought out a small blue gem, which glowed strongly enough to illuminate the far corners of this gray and dreary room.

"You must calm down," he said slowly. "Allista, you must be calm."

"No," said Allista. Her attention was drawn away from the gouts of blood from Harlan and drawn to Doric, who wanted to control her. To send her away! To destroy her family. "You can't have me, or my family!" Allista thrust her will at Doric, challenging him to best her. His will strove with hers, evenly, but then, he seemed to find new strength, and he forced Allista back. Something rent within her own mind. A deep cut sliced mercilessly through her innermost thoughts, striking at the very core of her soul. She struggled for balance in the mindfelt agony, desperate for some semblance of control, but the more she grasped at the shards of her jumbled thoughts, the more they fled from her.

Kaitura gasped and covered her face in her hands. "No!" she shouted. "By Avarra the Merciful, no!"

Doric, confused, dropped his attack and, suddenly aware of his vulnerability, Allista *pushed* against him as she had against Harlan. Her thoughts skittered drunkenly through every vessel, every organ, every fiber of his muscles. She was weakened and wracked with pain, but he was distracted and unable to resist. Doric fell to the ground, twitching, twin streams of blood pouring from his nose to join the growing puddle of Harland's blood on the flagstones. This time, Allista thrilled to see the blood. She was fighting to save her family from these treacherous guests. Let them bleed! Let them pour out their lives on the stones of the gatehouse!

Kaitura gave a small, heartbroken cry and dropped to her knees. "Doric? Doric? Speak to me!"

After a few moments, dark wrath settled on her face and she spat at Allista. "Threshold sickness or no, you disgust me! Will you kill me, too? Will you?"

The echoes of *will you will you will you* sounded among the peaks and echoed back to Allista. She raised a hand toward Kaitura, who shrieked and fled out of the gatehouse.

Allista stumbled after her into the courtyard, woozy and uncoordinated, still reeling from Doric's attack on her mind. The guests' three chervines stood, still saddled, in the center of the courtyard, uneasy and untended, as if they'd stood unwatered and unfed since they had arrived yesterday. But they hadn't been there minutes before, when she had crossed the yard after speaking with Ailos and Kaitura. Where had the animals come from? Had Doric done something to her mind?

"Ailos! Mother Rakhalla! Help me!" Allista ran up the stairs and through chilled corridors to the inner chambers where the mothers and fathers dwelt. Where was everyone? Had Doric harmed them from afar? How strong were these lowlanders, to be able to do such drastic things in so short a time? Allista shuddered at the thought. The family would be helpless to oppose them, no matter how much they wished to stay together. The lowlanders would have their way in the end. They were too strong.

Allista ran to the great hall to find half-eaten, near-rotted food on the table and no fire in the firepit. Frost coated the andirons and sparkled on the ceiling.

"Ailos!" He, at least, must still be here, must know where everyone else had gone.

A whimper from the corridor beyond prompted her to follow. Kaitura! The brown-haired woman needed to explain this appalling change in the keep. And when she had explained, Allista would turn her over to the fathers and mothers for punishment. And then they would put the keep back in order and continue their lives as they always had.

Panting and moaning came down the stairwell to the room at the top of the tower, and Allista hesitated. Her old fear of the stairwell almost held her back. Almost. But today, the old childhood fright could do no more than slow her down.

Allista climbed the stairs, round and round she went until she reached the top. She felt powerful, and more alive than she ever had before. If this was threshold sickness, let it come!

At the top of the stairs, the door to the tower chamber was open, beckoning her to enter and kill this lowland enemy. Triumphant, Allista stepped inside.

Kaitura huddled against the far wall, but between the other woman and Allista was a vision even more horrendous than anything Allista could have imagined. Ailos was here, but not as Allista had ever seen him before. His silver hair was dull, his eyes half-lidded and lifeless, his skin dried from the constant wind. Around him lay the others in the family—there was Mother Rakhalla, large with child but just as dead as Ailos. And even Granddam Catriona, who had always had time to tell stories before bedtime, the one who could muster the best singing voice to soothe a sick child in the night. The most beloved woman in the keep.

Fathers Rafael, Rumal, and Rorick, Mothers Ranila and Ruella, Grandsires Callum, Corinn, and Colton, and all of Allista's siblings, including the gentle Aberlain. Oh, who could harm such a gentle soul!

"No," whispered Allista. She knelt by his pitiful remains, which were still clutching his favorite toy in his mummified hands.

Her anger re-ignited through her shock and she stood and shrieked at Kaitura. "What did you do?"

A near-growl came from the cornered woman. "What did *I* do? I came to a madwoman's household and ate rotted food and spoke with the dead. *What did I do?* I did nothing. You are the one who has done this. Think, child. Think about this spring. Was it not harder than usual? Did you have more difficulty finding food? Did you ever see your family all together at once in the great hall?"

Allista closed her eyes and tried to summon her power to kill Kaitura, but the other woman's words were a goad that did not let her shove this nightmare out of her mind long enough to harness her rage.

Blue light played against her eyelids and Allista opened her eyes to see Kaitura staring into a blue crystal as Doric had done. "See what you do not wish to see, child. See and remember." Her voice was hard and unforgiving.

The blue light sank into Allista's skin, saturated her bones, penetrated her mind. And she remembered. *The family was dining and arguing, as usual for an early spring night. But this night was different. Allista felt odd, as if her veins were on fire. Anger kept bubbling up in her mind unbidden. It was frightening yet simultaneously beautiful. Allista wanted to hold onto it and let it wash over her just as much as she wanted to run from it. Ayella teased her once more about how tall she was getting, and suddenly, Allista could control her rage no longer. The room spun; her confusion seemed to color everything in fiery shades of red and orange and purple. Ayella noticed* her grimace, and laughed at her again. Laughed! The anger and sparks in her mind reached a critical level and Allista knew she could now use it. Any fear that remained was swept aside in a sudden wave of exultation and hate. She pushed against Ayella, and the older girl screamed and clutched her head. In horror, everyone else had turned to her, and Mother Rakhalla had shouted, "No, Allista!" But Allista could not be stopped; her anger was too strong, her senses overloaded with power and threshold sickness and adolescent fury.

The family fled to the tower, except Father Rafael, the strongest of the fathers and mothers. He stood between Allista and the others, hands outstretched, face contorted with the effort of calling his own anger against his daughter. Allista's rage did not care; she broke through his thoughts and struck at his mind. Father Rafael turned, and stumbled up the stairs, thinking Allista would not follow. Ahead of Father Rafael was Ailos, who had burdened himself with the lifeless Ayella in his arms. The family stayed together; no one was left behind. Not Ayella, not Aberlain, not Granddam Catriona.

Moans and screams came from ahead of her, but Allista's fury would not be stopped. She followed them to the tower room, where the entire family huddled and cried, and begged her to return to them and save them. And she had ignored their pleas, was unmoved by their tears. The rage-filled hell of her mind colored everything in its wake. Nothing breathed once she had gone by.

She had killed her family. They were everything to her, and she had killed them.

"You said you had the power to *see*," said Kaitura, "but the other side of that is the power to *unsee*. You did not wish to know what you had done while in the grip of threshold sickness, and so you undid it. You undid it with enough skill that even the three of us noticed only that there was a spell, but could not determine its nature. We spoke with your family, unaware they were mere phantasms that you offered up. But you were not strong enough to conjure them all, just a few. Enough to make it look like the family still lived here."

"No," said Allista, sick with realization of what she had done, wanting it not to be true. "I spoke with Ailos just this morning. I saw Mother Rakhalla at dinner last night—and you did, too!"

"And when was the last time you saw, what were their names, Alisande? Alcor? What of them? Have you seen them since spring?"

Allista thought hard. Of course they had been here; where else could they go? But when had she spoken to one of them last? When had she last laughed with Ayella or heard a story from the lips of Granddam Catriona, or been hugged by Mother Ruella?

Spring, spring, and spring. Always spring. Allista dropped to her knees, hugged herself with trembling arms.

"I will make sure no one ever comes here again," said Kaitura with a voice rough with grief and disgust. "You will starve to death and take this cursed *laran* with you to Zandru's hell." The woman nervously edged by Allista and fled down the stairs.

The gulf in Allista's heart was too big to allow tears or screams of protest. It was infinitely deep, and the pain of it was difficult to breathe around. Speech was out of the question. Allista reached out to touch the dried hair of Ailos, desperate to see any movement, any sign of life in those dried husks that had been eyes. He had to be well. He had to be alive. For her. They had to make the next generation. She would name her first child Tollan if a boy and Tierra if a girl.

"Ailos," she called. He had to hear her. Her entire soul longed to see him move, to smile, to be at her side once more. To be where he should be.

Slowly, she climbed to her feet and walked to the window. The green valley below was pleasant to behold and helped soothe her thoughts. She watched the grain bow and dance in the breeze. Presently, it seemed she saw a cloaked figure on a chervine departing the valley, disappearing over the saddle pass. The figure led two other chervines that were heavily laden with oddly-shaped burdens strapped across their backs.

"Have we had visitors?" she asked.

And then Ailos was there at her side, where he always was, and always would be. "Yes," he said. "But they are leaving now. They are nothing to us."

"Oh." She realized she was in the tower room where she did not want to be. "Let's go down and see what has been set on the table for our midday meal."

"An excellent idea," said Ailos. He kissed her on the top of the head.

Wordlessly, Allista descended the stairs. Her family waited below.

COMPENSATION

by Leslie Fish

One of the delights of editing is the discovery of "companion stories," tales that reflect, complement, continue one another. I think of Leslie Fish's "Compensation" as companion piece to "The Tower" by Jeremy Erman. The latter takes place a generation after landfall and this one not too long after Recontact, but each illuminates an aspect of the value of history...among other things.

Leslie Fish learned to sing and to read at a very young age, playing guitar at sixteen, and writing the first of hundreds of songs shortly thereafter, including settings of Rudyard Kipling's poetry and the "all-time most notorious" Star Trek filksong ever written: "Banned From Argo." She's recorded a number of albums and composed songs, both alone and collaborative, on albums from every major filk label. She was elected to the Filk Hall Of Fame as one of the first inductees. In college, she majored in English and minoring in psychology, protest and politics, joined the Industrial Workers of the World, and did psychology counseling for veterans. Her other jobs included railroad yard clerk, go-go dancer, and social worker. She currently lives in Arizona with her husband Rasty and a variable number of cats which she breeds for intelligence.

High summer in Nevarsin meant the growing season of the ice-melons, which absorbed the time of most of the monks who weren't teaching at the school. This left the ancient library empty and quiet, exactly as Brother Stefan the Librarian liked it. He paced silently between the tall stone shelves, automatically noting the dates on which the assorted volumes were due for re-copying, shamelessly enjoying the faint scent of the desiccant herbs and the fainter scent of aged vellum. He would admit gladly, to any who asked, that he loved the ancient books as if they were his own family.

Nay, more... he admitted to himself. His parents were dead these twenty years, had politely disowned him when he became a *cristoforo* monk, and he hadn't heard from his brothers and sister in longer years than that. Not that he blamed them, really: what other life was there for a youngest son of a poor branch of the Leynier family, one totally lacking in any trace of *laran?*

Indeed, the monastery school of St. Valentine-of-the-Snows was the one school on all of Darkover that taught no courses in control of the Gifts, did not recruit the Gifted, and generally ignored *laran* altogether. On the contrary, the skills it taught could be learned nowhere else on the planet. Brother Stefan was perfectly happy with that arrangement. When asked why, he had always replied cryptically that the blind hear better than the sighted. The better students would connect 'blind' with 'head-blind', and understand.

Just now, for example, he could hear hesitant footsteps—in monk's sandals, weight about 80 kilos, dragging the left foot a little—just inside the doors of the library. That was Brother Ian, secretary to the abbot, come seeking him. The matter was clearly important, or the abbot would have sent one of the lesser brothers. That could mean only one of two things.

Stefan padded quietly around the corner of the third stack and came up to the doorway. "So, Ian," he said casually, startling the secretary, "Is it bad weather or bad politics this time?"

"Must you always do that?" Brother Ian grumbled, straightening his robe. "There's no need for such silence, nobody reading here today."

"I'm sorry. It's force of habit," the librarian smiled. "But what's the problem severe enough for the abbot to send me his personal secretary?"

Mollified a bit upon hearing the trick explained, Ian sighed: "Politics. We have a visitor, whose name the good father did not give me, who has come to ask some peculiar questions."

Aha. The news from Caer Donn, Stefan deduced, automatically adjusting his breathing to raise his internal temperature slightly to deal with the chill breeze blowing in through the open door. "And is this visitor from Caer Donn or Thendara, do you think?"

Brother Ian raised an eyebrow in acknowledgement. Outsiders never seemed to realize that cloistered monks might notice subtle differences in dress, gear, gesture, and accent that told one Domain from another. Only a few of them realized that there were other means than Tower relays for transmitting information quickly. "Definitely Thendara," he admitted, "And from the highest house, if I am any judge."

"So the Hastur king is perturbed about the tales from Caer Donn," Stefan guessed, "And has sent a trusted messenger to us for confirmation."

Ian raised that appreciative eyebrow again. "Just so. There is no great trust between the houses."

Stefan could already make some calculations about the questions Hastur would ask, and the rank and certain gender of the trusted messenger he would send. "By all means, then, send the young gentleman in," he smiled. Then he thought to add, "Are any in his retinue discreet enough to carry home some pigeons?"

Brother Ian grinned back. "Certainly: his camp cook. Not a *cristoforo,* but a sympathizer—and a graduate. We will, of course, give him the usual gift of a pack-load of ice melons. No one will remark about a cage of pigeons also."

"Excellent." Stefan sighed. "And how are the fire-watch towers?"

"Reliably staffed."

"Good. We will need to know what transpires when Hastur learns the news he will not like."

"You're certain he will not like it?"

"The powerful love no changes that could threaten their power," Stefan murmured, looking up to the shadowed stone ceiling, "And this... It will change the world. Yes, send the young gentleman in."

By the time the leather boot-heels clicked cautiously through the doorway, Stefan had applied his breathing exercises and was calmly holding his mind blank. He felt the all-too-familiar headache behind his eyes, and knew that the messenger was psychically scanning him, and probably with a larger than usual matrix crystal. That too indicated something of the visitor's rank.

"Brother Librarian?" a moderately-young male voice asked, even as the pain withdrew.

"I am that," said Stefan, turning—finally—to look at his guest, noting the undecorated but finely-stitched boots and cloak, the characteristic hair and features. The tiny scripts the pigeons could carry rarely sufficed for accurate portraits, but Stefan had no doubts as to his guest's identity. *Hastur must be seriously frightened,* he guessed. "How may I serve you, milord?"

The incognito prince took a few cautious steps forward. "Good Brother, I have a question the abbot could not answer, so he sent me to you." The man's voice betrayed none of his anxiety; he had excellent control, no doubt Tower-trained. "Have you heard anything of the news from Caer Donn?"

There was, Stefan considered, no point in drawing this out. "Yes, milord. Even at Nevarsin we have heard of the strange visitors who claim to be from the stars."

The prince took a few steps more. "They are quite head-blind. They look like us, save for the coloration of some of them. Their speech is much like ours. They recognize some of our words—even the tunes of old songs. They..." His composure began to fracture, just the tiniest bit. "They claim we are related to them! That we are a...they call it a 'lost colony', and tell a fantastic tale of how the people of their world ventured out into the stars, in great ships, a thousand years ago, and some of the ships were lost, and one of them must have landed here, and...and we are their descendants. We—sir, I must know. Can this be true? Is there any evidence that it could possibly be true? We know your library contains very ancient manuscripts..." He paused, panting audibly.

And now the world changes forever. Stefan climbed slowly to his feet, feeling the weight of history on his shoulders. He took up his lantern, automatically checked the oil and the wick, and turned toward the long corridor between the shelves. "Come with me," was all he said.

The Hastur prince followed humbly at his heels, all the way down the long corridor, through the maze of shelf-lined tunnels, and off to the side-hall at the end, deep into the mountain where the temperature stayed always the same. On these shelves stood glass boxes with tight-fitting lids, sealed with clay or wax, containing the oldest books.

Stefan paused at the next-to-last shelf, pulled down one of the boxes, and carried it to the small reading-table near the end wall. He set the lamp into the waiting socket on the table, pulled out a pen-knife from his belt-pouch and began digging out the dried clay seal.

"This is not the original book," he explained. "That one was last copied and sealed over nine hundred years ago. This is, however, one of the oldest copies. You may be assured that it is absolutely accurate."

He felt that familiar headache again, and knew the man was scanning him for truthfulness. The scan was mercifully brief.

"We seal the books, with some desiccating and mold-killing herbs, in these boxes of cold, still, dry air," Stefan went on as he pried out the clay. "It preserves them from any form of rot, but that cannot be guaranteed if the glass boxes are opened often. Thus we make copies for common use... Ah, there we are. Now let's lift the lid carefully..."

"And what book is this?" the prince asked, peering closer.

"It is one of the journals of one of the first companions of Saint Valentine." Stefan carefully lifted the book out of its glass bed and set it on the table. "He feared that his and his ancestors' knowledge would be lost, so he wrote several books detailing that knowledge as best he could remember it. This is his book of history. The lettering is of an ancient form. Can you read it, sir?" He pulled the book open, and turned to the first page.

"Yes, yes," the prince muttered impatiently, leaning close. "I was schooled here, after all."

Of course... Stefan remembered him now. *Nearly ten years ago, and you weren't interested in books then. I daresay you will be, hereafter.*

Stefan watched as the prince read, knowing from the subtle shifts of his expression just what paragraph his eyes ran over. Yes, there was the puzzlement, the dawning understanding, the shock, the awe bordering on horror.

"It's true!" the prince gasped, slamming the book shut as if the sight of the letters burned him. "It's true! They are— Gods, we..." He turned mutely pleading eyes toward Stefan.

And he hates the thought. The librarian knew he could offer no pity, nothing that could muffle the truth. "We have changed much during all these generations on Darkover," Stefan said calmly. "I daresay our...cousins have changed also in the same stretch of time, but yes, we are of one source—and one blood." He leaned past the prince to pick up the book and set it back in its nest of dried herbs and glass. "For proof, you may take this copy with you..." He carefully closed the lid. "Take it back to Thendara to show to the king. Have it examined, authenticated, by the Tower there. Whatever the *Comyn* think of the truth, they must know and acknowledge it." *And I'd best have the box bound up in oil-cloth, and packed in a sturdy bag, to prevent too-opportune accidents. Perhaps another discreet word to the cook...*

Stefan took up the glass box in one hand, hefted the lamp in the other, and turned to go. After a moment's hesitation, the prince rose and hurried after him, unwilling to be left alone in this dark maze full of secrets.

"But why...why?" he panted after Stefan, "Why was this forgotten? Why did nobody know, all those years...?"

The answer to that was so bitterly easy that Stefan couldn't resist giving it. "For that we must ask fifty generations of kings and nobles, first struggling to survive on a hard new world, then backsliding into an old sin: enjoying their rule too much to give it up, deliberately keeping their underlings ignorant so as to maintain power. Do you know how few schools there are, in all the Domains? How few of our people can read at all? How few have any interest in history, let alone ancient history?"

"Those who are... Don't they come to you?" The prince was definitely not a stupid man. "How many of your monks know the secret?"

"Any who wish to stay for the love of learning," Stefan sighed, "For the love of knowledge alone."

"The teachers! The teachers at the school—Why didn't they tell us, when we were students here?"

"Ah..." Stefan turned at the doorway, setting down his lamp and facing his former student. "We *did* tell you. Once only. How many of you wished to know, or bothered to remember, or asked any further, or thought of the tale as anything but a *cristoforo* legend?"

The prince opened his mouth, paused, then shut it again, and blushed visibly in the light from the hall beyond. Stefan knew he was remembering those first few days in the school, in history class, when the young students were more concerned with the cold weather, the plain food, the loss of all the comforts and privileges of the houses they had come from, than with tales of ancient legends that no one cared about anyway.

Stefan refrained from pointing out that it was always the poor families' sons, used to being hungry and cold, with no expectations of great *laran* or great rank, who had looked to education to better themselves. They were the ones who listened keenly, remembered well, asked questions, and studied further. They were the ones who would accept the truth of the new people, who would make the transition most easily, and who would gain the most from it. He carefully wiped the thought out of his mind; there was always a chance that the Hastur prince might think to scan him again.

At the door Stefan stopped, handed over the glass box, and watched his visitor walk unsteadily away. He summoned Brother Ian, who had been waiting in the hallway, whispered some succinct words in his ear, and watched the monk pace silently after the prince.

The truth will reach the king, Stefan thought, stepping back into the library and pulling the doors closed behind him. Even if the one book were destroyed, there were over a hundred more copies waiting. There were also a host of defenses to keep anyone from breaking into the library and destroying them. The truth would make its way out, regardless of what the *Comyn* might wish.

...and democracy shall finally return to Darkover, after a thousand years of psionics-propped feudalism, he thought, turning back to his lamp.

The familiar pain in his head warned him. Stefan swore and set his lamp down again. "Narell," he called into the musty darkness, "Give it up. We're alone here, and you know that always gives me a headache."

"I'm sorry," the soft voice sounded from the empty air. Like a page in a book turning, the invisibility pulled away to reveal a tall, slender figure, wrapped in a soft gray tunic and cloak, silver of hair and eye, sexless in form. The only notable color about him was the blue stone pendant that hung from his neck. "I didn't mean to come so close, but I was distracted with following the Hastur prince."

"Let us all bend our efforts to make certain that the Hastur king does not suppress the knowledge in that book," said Stefan, drawing the bar across the doors. "Tell me, Narell-vye-Shath, did your folk draw the Terrans here again?"

Narell gave Stefan a startled look. "No," he admitted. "We knew they were coming in this direction, and did not...discourage them."

"Why?" Stefan turned around and put his back against the doors. "Why did you let them come?"

Narell almost flinched, then sighed. "New blood," he admitted. "Surely you—and yours—have noticed the tendency to inbreeding over the last few centuries."

"Human or *chieri?*" Stefan smiled with no humor whatever.

"Human," Narell smiled back equally. "Over the last millennium we've crossed our blood enough with you...aliens to have no further problems on that account, not among those of us who have been willing to crossbreed."

"Ah," *Which means that some faction of them insisted upon remaining 'pure', and have suffered thereby, but let that go...* Stefan calculated. "But the Dry Towners would rather mate with their first cousins than with the folk of the Domains, and the Domain people return the favor. Centuries ago the *Comyn* bred dangerously close for the Gifts; nowadays everyone breeds for wealth and power."

"The result is the same." Narell shook his head. "How many times will the nobles repeat the same mistake?"

"They might have learned from your folk, had you told them," Stefan reminded him. He took up his lamp and strolled to the small reading-table beside the door, and the cabinet above it.

"You know how humans would have treated us, had we revealed ourselves so clearly to them," Narell frowned, pacing after him. "It took work enough to keep them from exterminating the other non-humans. Is there some of your melon-wine in that cabinet?"

"Of course." Stefan opened the cabinet and pulled out a decanter, followed by two goblets. "The problem could have been avoided by ending the political power of the nobles—and changing the culture of the Dry Towns."

"The problem with the nobles was that their power was based upon the Gifts," said Narell, seating himself and taking up one of the goblets. "We had understandable reasons for encouraging the use of the Gifts."

"Indeed," said Stefan, pouring. "But didn't you just tell me that the *chieri* had enough crossbreed children to refresh your own gene-pool?"

"Technically, yes." Narell looked pained as he waited for his goblet to fill. "Still, you can understand that we wanted a larger reservoir. Also, I confess, we were fascinated with watching how you humans dealt with our ancient problems. Your folk did come up with some surprisingly original developments, you know."

"That explains your hands-off policy with the Domains," Stefan granted him, filling his own goblet, "But what of the Dry Towns? Why did you leave them to stagnate for a thousand years?"

"Why did you humans?" Narell raised an eyebrow and sipped.

"Insufficient resources to mount a major war." Stefan shrugged. "The only alternative was to go after them with *laran* weapons, and after the Ages of Chaos nobody wanted that. Human societies are capable of learning, given literacy anyway."

"Even where literacy—and the inconvenient lessons of history—are unwelcome." Narell tipped his goblet in salute. "We've followed the development—and survival—of the monastery library with great interest, I may add."

"Umhmm..." Stefan peered at the *chieri* over the rim of his cup. "Were your folk illiterate before humans arrived?" he asked. "And have you developed reading since?"

Narell set down his goblet and stared at the monk, open-mouthed. "How—" he started, then caught himself.

"Deduction," Stefan explained. "Consider our early discovery of the use of the starstones, which knowledge could only have come—so quickly—from the *chieri*. Consider the equally early eroding of literacy, which had been the pride of humanity since our most ancient of days—which could likewise have come only from subtle encouragement by your folk. Consider the common use of starstones to store memories. Add those facts together, and the conclusion is clear."

"Deduction..." Narell repeated, still staring.

"By the way, old friend, was it your folk who influenced

the first settlers to destroy their ship's computer, so as to leave them dependent on you?"

"Yes..." the *chieri* admitted, "Yes, we did. During that first Ghost Wind.... Stefan, you must understand how desperate we were! There were fewer than a hundred thousand of us left, in all the world—we were *dying*, Stefan!"

The monk felt that familiar headache again, and saw that Narell's hands were nowhere near his starstone. *Driven by pure emotion...* "I understand," Stefan said soothingly, rubbing a surreptitious hand across his forehead. "No one could blame you for that, nor, ah, for making use of that first Ghost Wind to mate as many humans as possible. Neither have you done so badly by us since, really. Most of our subsequent sins have been primarily our own doing."

The headache vanished and Narell slumped visibly. He had really been concerned over that.

"But the Dry Towners?" Stefan nudged, not about to let Narell evade that point.

The *chieri* took another mouthful from his goblet. "To be honest, we didn't know what to make of them. Not being bound to any one gender, we had never had experience of...enslaving one group according to gender, let alone mythologizing the reasons for it. Still less did we understand turning away from both the *chieri* Gifts and..." He waved his hands vaguely. "Your peculiarly human abilities for...literacy, deduction, elaborations of logic...the bizarre way you mind-blind humans think, Stefan. We left them alone to see what they would do—an experiment, you might say."

"Ah," Stefan calculated further, "As you did with us, the brotherhood of St. Valentine—until we deduced your place in our history, and came seeking you."

Narell got that stunned look again. "The way you humans think, in the absence of *laran!*" He reached for the goblet and took a quick swallow. "Your 'computers,' your libraries, your...elaborate logic, your 'deduction'—you can think five or six steps ahead, and—and sideways at the same time. A thousand years, and we still don't completely understand that, Stefan. And we need to understand it!"

"So you let the other humans come," Stefan made a good guess, "Also because you guessed that some few among them would have at least a touch of the Gifts, but no training in using them, so you could observe their minds in action without being noticed."

Narell nodded mutely, and peered into the goblet to see how much was left in it.

"Finally," said Stefan, lifting his own goblet, "You need the Terrans because you know that, in future years, your people too will need to go out among the stars—if only to escape our slowly-dying world, under its slowly-dying sun."

Narell only drained his goblet.

"I will help, of course," the librarian added, "And most of the Brotherhood too. We have known, for a very long time, that all of Darkover needs new blood. The stagnation must end." *I could almost pity the Dry Towners what will befall them, though they've brought it on themselves....*

"I hope to all the stars," Narell murmured, rising, "That this peculiar human Gift is—as you've so often told me—a skill that can be learned, not just a peculiar compensation for the lack of *laran.*"

"It is," Stefan reassured him. "It only takes practice."

With no further word, the *chieri* went to the doors, pulled down the bar, opened one leaf a little way and glided out.

He'll be back, Stefan knew. *Perhaps next time I can begin teaching him chess.*

The librarian finished his own goblet, took up the lamp and paced back down the book-lined corridor, taken with the quaint notion that he was a thought wandering through an enormous brain, noting memories in passing.

One particular memory snagged his attention; humans had always had the capacity for *laran,* but had never developed it until assisted by the *chieri.*

Or had they?

There were mentions in those ancient journals, myths of an even more ancient time when humans—some humans—possessed psychic Gifts long before the species ever left its original home. Had that been true? If so, then what had happened to those Gifts?

Had they been suppressed—deliberately—just so that humans could develop these other uses of the mind? Observation with the common senses, deduction, logic—those were skills, as he'd told Narell, that anyone could learn with practice, not dependent upon a degree of inherited talent.

Skill is democratic; talent is random, he realized. And a useful talent, as Darkover's history showed, could be used to create horrors, slaughter, tyranny, and a withering stagnation. Of course the same could be said of any skill, but—as the vast number of books in the library showed—skill was much harder to keep in the control of a privileged few.

Stefan realized he had come to that treasure-house at the end of the corridor, and he was looking into two of the ancient journals. He didn't need to read the faded labels to know what they were.

Principals of Logic was the first one. The second was a thick volume of logic puzzles, meant as amusement or exercise but above all as training for the mind.

Laran or logic, which is the greater Gift? Stefan pondered.

He knew that, born lacking the one and having perforce devoted his life to the other, if only as compensation, he was not a disinterested judge.

But still, the experience of both humans and *chieri* gave strong evidence as to what the decision should be.

GREEN IS THE COLOR OF HER EYES SO BLUE

by Deborah Millitello

From the frozen peaks of Nevarsin to the arid sands of the Dry Towns, gifts can be found in unexpected places. Some we can accept, in sorrow or gladness, but others we must pass by.

Deborah Millitello published her first story in 1989 in Marion Zimmer Bradley's Fantasy Magazine. *Since then her stories have appeared various magazines such as* Dragon Magazine; *Marion Zimmer Bradley's Fantasy Magazine, including the third-place Cauldron winner "Do Virgins Taste Better?";* Science Fiction Age; *and anthologies such as* Aladdin Master of the Lamp; Witch Fantastic; Sword and Sorceress; Tales of Talislanta, *and* Bruce Coville's Book of Nightmares. *Her first book,* Thief's Luck, *a YA fantasy mystery, is out from Double Dragon Publishing, and a YA fantasy novel,* The Water Girl, *will be out in February 2015 from Word Posse. She spends her free time baking cookies, cakes, and pies, making gourmet jams such as strawberry lemonade jam, lemon blueberry jam, and tangerine marmalade, knitting & crocheting, and growing herbs, vegetables, berries, and orchard fruit. A member of the Alternate Historians writers group, she lives in southern Illinois with her husband Carl (who has put up with her writing obsession for over forty years), has three children, nine grandchildren, and one great-grandchild on the way, and works at a doctor's answering service as her day job.*

Dry Towners didn't have *laran*—that was a well-known fact. Only settlers who lived in the Domains and the native *chieri* possessed various psychic talents. So why did Gareth Marius-Danvan Elhalyn y Hastur sense the touch of someone with *laran* as he approached Shainsa, one of the largest cities in the Dry Towns?

The red sun of Darkover had just climbed above the horizon, revealing the bleached walls of the desert city and the cliffs beyond that had been quarried for building stones. Huts, hovels, and tents huddled outside the city walls where those who couldn't afford the gate fees struggled daily to find food and water. Dozens of people, wrapped in rags, peered out from their makeshift abodes, staring at him and the caravan he traveled with. And somewhere in that squalid mass of the poor was one person with power.

Gareth slowed his horse to a bare amble, lightly grasped his starstone amulet to strengthen his *laran*, and searched for whoever had touched his mind. The feeling had the same intimate sensation as *laran*, but it was subtle, subdued, and very faint, like the sound of a distant dove cooing. It also felt unlike any talent he'd ever encountered. Halting, he glanced across the people peeping from their wretched shelters, but he couldn't determine the origin of the power.

"Why are you stopping here?" Rahelle asked, reining her horse beside him. "We're almost at the gates. The horses and even the pack *oudrakhi* are straining to get to water."

Gareth gazed at his wife a moment, then scanned the faces staring at him. "I'm not certain," he said, just loud enough for her to hear. "There's something...unexpected."

"Unexpected?" she said.

Gareth nodded. "Someone here has *laran*."

Rahelle raised her eyebrows and blinked her dark eyes slowly, just once. "That's impossible."

"I know," he said, still searching for the source of the impossibility.

A group of ragged children came running up to Gareth. They held out their hands and chattered so fast, he could barely understand them, but he was certain they were begging for money. He pulled out a few coins and tossed them to the beggars.

Suddenly, he noticed a slight figure, dressed in rags from head to foot. Even the child's head was covered so that only bright blue eyes were visible. A knotted strip of cloth stretched from one wrist to a cloth belt then to the other wrist. *A little girl,* he thought. *Even the poorest girls are shackled in the Dry Towns.*

She held two small melons that seemed to grow larger as Gareth stared at her. The girl looked startled as she gazed at him. For a moment, just a moment, he thought her eyes changed from blue to green.

The sun rose higher. The girl shuddered, turned, and fled into the narrow paths between shacks and tents. Gareth started to climb down from his horse to follow her, but stopped.

Rahelle grasped his arm. "What?"

"It's that girl," he said, his hands tightening on the reins, "the one holding the melons. I'm sure she's the one with *laran.* But I can't go after her right now. I have to present myself to Lord Dayan before we do anything else. The last thing I want to do is offend his *kihar,* his honor, before we begin negotiations. I don't want to fail in my first mission as ambassador for the Domains."

"You won't," Rahelle said, smiling at him. "I have faith in you. We're here for at least seven days, probably much more considering how difficult making a treaty with Lord Dayan will be. Plenty of time to find the girl."

Gareth scanned the camp, trying to catch sight of the mysterious child, but didn't see her. "All right," he said, smiling back at his wife. "Let's go pay our respects to the Lord of Shainsa. Are you going to dress for the occasion?"

She laughed. "Yes, just for Lord Shainsa I'll put on my gold chains."

Gareth laughed, then urged his horse toward the city gates. He stopped at the market plaza inside the gates where Rahelle gave her half-brother Alric charge of watering the animals at the ancient well, setting up tents, and preparing booths to display their goods. Gareth looked back at the huts outside one last time, then he and Rahelle rode toward the center of Shainsa to the Great House, Lord Dayan's home and seat of his power, to pay respects to the lord as was required by law.

The Great House was built of salt-pale rock and had no windows on the first two floors, but Gareth noticed that another story had been added since he had last been to Shainsa. Narrow balconies hung on the right and left sides of the front wall. Four stone-faced guards, dressed in purple and gold, stood before the double doors.

Gareth dismounted before the house, as did Rahelle, and they handed the reins to a servant waiting by the steps. Mounting the steps, Gareth said, "I am Gareth Marius-Danvan Elhalyn y Hastur, ambassador from the Domains, and this is my wife, Rahelle of Carthon, caravan master, come to pay our respects to Lord Dayan of Shainsa."

The guards studied them for a few moments, then the largest guard opened a door and let them enter. They were met by two more guards and escorted down a hall, past a dust-covered guard leaving the Great House, and into Lord Dayan's presence. The hall was empty of all but a few servants and two other guards. The Dry Town lord looked much older than when Gareth had last seen him. Dayan's hair was almost white, and his face was crinkled and as brown as his leather boots.

Gareth bowed. "Lord Dayan."

"Gareth of the Domains." Dayan's voice sounded gravelly. "It's been five years since I last saw you. The gods have been kind to you."

"And to you," Gareth said. "This is my wife, Rahelle of Carthon, daughter of Cyrrilon."

Dayan didn't acknowledge Rahelle.

Gareth stiffened for a moment but let the lord's dismissal of Rahelle pass. She was a woman, and in the Dry Towns, that meant she was unimportant. "I come to seek a treaty between your people and mine."

Dayan gazed at him silently for a long while. "A treaty. Between the Domains and the Dry Towns. An unlikely idea. But we will see. And you must stay in my house. I will have rooms prepared for you."

Startled and a bit unsettled, Gareth glanced at Rahelle,

then bowed to Dayan.

Gareth opened his eyes again to the darkness of the bed chamber. Lord Dayan had given them a room on the third floor, one with a balcony. Rahelle lay beside him, sleeping soundly. He envied her. His thoughts kept him awake. He was trying to forge a difficult alliance with the lord of Shainsa, but although the agreement was the reason he had been sent to the Dry Town, it wasn't the reason he couldn't sleep. The girl—the strange sensation she evoked—that kept his mind churning with questions.

Suddenly, he felt someone watching him. For a moment, fear chilled his heart, considering the enmity that had always been between the Domains and the Dry Towns. But he sensed no hostility, so he relaxed but remained alert. Keeping his body completely still, he glanced around the room until he saw a shadow at the small balcony. The shadow moved with less sound than a whisper. Eyes that glittered in the moonlight, blinked once, then seemed to search the darkness in the room.

Rahelle stirred and rolled onto her side, her back to Gareth. The shadow shrank back, but Gareth didn't move. It was the girl; he could feel that same sensation as when he'd first seen her. He waited silently, wondering who she was, how she had entered the city without money, and how she had climbed to the third floor of Lord Dayan's house— the most guarded building in Shainsa—without being seen. And most of all, what was this strange power that emanated from her.

Slowly, the girl took a step into the room.

Gareth inched his hand toward the amulet that held his starstone, until his hand closed around it. Instantly, his *laran* grew stronger, and he concentrated his thoughts on the girl. "My name is Gareth," he sent to her, "and I will not harm you."

The girl stiffened, then fled the room.

"Wait! Don't go!" he sent to her, but she disappeared. He leaped from bed and ran to the balcony, but she was nowhere in sight.

"You frightened her," Rahelle said, turning over to face him.

"I thought you were asleep," he said.

"I heard her climb onto the balcony," she said. "I thought if I pretended to be asleep, she might be less scared." She paused, then said, "Next time, just talk to her."

"You think that would make her less afraid of me?"

"Of course." Rahelle stretched, then closed her eyes. "When would she ever have heard someone speak to her mind?"

Gareth thought for a moment. Of course, he'd frightened her. He remembered the first time his grandmother had entered his mind. He'd given her permission during their training session, but still it had been startling, almost overwhelming. This Dry Town girl could have had no idea what *laran* was.

"Yes," he said, mostly to himself, "next time I'll just talk to her."

Mornings and afternoons were spent hammering out a treaty with Lord Dayan. Gareth soon realized the negotiations would take much longer than a week. It was hard, trying to overcome years of distrust, but gradually, they made small agreements. Evenings, when the red sun was still above the horizon but the day was cooling, Gareth and Rahelle walked to the market near the city gates. Rahelle checked on how well her brother was handling the trading, seeing what goods were for sale from other venders, what items seemed coveted by the shoppers, and what products Rahelle might choose to bring on her next caravan.

On the fourth evening, Gareth and Rahelle casually walked outside the city gates to the collection of tents and shacks. Gareth offered a few coins to the children who swarmed around them, begging for money. He clutched his starstone and tried to sense the girl's location, but felt no trace of the *laran*. Rahelle talked to the ragged people, since she was from the Dry Towns, although he understood most of what was said.

"I don't know who you are talking about," one boy said, then backed away and fled inside a shaky house.

"There are many girls here," a woman said, her voice as harsh as a sand storm, "but none like the one you described. And none that would have you or that we would let you have."

"Go back to the city," an old man said, anger glinting in his pale blue eyes. "Leave us alone. Just leave us alone!"

Gareth wanted to press them for answers, but his wife held him back. She nodded toward the gate, and Gareth glanced that direction. The city guards were watching them intently.

"Let it go for now," she said quietly. "Lord Dayan might take an interest in what we're doing. And why. Do you want him to discover this girl before we do?"

"No. She would never be safe then." He turned back to the old man. "If you see her, tell her we will wait for her to come to us. We would never hurt her. Please tell her that."

The old man glared at them, but didn't reply.

As nonchalantly as possible, they walked back through the gate as the sun reached the horizon and drenched the world in a crimson glow. The guards closed the gates for the night, but Gareth noted that one of the guards was missing. Looking askance at Rahelle, he knew she was thinking the same as he was: Lord Dayan had been informed of their actions.

Several nights later, the girl came back. Gareth sat on cushions on the floor halfway between the bed and the balcony, trying to keep his eyes open and hoping she would come. He was just nodding off when he felt the light, gentle sensation that came from her. Opening his eyes but remaining completely still, he waited until the girl's shadowy figure crept to the doorway. When she was standing just inside the room, he spoke aloud.

"I am Gareth," he said softly, hoping he wouldn't scare

her. "Who are you?"

The girl stiffened, and for a moment he thought she might bolt. She didn't, but she stayed in the shadows. "I am Aniella," she said, her voice as quiet as a night breeze. "Your voice—I felt it—in my head—the last time I was here. How did you do that?"

"I am from the Domains," he said, staying seated on the cushions. "Some of us have the ability to speak thoughts to others, who can hear those thoughts."

"But how did I hear your thoughts?"

"You have that ability, too."

"But I never heard anyone's thoughts before."

"No one in the Dry Towns has ever had *laran*—that's what we call the ability. No one—until now. Until you."

She was quiet for a while. "But how?"

"I don't know," he said. "Can you do anything special? Something no one else can do?"

"It's a secret," she whispered. "Father told me never to tell anyone."

"But I shared my secret with you. Won't you tell me yours?"

She shuffled a bit, although her feet made no more sound than a moth's wings. "I... I can make things grow," she said.

"Grow?"

"Plants. Fruit, vegetables, grains, herbs. I can make them grow faster."

"How long have you been able to do this?"

"Since I was very young." She hesitated and fidgeted with a woven string around her neck. "Since my father gave me the crystal."

"A crystal?" Excitement thumped in his chest. He clutched his own starstone and felt his *laran* increase. "What kind of crystal?"

Slowly, she pulled the string from under her ragged jacket. Hanging from the end was a round disk that rotated left then right. In the center of the disk was a gem that glowed green in the moonlight. Gareth had never seen anything like it. Even though Aniella was at least four arm-lengths away, he could feel her power, strong and pulsing.

"Where did you get that?" he asked.

She rubbed her small thumb across the surface of the gem. "Father found it long ago, when he was on a caravan. He never told me where."

"Where is your father now?"

"Dead."

"And your mother?"

"Dead, too."

"Who do you live with?"

"No one."

"No family at all?"

She shook her head.

"But where do you live?"

"I used to live in a cave near a small village farther out in the Dry Lands. But when Mother died, Father brought me here. He thought it would be safer in a city. He even found a cave we could stay in. But he died only weeks after we arrived. Now I live in tunnels and the cave."

"Tunnels and a cave? Why not here in the city? You seem to come and go as you wish. The walls and gates don't keep you out."

"I have no one to stay with here, and I can't bear the sun and the heat. So I stay underground during the day and come out from sunset to sunrise."

"How long have you been in the shanties?"

"Four years. Since I was ten."

Thoughtfully, Gareth studied the green shining crystal, wanting to know its secrets. "May I hold it?"

"No," she said and quickly slipped the disk back under her jacket. "It's mine."

Gareth smiled at her. "I would not take it from you. I have my own stone." He held out his starstone.

"Would you let me hold yours?"

He shuddered slightly. To let another person touch one's starstone could cause pain. He'd never willingly let someone else handle his stone. "No," he said reluctantly.

"So," she said, folding her arms.

She seemed less timid than when she'd first stepped into the room. He wanted to keep it that way.

"Would you like to meet my wife Rahelle?" he said. "She comes from the Dry Towns, too."

Aniella's eyes widened, then narrowed slightly. "The why doesn't she wear shackles like all Dry Town women do?"

Gareth smiled, remembering the first time he saw her wearing chains. She had taken him by surprise, using the chains on her wrists to attack and disable him in moments. "She does sometimes. When she chooses. She just doesn't choose to right now. So would you like to meet her?"

After a few moments, the girl nodded.

Rahelle got out of bed cautiously, straightening her sleeveless nightgown. "Moonlight is lovely but not very bright. May I light a lamp?"

"No!" the girl said, her voice hissing like a snake. "I don't want you to see me."

"But why?" Rahelle said. "We have seen you before."

"I ... I am different," she said slowly.

"Different?" Gareth said. "We are all different."

"Not like me. No one is like me. You would be afraid of me."

"No, I wouldn't. Believe me. Let my wife light a lamp."

The girl shivered visibly, wrapping her arms tightly across her chest. "All right," she said, but she kept her head bowed.

Rahelle lit a brass oil lamp and carried it over to where Gareth sat on the cushions. "Come, sit with us," she said, moving a cushion in front of Gareth so the girl would be facing them.

Aniella hesitated, but finally sank down on the cushions. Gareth noticed she still had the cloth strip tied to her wrists.

"See," Gareth said, "we aren't afraid of you."

"You haven't seen me yet." Gradually, she unwound the rags that covered her face and head.

She was much slighter than Gareth had expected. Her

face was thin and extremely pale though the skin was mottled a light red. Her jaw came to a point at her chin, jutting out, and her teeth were bare nubs and crooked. Her nose bent down. The deep blue eyes had no lashes. She had no eyebrows and only a few brittle, short strands of hair on her head. As she unwrapped her hands, Gareth saw she had almost no fingernails and her palms were red, cracked, and in some places raw.

"What caused this?" Rahelle asked gently.

"I was born this way," Aniella said. "It's why I have to live in a cave or underground where it's cool."

Born this way, Gareth thought. *Maybe that's why she has* laran. "Could your father use the crystal?"

"No. Only me. He didn't know it was anything but pretty. But I knew when I first touched it, it was special. I felt seeds sprouting, sending down roots, sending up stems, growing in the earth. I knew how to make them grow."

"Maybe you could use the crystal because you *are* different." Gareth looked askance at Rahelle. "Would you let my wife touch it? Not hold it. Just put her finger on it. I want to see if another Dry Towner could feel the power."

The girl frowned, then nodded. "But only if I hold the disk."

Gareth nodded.

Grudgingly, she pulled out her amulet. In the lamp light, Gareth could see the disk was made of dried clay inserted in a metal casing. The green gem was round and smooth, the size of a large pea, and even in the lamp light, the stone seemed to glow brightly.

"May I?" Rahelle asked.

Aniella cupped the disk in her hands like a clam shell and held it close to her chest. She took a few quick breaths, then opened her hands and held the disk out to Rahelle.

Rahelle stretched out her first finger and cautiously stroked the green crystal.

"Do you feel anything?" Gareth asked.

"No. Nothing. It just feels like an ordinary gem."

"So it isn't because she's a Dry Towner." He turned to Aniella. "Please, may I touch it, too, the same way my wife did?"

The girl held the disk tightly, then nodded and held it out to him.

Taking a deep breath and blowing it out, he reached out his first finger to contact the gem. It felt as smooth as glass, but that was all he felt. He pulled back. "Nothing. I didn't feel any power. I think only you can use the crystal—because you *are* different, unique. But your father was right. Tell no one else about your gift. Some might try to control the power by keeping you a prisoner." He paused. "What do you use it for?"

"I feed the ones outside the gates. They never have enough to eat. So I scavenge for seeds in the rubbish heaps, and I plant and water them. Then I put one hand on the soil and hold the disk with the other. By the next day, the seed has sprouted and the plant is growing large. Within a week the plant produces fruit. I share it with the outside people."

"Do they know about your gift?"

"No. They only know I bring them food. They think I steal it."

"That's why they tried to protect you when we came searching for you. Can you show me what you do?"

"I don't have any soil to plant a seed." She thought a moment. "Do you have any water and a cup?"

"Yes." Rahelle rose, went to a small table beside the bed, and brought back a ewer of water and a metal cup.

"Fill the cup halfway with water," Aniella said.

When Rahelle finished, Aniella took a large corrinfruit seed from a jacket pocket. Placing the seed in the water, Aniella placed her thumb on the crystal and put the fingers of her other hand in the water. The stone began to glow brighter, and as it did, Aniella's eyes turned from blue to bright green. The seed's hard shell broke open, and a slender root snaked out. A thin stem with tiny leaves uncurled from the seed and stretched out of the water.

Gareth stared, amazed, as the plant grew nearly as long as his forearm before Aniella set the cup down. Her eyes turned blue again, and her shoulders slumped forward as if she were fatigued.

"I have never seen anything like that," he said, almost breathless. "I don't want to expose you. We will not walk outside the gates again. We won't betray you, but if Lord Dayan learned of your power, he would find a way to use it and you wouldn't be safe. Even now he may suspect something. I'm sorry if we put you and your people in danger. It might be better if you don't come here again. I wouldn't want you to be caught."

Aniella looked surprised, glancing back and forth at Gareth and Rahelle. "Will you be here many more days?"

Gareth sighed. "Maybe another week. I've nearly completed as much of a treaty as I'm likely to get with Lord Dayan. Then we'll go home."

The girl looked pensive. "What is your home like?"

"Which home? I have one in the Dry Town city of Carthon. And one in Thendara in the Domains. And my family home at Elhalyn Castle."

Her mouth dropped open. "More than one home? You must be very rich!"

Gareth' dark brows furrowed, then he smiled. "I guess I am."

"Is it cool where you live?" she asked. "Is it cool and green, shaded from the heat and the sun?"

"In Thendara it is, and in Elhalyn Castle."

She sighed. "I would like to see a place like that, a place so cool I could go outside during the day."

"Would you like to come with us?" he asked.

Her eyes suddenly lit up, and she smiled. Just as quickly the smile disappeared, and she looked troubled. "But who would take care of my people? How could I leave them?"

Gareth turned to look at his wife, who shrugged.

"Just think about it," he said. "You can let us know later. Come and visit us whenever you like. We should be here for a while yet."

"All right," she said pensively.

"If we need to speak to you, we'll stand at the city gates, and Rahelle will be holding a flower in her hands."

"I will have my friends watch for you."

She rose, slipped her disk inside her jacket, and began rewrapping her head and face, then her hands.

"Here," Rahelle said, handing her the cup with the corrinfruit plant in it. "Take this with you."

Aniella soaked a rag with the water still in the cup, then wrapped the rag around the plant's root, and carefully placed the plant in one of her pockets. Walking to the balcony, she stopped and turned. "To live in a place that is cool and green," she said softly. "That would be like my heart's dream." She bowed to them, then soundlessly slipped over the railing and disappeared into the night.

Aniella visited them every night, and she eagerly listened to Gareth's descriptions of Thendara and Elhalyn Castle and the Yellow Forest of the *chieri*. "Trees as tall as the salt cliffs," she said, her eyes wide with amazement. "And cool winds and rain. I've heard of rain but I've never seen it. What does it feel like? And smell like? And taste like?"

"It feels cool like water from the deepest well," Gareth said, "with a slight metallic scent. And the taste—there are no words to describe it. You would have to taste it for yourself."

Aniella hugged herself and rocked back and forth on her cushion. "So many things my eyes hunger to see. So many."

Gareth started to ask her if she had chosen to come with them, but Rahelle shook her head. *Too soon*, he thought. But each time Aniella came, she seemed more excited by the places he told about, the plants and flowers and fruits that grew in the Domains, the sight of snow glittering on mountains. *She'll come with us*, he thought. *I'm sure she will. And she'll be like our daughter.*

The treaty was finished four days later, not the best of treaties, but it was a start. Lord Dayan had his scribe make two copies and signed them both. Gareth was relieved he had accomplished his mission. *Hopefully, there will be peace between the Domains and the Dry Towns now,* he thought.

When the scribe presented the signed copies for Gareth to take back to the Domains, Lord Dayan called for wine to celebrate. "Let us drink to our alliance," he said as a servant handed him a golden goblet, then another to Gareth. "And to prosperity for both our people."

Gareth raised his goblet. "Long life to you and peace."

They both drank, then Dayan said, "I have heard that you were..." he paused, "curious about those living outside the walls of Shainsa."

Gareth's heart beat with fear. Dayan was subtle, never letting his true thoughts be spoken. But Dayan suspected there was something hidden in the shanty town, something important in the camps outside the walls. Gareth sensed it in the lord's voice.

Taking another sip of wine to give himself time to think, he said, "This wine is very good. I must tell my wife to purchase some for trade. She's always looking for exceptional goods." He took another sip. "And yes, we were curious about the outside people. My wife was looking for a girl or young woman for a house servant. She is gone from our house in Carthon so often on caravans or visiting with me in the Domains that she needs someone to help with running the household. She thought she might find someone willing to work. We talked to a few but didn't find anyone suitable." He took another sip. "This really is excellent wine."

"That is interesting," Dayan said. "I was told you were asking after a particular girl."

"Well, there was one girl Rahelle seemed to think might do. We only saw her once, but after that we couldn't find her. She was obviously unreliable."

"Ah. Your wife must be disappointed."

"Yes, but we'll look in Carthon. I'm sure we'll find someone there who is willing to work."

"Perhaps I could help you find this girl," Dayan said.

"I'm certain my men could search for her. What did she look like?"

Gareth took another sip, his stomach beginning to slosh nervously. *He knows*, he thought. *Somehow he knows there is something special about her. He just doesn't know exactly who she is.* "It is kind of you to offer your help, but all we saw were her eyes—blue, like most of your people. And besides, she wasn't interested in working for us."

Dayan smiled, but the smile lacked any warmth. "Perhaps you will see her again. She might change her mind."

Gareth smiled back as well as he could. "Possible, but I doubt it." He handed the goblet back to the servant, bowed to Dayan, then turned and left.

Rahelle returned from checking on the caravan not long after Gareth entered their room. He quickly embraced her, and whispered in her ear, "We have to warn Aniella."

"What—" she started to say, but he kissed her to silence her.

He held her close and whispered, "Someone may be listening to us. I think Dayan knows about Aniella."

"But how?" she said.

"I don't know. He's not certain what she can do, but he knows we want her, so she must be important."

Rahelle inhaled sharply. "He's had guards following me when I was at the market. They tried to be subtle about it, but they were watching me."

"He'll search the camps until he finds her. We have to get word to her that she and her people are in danger."

"What can he do?" she whispered back. "She hides underground during the day. He won't be able to find her."

"If he offers enough money to enter the city, some of the people there might be persuaded to tell the guards where to find her. And if money won't loosen tongues, other kinds of persuasion will. And Dayan is not above using that kind of persuasion. How can we get word to her?"

"A flower at the gate. That was our signal."

"Is the caravan ready to leave?"

"Tomorrow evening."

"Good. Let's go buy some wine."

The sun was in the far west as they strolled to the market plaza. Several guards accompanied them "for protection," Dayan had said. Rahelle located a wine merchant and bought several barrels of the same vintage as Dayan had offered Gareth. They checked with Rahelle's brother Alric to be certain the caravan would be ready to leave at sunset the next day. Gareth located a flower seller and bought Rahelle a single pink rock rose. As they ambled around the market, they finally reached the city gates. Several children crowded near the gate, hope in their faces as they chattered and held out their hands. Gareth tossed some coins to the urchins. They scrambled to snatch the treasures in the air or on the ground, then ran back to their huts.

One little girl wasn't quick enough to catch a coin. She started to cry, tears streaking her dusty face. Gareth gazed at Rahelle and smiled, then the two of them walked out to the little girl. He gave her a copper coin, and Rahelle gave her the rock rose. The little girl wiped her face on her sleeve, smearing dirt across her cheeks, then she smiled and hurried back to her home.

The setting sun painted the world crimson and black as they gazed at the outsiders' village. He looked at his wife and smiled. "Message delivered," he said softly.

They waited in the dark room until Aniella's shadow climbed onto the balcony. Rahelle lit a lamp, and they sat on cushions as far away from the door as possible.

"What's wrong?" Aniella whispered as she unwrapped her face.

"Lord Dayan knows about you," Gareth said, leaning in closely. "I don't know how much, but he was questioning me specifically about you today. He said he could have his men search the camps. I'm afraid your people might get hurt."

Aniella gasped. "But they don't know where I hide. All they know is I bring them food."

"He might hurt them, just to make you reveal yourself," Rahelle said.

"But they've done nothing. Why would he do that?"

"Because he can."

The girl's lips quivered, and she swallowed hard. "What can I do?" she said, resting her face in her hands. What can I do?"

"You can come with us," Gareth said. "We will leave just before the gates close at sunset tomorrow so we can travel in the cool nighttime. Wait for us at the edge of the outskirts. We will look for you there. And we will take you to the place of green grass, tall trees, and cool breezes. And you will be safe. With us."

When she looked up at him, her eyes were red but there were no tears in them. "Yes," she said, smiling. "Yes, I'll go with you. I want to see all the places you told me about. I want to see those trees. And most of all, I want to stand in the sunlight, if only for a while."

Rahelle leaned over and hugged her. "You will be a daughter to me."

"And I will be your father," Gareth said.

"And I will have a family again." Joy sparkled in her eyes. "I have few belongings, so I won't need to take much with me, mostly what I'm wearing." She felt around in her pockets. "Just a few seeds. And a pebble. And—" She pulled out a rock rose, the one Rahelle had given the little girl. Standing up slowly, Aniella stared at the flower. She rewrapped her face with rags until only her eyes were visible, and she shuffled slowly to the balcony, then stopped.

"The little girl who gave me the flower," Aniella said as she caressed the petals of the flower, "she only has a grandmother to care for her. They have little to eat and only survive because I give them food. And the other children—they only survive by begging and the extra fruit and grain I bring. Their lives depend on me, on what I can

161

do."

She slumped against the door frame and shook as though she were sobbing. "I can't abandon them. I can't. I couldn't enjoy the beauty and comfort you offer, knowing I'd left them with nothing. I can't go with you, no matter how much I want to. I'm sorry. I'm sorry. And thank you. Thank you for everything."

She climbed over the balcony and disappeared into the darkness.

"Wait," Gareth said as loud as he dared and ran to the balcony. "Don't go."

But he couldn't see her anywhere.

"Maybe she will change her mind," he said. "Maybe she just needs to say goodbye to her friends."

"Maybe." Rahelle took his hand, entwined her fingers with his, and leaned her head against his shoulder. "Maybe. Come to bed now. Tomorrow will be a long day."

The sun was nearing the horizon and the heat of the day was diminishing when Gareth and Rahelle rode from the Great House to the market plaza, followed by half a dozen mounted guards. "An honor guard," Lord Dayan had said.

All the pack *oudrakhi* were loaded and ready to leave. Alric mounted his horse, as did the drovers and guards. Rahelle nodded to Alric, who led the caravan through the city gates.

Gareth and Rahelle rode at the back of the caravan instead of at the front where they would normally be. They kept watching for Aniella, hoping she'd changed her mind. Hoping she would be able to slip into the caravan without Dayan's guards seeing her, especially as sunset left shadows on both sides of the trail as well as the road. Hoping she would leave the danger behind and come with them to the safety of the Domains. But there was no sign of her.

They reached the last tents of the outskirts before Dayan's guards turned back to the city. Gareth was relieved but terribly sad. Aniella had not appeared. Maybe she had been unable to sneak out to meet the caravan with the guards so close and watchful. He kept his horse at a slow walk, still hoping she would appear.

A few lengths from the edge of the outskirts, he halted and stared at the side of the road. Rahelle reined in her horse beside him.

"What is it?" she said.

"Look. There. Beside the road." He nodded toward the right side of the trail.

Small white rocks lay in a hand sized circle, and in the center of the circle a pink rock rose was stuck in the ground, its petals faded and limp. Aniella wasn't coming.

Rahelle placed her hand on his arm. "She chose to stay with the people who needed her and protected her."

"But she won't be safe," he said, his throat tight.

"Perhaps not," she said, giving his arm a gentle squeeze, "but it was her choice to make."

Disheartened and anxious, he clapped his legs against his horse's sides. As he rode beside Rahelle, he suddenly felt a faint tingling sensation. He glanced over his shoulder toward the city, and the rock rose caught his eye. The flower seemed to glow for a moment, then the petals revived. The stem began to grow and twine until it was nearly knee-high and a dozen blossoms opened. And for a brief moment, he thought he saw green eyes glittering in the shadows.

RENEGADES OF DARKOVER

by Robin Wayne Bailey

Early Darkover novels focused on the melding—and sometimes the violent clash—of cultures, the low-technology yet psychically advanced Darkovans opposed by the highly industrialized space-faring Terrans (first as an Empire, then a Federation, now a fractured Star Alliance). Of course, not everyone on both sides is happy with evolving cooperation and understanding.

Robin Wayne Bailey is the author of numerous novels, including the Dragonkin *trilogy and the* Frost *series, as well as* Shadowdance *and the Fritz-Leiber-inspired* Swords Against The Shadowland. *His short fiction has appeared in many magazines and anthologies with numerous appearances in Marion Zimmer Bradley's* Sword and Sorceress *series and Deborah J. Ross's* Lace and Blade *volumes. His novelette, "The Children's Crusade" was a 2008 Nebula Award nominee. Some of his stories have been collected in two volumes available from Yard Dog Press. He is a former president of the Science Fiction and Fantasy Writers of America and co-founder of the Science Fiction Hall of Fame, now located in Seattle, Washington. He lives in Kansas City, Missouri, and denies that he ever went undercover as a pink flamingo in order to research his stories.*

Donathan Storn strolled through the markets of Thendara with his gray hood drawn up and his cloak wrapped closely around his shoulders against the cool air of twilight. As he walked the streets, he appeared to study the produce in the fruit stands, the breads in the bakers' stalls, a potter's fine ceramics, and other wares, but that was a pose, a ruse. He focused his true attention on other matters, studying the shoppers, pedestrians and merchants, noting their expressions and memorizing their faces as he avoided their eyes.

Carnival Street at dusk was already alive with the nightly celebration that accompanied sundown. Acrobats turned flips, mimes worked their art as jugglers juggled, and minstrels sang their baudiest ballads for coins. Young men and women flirted with abandon in a casually sensual mood. A young, red-haired youth touched Donathan Storn's arm in a suggestive manner and sought to make meaningful eye-contact. Storn ignored him and turned away. He might have found the youth attractive, but he hadn't come to Carnival Street to indulge his passions. He gazed upward over the heads of the laughing throng to the spectacle of the four Darkovan moons as they approached conjunction.

Let them celebrate now, he thought. *They will know soon enough. Soon enough, they will see!*

The four moons drew closer together. Blue Liriel overtook the shimmering emerald that was Kyrrdis. Pale and small Mormallor raced to catch the soft disk of Idriel, the largest of the four. Like shining magnets, they drew together and for one brief moment they hung as if impaled on the black spire of Asharra's Tower.

Donathan Storn smiled to himself.

An explosion suddenly rocked the street. Flame and smoke and bits of rubble erupted outside the gates of Comyn Castle one block over. Almost simultaneously, a second blast shook the street, causing fruit stalls to collapse and pottery venders scrambling to save their products. At the opposite end of Carnival Street a second fountain of fire and smoke shot upward with such force as to obliterate the entrance to Thendara House.

The sounds of celebration turned to screams. In the four-moon glow, Donathan Storn flung back the folds of his cloak. With arms full of leaflets, he leaped upon the restraining wall of a public fountain and flung his pieces of paper into the air. The leaflets scattered like frightened birds as the evening breeze blew them down the street, plastered them against shop windows, and lifted them over the walls of private homes.

In such an atmosphere of terror, few paid attention to the flyers. By morning, that would change. Donathan Storn pulled his cloak close again and, tugging his hood over his face, he hopped down, slunk off and blended into the panicked crowd.

"Four bombs!" Jean Ardais addressed the emergency meeting of Comyn representatives, his plump face red and sweating, his fist drumming incessantly on the table. "And I have heard as many as six!"

The Aillard representative looked bored. "Two bombs," he corrected as he yawned. "The Ardais clansmen are always over-reacting."

Tomas Alton stretched his lanky body in his seat and folded his hands behind his head as he watched the squabbling. There hadn't been time to assemble a full Council, nor did everyone agree that was yet needed. Two bombs had erupted in very public places with numerous injuries, but no deaths. It appeared the bomber had been careful. *Or bombers*, he corrected himself. *Nothing can be assumed.*

He fingered the folded leaflet that one of the castle guards had given to him. He had lost count of the number of times he had read the document. More than the actual bombings, the leaflet fascinated him. *Cieloslibertat!* it proclaimed, but what was that? A call to action? The name of a group? He recognized the corrupted forms of two Old Terran words in this new one, but what did *sky* and *freedom* signify in the context of this terrorist attack?

A brief scowl flickered across his face as he glanced around the room. Telepathic dampers in the ceiling nullified his *laran*, but he didn't need psi abilities to read the expressions of the Council members. With a small flash of insight, he realized that few Comyn were good at masking their emotions. Perhaps it was an unacknowledged side-effect of *laran*. He saw the fear on some faces, and the worry. On others, he noted consternation, anger, and outrage. On still others, he saw suspicion and that surprised him, that they might distrust each other even on a matter such as this. Still, the men in the chamber were the privileged elite of their society, and if they could agree on nothing else at the moment, they agreed on this, that someone had just challenged their privilege.

Like wasps, they were stirred up.

He sat through the meeting as long as appearance required, but when Ardais took the floor again to spew his same ridiculous allegations, he rose, stretched and yawned noisily to express his boredom, and departed the chamber. Free of the telepathic dampers, he paused and rubbed his temples. The dampers always caused him headaches.

He would have to make a report to Armida soon and preferably before any wild rumors reached his home. First, however, he wanted to do some checking of his own. If the bombings were the work of a single madman, there really was little to worry about. The perpetrator would be found and taken care of in a quiet manner. Yet, if there was something more to *Cieloslibertat*, if it represented some actual threat, then as an Alton telepath, he had the means to discover it.

The Alton family maintained a well-appointed suite in Comyn Castle, and Tomas Alton, who had come to Thendara some days before on a trade mission, had installed himself there. Esmeralda, an elderly servant woman, greeted him and hurried to set out a tray of fruits, cheeses, and fresh hot fry-cakes. "You neglected breakfast, my lord," she reminded him, "so I prepared this myself over a hot stove in your absence."

The slight scolding in her voice amused him, so he humored Esmeralda by wolfing down two of the quite delicious fry-cakes and a single piece of cheese. Then, under her stern scrutiny, he made a show of pocketing an apple. "A ward against starvation," he told her with a grin. He stopped by his quarters long enough to strap on his sword and don a thin cloak. He took a quick drink of water from a crystal goblet by the tray and set it down again. "Now, a kiss for Esmeralda," he said as he took her veined hands in his and pressed his lips to her forehead. Ignoring her blush, he moved toward the door. " I may not be home for dinner, so stay away from hot stoves in my absence." He gave her a wink as he departed.

As he strode through the corridor, he fingered the hilt of his sword. It was a thin blade, a gift from his father, and his most prized possession, coldly utilitarian in appearance, unlike the ostentatious blades so many other Comyn carried to proclaim their rank to the public. He disliked making a show of himself in the streets, preferring a nondescript appearance as he moved among other citizens.

He went first to the damaged Comyn Castle gate. There were numerous gates into the castle, and the gate on Carnival Street was not the main entrance. In the press and chaos of the celebration, anyone might have left a package beside it without being noticed. Already, workmen had cleaned up the worst damage. He paused to watch as carpenters labored to build a new gate right on the spot and to observe a pair of young men busily whitewashing away the smoke and residue on the walls.

As he watched, he opened his mind, turning his telepathic sensitivities on each laborer in turn. The carpenters went about their work, unaware of his presence, grateful for their jobs, content with their lives, focused more on hinges and lathes and the music of saws and hammers than on the bombing. He found the same to be true of the two young painters, although one seemed not so unaware of him. That one paused and put his brush into the whitewash, then looked around, finally gazing directly at Tomas Alton.

Tomas drew his hood a little closer about his face as he probed that young man with keener interest. *Mikal* was his name. His parents were cloth-merchants on Weaver Street, and he had never been in any trouble. Still, Tomas Alton made note of these details, Mikal was not, himself, a telepath, but he had a strong latent potential for it, strong enough that the Comyn should know. It interested Tomas greatly to discover such a talent so close to the castle.

After a time, Mikal frowned and scratched his head, then picked up his brush and went back to work. Tomas also turned away. The boy, although a curiosity, knew nothing useful.

Despite the early hour, small throngs of shoppers moved up and down Carnival Street. They milled among the candle shops, bakeries and candy stores, eyed colorful scarves and kerchiefs in store windows, savored various fruits and snacks offered by street merchants. Tomas set aside all his rigid training, all his psychic barriers, and kept himself open to stray thoughts and random impulses as he strolled at the sides of the road. It didn't surprise him too much to realize that most of them weren't interested in shopping at all. Their curiosity had drawn them out into the day to see what they could see and to gossip and pick up news.

But there was more, as well. Among the many minds he brushed over, he felt something that genuinely startled him and even touched him with a small fear—a passive but smoldering resentment against the Comyn.

A cloak-maker leaning in the doorway of his shop gazed up and down the street. He greeted the passersby, made his attempts to lure them in to examine his wares, and quietly made plans for his lunch and dinner. Yet, in the back of his mind was a word—*Cieloslibertat*—and folded in his pocket he carried a flyer he'd found in the gutter.

On the other side of the street a pair of matronly women walked together with their packages. They kept their voices low, but they couldn't hide their thoughts from an Alton. They were also chatting about the bombings. One of them muttered *comeuppance,* and her companion nodded agreement.

The biggest shock, however, came from a group of children. As they ran squealing and playing across his path, he realized they were acting out the events of last evening. "I want to be the bomber!" one of them called. "Let me!"

Tomas Alton stopped in his tracks, shaken. To these children, the terrorist was some kind of a hero.

All of Tomas's barriers slammed into place again. Disconcerted, he moved away from Carnival Street and made his way to Commercial Street, the city's primary thoroughfare. There, he turned toward Thendara House. Gradually, he shrugged off the sense of hostility he had found on Carnival Street and cautiously opened his mind once again to the thoughts of those around him.

Things seemed calm on busy Commercial Street. The pedestrians were focused on their immediate tasks, their shopping, their jobs, or on practical matters such as lunch. The bankers thought only of their banks and their money, the lawyers of their clients. A small group of Terran workers from the spaceport discussed new overhauls and upgrades to their ship in port. A young woman worried secretly about her upcoming wedding as she gazed into a shop window.

Tomas stopped at a street side food stall and ordered a biscuit stuffed with cold meat. As he paid for his meal, the vendor looked up at Tomas and Tomas plainly saw his thoughts. *My red hair and my height. He recognizes me as an Alton—and fears me.*

The biscuit broke in Tomas's hand, and the meat slipped free and fell to the ground. The vendor reacted with shock and apologized profusely, although the fault was Tomas's. With a trembling hand, the vendor hastily pushed a second sandwich toward Tomas, who also apologized and tried rightfully to take the blame and calm the vendor. "Forgive my clumsiness, my friend," he said conversationally. "I'm distracted by this beautiful day and the charms of this city." Accepting the replacement biscuit, Tomas moved on.

The encounter with the vendor troubled him, however. The man feared him groundlessly simply because of who Tomas was. But it wasn't just Tomas he feared. It was all the Comyn. It was not a reaction he had encountered before, although he had to admit that his position and status had perhaps sheltered him. He had too seldom taken walks like this among the city folk and common people.

"You seem surprised."

Tomas stopped and turned around with his mouth full of biscuit. A dark-clad man with a handsome face and a broad grin stood directly behind him. Tomas hastily swallowed. "Were you addressing me, sir?"

The speaker stopped and adjusted his backpack on his shoulder. "Indeed, young Alton," he answered. "I don't have to be a telepath to understand the expression on that poor man's face—or on yours."

Tomas took a quick look into the grinning man's mind. The stranger really wasn't a telepath, yet his mind was strangely difficult to penetrate, not shielded in any manner that indicated training, just inscrutable and vaguely chaotic. "I'm sorry, do I know you?" Tomas felt awkward with his sandwich in hand, but more, the man's grin annoyed him.

"Apologies," the stranger said with a slight bow. "I'm not following you, but we seem to have been on parallel paths for the past few blocks. On these streets, I noticed you right away.' His grin faded, and he looked directly into Tomas's eyes. "You're very easy to notice, young Alton." He offered his hand. "My name is Robert Barron, and I'm on an errand to Thendara House. If you wish, we could walk together." His grin immediately returned. "But please, finish your lunch."

Tomas's annoyance faded, as did the tension in his shoulders. He hadn't realized how intensely the open reading of so many minds had affected him, put him on edge. He looked at the stranger with new eyes as he accepted the handshake. In fact, that easy grin was somewhat charming. "I welcome your company," he answered, "but tell me, as you're obviously so observant, why would these people fear me? What do they have against the Comyn?"

Robert Barron shrugged and adjusted his backpack again as they started side-by-side down Commercial Street. "Why would they not fear you?" he answered. "You are a superman to most of them. Your powers elevate you above them. You can see their thoughts, their fears, their secrets as casually as they might watch a bird fly or a leaf fall. That alone makes many of them feel unsafe."

Tomas frowned. "I can't help what I can do any more than they can help seeing with their eyes or hearing with their ears."

"On the contrary," Robert Barron said, shaking his head. "You are born with your abilities, but you take special training to strengthen and expand them, and you do that in secret places like that." He stopped, turned and pointed back to the high tower of Comyn Castle. "And that." He turned again and pointed across the rooftops to the soaring pinnacle of Asharra's Tower. "Places reserved only for Comyn and off-limits to ordinary men and women. Taller and grander than any other structures in the city, they are constant reminders—almost thorns, you might say—to prick the fears and jealousies of lesser Darkovans."

"That's preposterous," Tomas replied, sputtering mouth full of biscuit crumbs. Yet, as he gazed toward Asharra's Tower rising above the rest of the city, he felt a moment of doubt and even some sympathy for Robert's assertion.

"Is it?" Robert persisted. "Let me ask this—who controls the starstones? Who grants access to them? How many of these shop-keepers and vendors and merchants, each possessing at least some small degree of latent psi-ability, might benefit from the awakening of those abilities if such access was granted in more democratic fashion? But the Comyn, alone, reserve to themselves the right to such access, and the commoners are held back. Can you not see how that might breed resentment?"

Tomas shook his head. "But the Comyn take care of the people! We use our *laran* in their best interests."

Robert Barron brushed his hand against Tomas's hand and gave him a sidelong look. "I think you're a good man, Tomas Alton, and you sincerely believe that, but you're young and your eyes not yet fully open. The Comyn are an oligarchy. They rule Darkover for their own interests. If those interests also appear to benefit non-Comyn, that's purely a secondary benefit. Think back over history. All this planet's wars have been fought among the Seven Domains. The Comyn, with *laran* and exclusive control of the matrix crystals, have ravaged Darkover many times over. Those wars were not fought for anyone but themselves." He sighed as he looked away from Tomas to gaze ahead down the street. "And consider that perhaps not everyone wants to be *taken care of.* Consider how paternalistic that sounds."

Tomas felt a defensive flush of anger and considered walking away from Robert Barron, whose comments bore more than a hint of insult and disdain. Tomas thought his must surely be a misinterpretation of events and history and a twisted misunderstanding of the Comyn. He knew he should have arguments to counter every statement Robert made.

Yet, these were views he had never heard before, certainly not in the training halls or towers of the Comyn. Based on the animosity he had sensed on Carnival Street and the vendor's fear, he had to concede that perhaps there was some validity in Robert's words. He watched the passersby and window shoppers nearby. "Everyone seems content," he muttered to himself.

Robert still heard. "On this street and for the moment," he suggested. "Between Comyn Castle and the Terran spaceport lays the best part of Thendara. Everything appears clean and bright on these streets. But there are older parts of the city, darker places where the poor live, and the poor always outnumber the wealthy and successful. Every city, even this one, has its slums and tenements, places that you, young Alton, never see and never go."

"Then I will go someday," Tomas affirmed. Unconsciously, he tried again to probe Robert Barron's thoughts, but all he read were surface impressions. Among those impressions, one surprised Tomas. Robert Barron found him attractive. Tomas blushed and quickly retreated from Robert's mind. "Have you ever heard of

Cieslibertat?" he asked.

The grin returned to Robert's face. "A word spoken only in whispers," he said with mock gravity and one hand to the side of his mouth. "Their pamphlets and flyers are all over town. Rumor is, in other cities, too. Word on the streets is that they're renegades. They staged last night's attacks."

"I don't know if I'd call them attacks," Tomas said. "More like acts of vandalism."

"Now that is the view of a Comyn," Robert snapped. "You weren't among those injured in the blasts."

The charge stung Tomas like a slap, and again he considered walking away from the aggravation that was Robert Barron. Yet, he heard an echo of truth in Robert's words or, at least, truth from a certain perspective. "If you find me so offensive," Tomas said as he stared straight ahead, "why do you walk along with me?"

Robert stopped still and looked surprised. "I don't find you offensive," he answered. His dark-eyed gaze lingered on Tomas's face. "Quite the contrary. I find you very pleasing company. But you've asked me some difficult questions. Can one hope to lie to an Alton telepath?"

Tomas pushed back his hood and welcomed the touch of a cool breeze on his uncovered head. Robert's response confused him just as everything he said confused him. Yet again, he tried to probe his companion's thoughts and encountered the same churning fog of surface impressions and contradictory patterns. He understood none of it, and that, too, confused him. Only one thing stood out—Robert wanted him.

A hot blush colored Tomas's face, made all the redder by the ginger color of his hair. He contemplated something he had seldom done and, admitting his reciprocal desire, he lowered his voice, looked around, and then spoke. "We Altons keep a private residence near Thendara House for times when Comyn Castle would be inconvenient. Would you like to join me there?"

Robert smiled and adjusted his backpack again. "I have

much to accomplish today and little time," he answered. "But I would join you for a while." His smile turned into that now-familiar grin. "Will there be wine?"

Tomas laughed for the first time all day. His decision might be impetuous, but he wanted to know more of Robert Barron, much more. He could visit Thendara House later. He still wanted to see the second blast site and dig around a little. His parents would want a first-hand report of the incidents and *Cieloslibertat*, whatever it was, when he returned home.

But he still had time for Robert Barron. Robert had opened his eyes to some things. Tomas felt sure there was more to learn.

The Alton residence lay another block off Commercial Street on Fountain Road. Its high, vine-covered walls concealed a veritable paradise of small fountains, shrubs and rare flowers, all carefully landscaped and arranged for calming meditation and contemplation, a refuge from the rest of the busy city and the affairs of the world. Tomas had been here only once before, but he loved the place. Everything about its architecture and furnishings were designed to foster an attitude of rest and peace.

"Impressive!" Robert said as he passed through the gates and looked around.

A serving woman and a caretaker hurried to greet them as they approached the house. After acknowledging their greetings, Tomas waved the caretaker back to his duties and instructed the serving woman to bring food and wine to the master suite. "Follow me, my friend," he said to Robert as he entered the house.

Robert walked inside. As they approached a staircase to an upper level, he paused to unsling his backpack. "May I leave this here?" he asked as he set his burden on the floor by the lowest step. "It contains my day's work. I mustn't forget it when I leave."

"Set it wherever you like," Tomas answered. "No one will disturb it. Except for the small staff, we're entirely alone here."

They went upstairs together, and as they entered the master suite, Tomas hesitated, suddenly nervous, and licked his lips. Second-guessing himself, he wondered if he had made a mistake bringing Robert here. He knew so little of the man, only that he found him fascinating and disquieting. Before he could change his mind, however, Robert touched the back of his head and kissed him lightly on the mouth.

After that first kiss, they wasted little time. Ignoring the food and selection of wines the serving woman had brought before them, they found the bedroom, stripped each other wordlessly, and plunged beneath the piles of fine blankets to explore each other's bodies.

Tomas forgot all his doubt and hesitation. He had been right about one thing—he had a lot to learn from Robert Barron, and Robert proved an exquisite instructor. At the end of an hour, Tomas sank into the crook of Robert's arm. They had kicked away the blankets, and the sheets were drenched in sweat. Exhausted, Tomas curled up close to share the warmth of his companion.

Robert hugged and kissed him, then rolled off the bed. "You promised there would be wine," he grinned, "and I saw wine on the table. I think we could both use a glass."

Wine did sound good. Tomas stretched as he watched his naked companion walk from the bedroom and return a few moments later with two delicate glasses of deep red beverage, a Terran import of intoxicating color and bouquet. *A luxury for Comyn*, Tomas thought, reflective and a little guilty as he took his first sip and leaned back. *Something not for the common people.* He stared into his glass, then set it aside as he contemplated his surroundings—the magnificently polished wood that made the bed, the expensive blankets and quilt lying in a tangle on the gleaming tiled floor, the richness of the Alton estate, itself, his entire pampered life of privilege.

He looked over at Robert. His lover wore a relaxed expression, his eyes lightly closed, wine glass balanced precariously on his bare thigh. Tomas reached over to touch Robert's hand. At the same time, inadvertently, he reached out to touch Robert's thoughts.

For the first time, he penetrated the fog and chaos of his lover's mind. It happened with such unexpected ease that it startled him. The bed creaked as he sat up suddenly. Hearing the sound, Robert snapped open his eyes and stared at Tomas. "What have you done, young Alton?" he said with a curious glance.

Tomas rose from the bed and backed away. "Who is Donathan Storn?" he whispered. Confused, he stared at Robert. "Who are you?"

A change came over Robert's face. His jaw tensed and his brow furrowed as he ran one hand through his hair, pulling some strands of it down toward his eyes. The change to his appearance was pronounced and remarkable. He was still Robert—but he wasn't!

"I am Donathan Storn," he answered in a deeper, rougher voice. "And Robert Barron. And if you push deeper into my mind, you'll find many others. As they say, I am Legion. And I am the Renegades of Darkover."

Tomas saw it then, the truth; all the multiple personalities layered one over another, the chaos of broken thoughts that had prevented him from reading Robert's mind. As Robert Barron fell asleep and the Storn persona prepared to emerge, he saw the horror of it all.

Donathan/Robert slowly grinned and raised his glass to Tomas. "I shouldn't have let my guard down. I'm afraid I've overstayed my time."

Tomas got one more brief glimpse into the mind of the man in his bed. He saw the backpack at the bottom of the stairs. Too late, he rushed for the door, calling for help.

The explosion rocked the Alton mansion. The stairway erupted in splinters amid a shower of shredded leaflets and pamphlets. A ceiling collapsed. Plaster and stone fell, and a wall crumbled into dust. The force of the blast flung Tomas off his feet. He struck his head on the table, sprawled over the food and wine, and rolled to the floor. Barely conscious, he saw Donathan/Robert step from the bedroom, still naked, just as the ceiling came down upon them both.

MEMORY

by Shariann Lewitt

In the Introduction, I wrote about how fans who became fine writers in their own right viewed Darkover through their own creative imaginations. Nowhere is this more evident than in the many explorations of the psychic talents called laran. Marion Zimmer Bradley hinted that these talents were developed in many forms, some dangerous, others highly beneficial. I leave it to you to decide which one Shariann Lewitt's heroine possesses.

Shariann Lewitt has published seventeen books and over forty short stories under five different names. When not writing, she teaches at MIT, studies flamenco dance, and is accounted reasonably accomplished at embroidery. She adds that, much to her regret, "flamingos, pink or otherwise, tend to be very unhappy in New England." She compensates by owning two parrots.

I want to preserve memories. My mother could neither read nor write and so I have only the shreds of her memories plucked from her mind. My *laran* I had from my father, a man she had enjoyed one Midwinter festival in a poorly lit room. Yes, his clothing had been very fine, but she had paid more attention to the dimple in his cheek as he smiled at her and called her a beauty, to the rippling muscles of his chest as he had pulled a finely embroidered Festival shirt over his head, to the desire in his hands as he ran just the tips of his fingers over her firm young breasts.

This I knew because I read it in her mind when I asked who he was and she told me she did not know. She had never asked his name, had not noted the colors of his clothing, had not cared about anything but the passion

179

rising in her skin and between her thighs. She did not know to shield and I did not know either, and so I saw them together and felt the heat and joy of them and I turned bright red. I had been no more than twelve years old at the time.

That was when my mother knew, or rather, could no longer pretend she did not. The next rest day she dressed me in my better dress, the one that had no patches or stains and had even a touch of embroidery around the neck, and we started out on the long trek from our neighborhood in Thendara to the Tower of Hali.

That day I remember her back held proud in her faded brown dress, her good one, as she marched up to the gate of Hali Tower. She did not turn around when she shoved me forward just a bit and told me to follow the *vai leronis* and do as I was bid.

A lady in a white robe invited me in and led me to a small chamber. She asked me permission and I gave it and I felt—how do I explain how it felt, as if I had been turned inside out, sifted through, and yet nothing remained of that sifting, not even the memory.

An untrained telepath is a danger to herself and everyone around her.

I was that danger, and so I was told that I would now live in the Tower and learn to use my gifts. I ran downstairs to tell my mother, to say goodbye, to ask when I would see her again, but by the time I raced to the bottom of the stairs she was a distant brown mark well on the road back home.

The monitor that first day was one of the best, and she had not only identified my Gift, but my father and my mother's genome as well. "Your father is Coryn Hastur," the monitor told me gently, "and your mother has Aillard blood. If your *laran* were minor, we would not have taken you from her, but as it is..."

As it was, I was *nedestra* Hastur, and Hali belonged to the Hastur. Unlike the Comyn youth who arrived when their *laran* flowered and they were already fully prepared for their world, I had no letters, no knowledge—and far more *laran* than I should. Far more than most of the Comyn youth who came to Hali for their season.

I studied hard and learned to use the starstone easily, as if it were a part of my body I had been missing, but I never quite belonged.

Working in matrix research meant that I could stay away from the others' taunts. In the workroom the substance of the matrix itself absorbed me, and if I found no acceptance at least I had made some kind of place.

In my seventh year at Hali, King Raimund died, quite suddenly, though the monitor who examined him said that his heart had been weak for years from too much rich food and drink. So Lorenz, lovely laughing Lorenz took the throne. We all loved Lorenz and celebrated his coronation with great hopes.

None of this mattered to me beyond the usual Tower gossip, for Hali was full of political rumor. I withdrew to my workroom with my amber matrix memory stones.

"There are rumors about King Raimund's death. People are content now, but we may need to support these facts in the future. We need a way to preserve a memory and prove it is true," my Keeper said to me the evening after the coronation. We had risen late, having attended celebrations all the day before and then worked deep into the night. Now the Tower workers had begun to stir as the sun set over the trees, casting a lavender violet shadow over the rustling leaves. "You have made great progress in putting memories into those yellow stones. Can you seal them with truthspell? And perhaps lock it to someone's *laran* as well?"

As soon as he said the words I knew this was what had been missing from my memory stone. But precisely how to make it work? The lock I understood in principle. We created such locks frequently, both for privacy and also safety. All aircar controls had such locks so that only authorized pilot-*laranzu* could use them. Before such locks, many young Comyn had killed themselves trying to fly the intricate machines, thinking them not terribly more complex than children's matrix kites. And locking a truthspell into a stone, that was new to me.

Interesting work could distract me from my loneliness, and this idea intrigued me. I wanted to talk to someone who would listen to me, someone I could trust and who also understood the technical problem. Only two people made me feel completely accepted and at home. One was my Keeper, but he was no researcher. The other was Felix of Neskaya, who I knew only in the relay screens.

Even among the technicians I knew, Felix was special. No one at Hali got lost in the intricacies of mutating crystal structure the way I did with him. I was certain he must be far older than I, for he was so experienced with both the technology and had such great insight.

"Hali greets Neskaya," I said formally before we began our exchange that evening. "Do you have any news for us?"

"Important news here, Carla of Hali. Two calves were born with spotted hindquarters and we still have not resolved that dispute over the rights to the Sweetwater mill." And then he laughed, like a deep running brook dancing through the great matrix screens. "I am sure you do not have such excitement. How is your memory project progressing?"

"Very well," I told him. "But I want to work on a long-distance lock, and also truthspell."

"Hmmm." He paused. "Do you know how long your alterations last? I've had trouble with that when working with amber matrix. It is weak so it takes the changes very well, but it also seems to revert. You might want to think about that. As to the locking, can you use the signature from the memory itself?"

I could feel his interest as if he had been in the room. His keen curiosity and expertise inspired me and somehow always made me think more clearly. In those moments of relay rapport I could feel his deep knowledge support my creative thought so that together it felt like flying. When the depth of contact faded I understood just how to work with the memory signatures.

"Be sure to let me know how the experiments work," he said.

"Of course."

I was about to end the contact when he interrupted. "One last thing. Do you have any word on the breeding program matches? Not that our young Comyn here are anxious to go to their fates. They would prefer to dally with their current favorites as long as possible, but still, we do need to have those arranged some time."

"Indeed. I have not gotten any word from those who work with the breeding program, but I will inquire and make a point of relaying your need."

"Thank you." I could feel his smile without any sight of his face. "And let them know that we have plenty of firefighting chemicals and charged batteries ready to pay for the trouble. When they are ready, of course."

"Of course." For Hali has always been the center of the breeding program, with the books that record the lineage of every member of every noble house and every *nedestro* who carries *laran*. I even found my mother's name there, along with my own.

Because of that program I would never have a partner or a child. My genes were too mixed, too "coarse" to be properly entered, and those who were in charge of the program did not want any loose *laran* among the peasants.

I pushed that thought aside. I had no other choice but to remain a technician at Hali for the rest of my life. Felix must have read some of that from me as we were in a light rapport and I was not at all shielded from him. But, kind as ever, he withdrew carefully and did not intrude.

Much as I enjoyed the time spent with Felix of Neskaya, I was impatient to get to my workbench and see what I could do with a truthspell, a memory and a bit of yellow matrix.

I barely noticed the arrival of Camilla Hastur at Hali. Why should I pay attention to yet one more pampered princess who, no doubt, would spend her season among us and then go off to the marriage we'd arranged and the political infighting that I ignored? Even if she was my own half-sister. Yes, I was curious about her, about my Hastur family, but I had known plenty of others like her.

I would have ignored her entirely had not two other things happened the same morning that she arrived. First, word had come through the relays late the night before that King Lorenz had been attacked by a catman near the Hastur hunting lodge and lay near death. Two of the best monitor healers of Arilinn were with him, but his condition was grim.

Second, Camilla was a walking pillar of terror.

I had never felt such fear as I felt from her. Even my mother, with nothing in the house to eat and no hope of work for the next two days, had not quivered with panic the way this Hastur daughter did.

"What of this Hastur lady who we hear has arrived at Hali?" Felix asked that night when I met him in the relay.

"What of her? She is afraid of something, terribly afraid," I told him. "I cannot imagine what."

"And I can imagine a great deal," he said, and then there was some silence on his end. "And the attack on Lorenz, what are they saying at Hali?"

I was confused. "What can we say? We are sending another healer, but we're afraid we may too late. He was always a favorite with us, for all he did his training at Arilinn."

"We at Neskaya are nearer to the range of the catmen than you are, and we think it strange that any should be so far from home. That is not cavern country and they don't like to range across open land. Who is saying that it was a catman? What do we know of his injuries? We would be happy to send a healer who is familiar with catman injuries, but no one has contacted us. Why have they not asked for our expertise and our experience, either to help King Lorenz or to track down his killer? That is what we are asking in Neskaya, Carla. We may not know what happens at Comyn Castle and the Council, but we know something of catmen and this does not smell right."

"I had not thought of that, Felix," I admitted. "We know little of catmen here except that they are dangerous killers."

Although I could not see him I could feel him nod. "Exactly. But we do. We have healers here, matrix mechanics from Serrais and Armida where catmen sometimes have threatened human settlements. Some of us have even hunted them in the past. Something here is very wrong. Will you tell me if you hear anything?"

"Of course I will tell you, Felix. You know that. You need not ask."

King Lorenz died a tenday later without ever regaining consciousness. Kyril Aillard, the most senior of the seven Keepers of Hali, stood up in his formal red robes and made the announcement during dinner so we knew it was true. "The Council has named Coryn Hastur as Regent, until such time as Mikhail Elhalyn y Hastur comes of age and is confirmed as King of the Domains."

My father. Much as I barely knew him, I could not avoid the thought that my own father was now Regent.

A thin wail came from behind my left shoulder. Camilla Hastur had doubled over and clutched her arms around her stomach as if trying to hold her fear and grief inside. Instead it spilled out in great engulfing waves, overwhelming all of us. This distant political event that had elevated her family had brought on shattering emotion; I was so overwhelmed by her terror that I could barely lift my head.

Fingers gripped my hand. This was not the feather-light brush of a telepath's fingertips against the back of my wrist, but a crushing hold that threatened to break bones. I had never imagined such strength in that slender, delicate hand. As she held on to me I was beaten with images of people I did not recognize though through Camilla's mind I knew them to be the family I had never met.

My father, Coryn Hastur, was Regent. He had sent me a stipend when I entered the Tower and acknowledged me. He had even sent a polite, though formal invitation for me to attend my first Midwinter Festival at Comyn Castle. We had had a stiff interview where he had asked me questions about my work at Hali over cups of *jaco* and a plate of pastries. The meeting became a ritual once a year that I assumed was an uncomfortable duty for us both.

SISTER! Help! We must make him stop!

I don't know if I heard actual words or if the meaning overwhelmed me. I did not understand what she meant—except the acknowledgment of our bond. Mind to mind, our shared blood made our rapport unlike any I had ever experienced.

She clung to me, hand and mind, and I could not assert myself or get free from the flow of terror and images that made no sense. At that moment, I believed myself truly mad.

Then I thought of my mother, of laundry, took a deep breath and centered myself.

I will help you, I promised her, *but you must become calmer. I cannot help you like this.*

The knotted fear that had been all we had known of Camilla softened and suddenly there was a person under all that thundering emotion. She reached out to me gently, tentatively, and touched my mind while a monitor kept her systems clear and emotions composed.

Breda.

I loved Camilla at that first true experience of her. For all she was a gentle soul, she had a sharp sense of humor and a clear-eyed vision of those around her. She saw their faults but did not think ill of them for their limits. Always she had appeared the dutiful and obedient daughter, supple as the grass, doing whatever was required of her. Others, she knew, saw her as weak, a pawn to be used in the schemes of the Council.

And yet I felt deep within her the same strength that had enabled me to survive and grow, even as I had to struggle to find and define my place in Hali. Camilla also had had to assert her place as Hastur, though she, like me, hid much of herself.

The next two nights were long hard ones for me. The Second Circle was quarrying a small vein of bluestone, and while I wondered about what had brought my sister to such terror, hard work and exhaustion overcame any further curiosity I had.

I came famished to the rich meal after our working session, my only desire to assuage my raging hunger and then fall directly into my bed. Nut bread hot from the oven spread with Fiona's special berry jam that went very nicely over the juicy haunch of roasted rabbit-horn too, a thick slice of hard salty cheese (also lovely with that jam) and two—make that three—of Fiona's honey cakes crowded my plate and I had eyes for nothing else. So I was taken by surprise when her voice came at my shoulder.

"Sister, will you walk with me?"

I turned, my mouth full of rabbit-horn and jam dribbling down my chin, to find Camilla Hastur seated beside me. I did not want to walk. I wanted only to fill my belly and collapse into bed. But she was balanced at the edge of her courage and was finally ready to tell me the reason for her fear.

"Oh, finish your food," she said, and attempted a smile.

I wolfed down the last of the meat. The cheese I put on the bread and held in one hand, the cakes I took in the other. "Lead on," I told her. I could eat as I listened.

She said nothing as I followed her along the path to the lake. She led me through the heavy, thick mist that pulled at my hem. The vapors of the lake tugged at the heart as well as my feet. Soft mist rose so that I could not discern a clear border between lake and air. Camilla still led on, unwavering, and finally indicated a place where a few boulders rose above the mist. I turned and saw we were a fair distance from the shore.

"We are safe here, I think," my sister said, but the fear did not leave her. Indeed, it seemed to wrap around her like a shawl and she seemed huddled within it.

I offered her a cake, but she shook her head. Hungry as I was, I urged her to take it. She was pale and, now that I could study her closely, far too thin. She looked a wraith barely more substantial than the mist of the lake itself.

"I came to Hali because I thought I might be safe, at least safer than in Hastur or Comyn Castle," she began.

"Why would you not be safe at Comyn Castle?" I asked, trying to keep any surprise from my voice.

Her eyes flickered over to the shore, which was empty of all life. "I know... He killed..." Her words drifted off into the lake, as insubstantial as the mist itself.

"Did our father kill King Raimund?" The words came out of my mouth but they were not mine. I had never even thought of Coryn Hastur as my father, let alone referred to him as such.

The shadow of the Hastur princess came over her. "No," she said, and this time strength touched her voice. "No, it was Lewis-Gabriel. Our brother. Father doesn't know. Lewis-Gabriel also killed Lorenz. I think his plan is that now Father is Regent, he will try to kill Father and take his place. Then, when Mikhail dies of threshold sickness, or appears to, Lewis-Gabriel will become King. We must stop him."

"And we must escape," I added.

She sat straighter on the rock, her mouth drawn firm. "That is less important. Lewis-Gabriel must be stopped. I am willing to kill him if I must. Will you help me?"

"How do I know what you say is true? Do you have proof?"

Camilla looked at me with those matrix-blue eyes, took my hand, and lowered her shields. I could feel the effort it took her, the determination and strength of that action. I touched her mind with a delicate, monitor's touch and found myself melting into her.

Breda.

We could have lingered in our shared delight of discovery, but something more important called.

Knowledge. Proof. I merged into her memories and they were mine.

Lewis-Gabriel. He believes I/we have so little laran *that I don't matter. He is not fond of me, but he is not fond of anyone. Something is missing inside of him. Empathy. Compassion. Love. He had none for any living being and never had.*

Father tries not to know, and Mother—he killed Mother. My/our mother that is. His own mother died earlier and my mother knew him for what he was and so he killed her. He made it look as if she died in childbed with my stillborn brother, another victim of our breeding program.

I felt my mother die. I knew. That was when I began to shield and let no one know how much laran *I have. My mother knew he murdered her. Lewis-Gabriel wanted her to know.*

He tried to make me kill the king. I had to seek shelter in Hali until I could find a way to stop him.

King Raimund was twice a widower with four living sons. My eldest brother came to me while I sat in the solar working on a difficult passage on the ryll. I am accounted a good player and wanted to master this piece, so I did not notice his arrival until he tore the music from the stand.

"Camilla, I have a charge for you. You are to sit next to King Raimund at the Feast of Evanda and put on your prettiest manners. If you do, you may be Queen."

I was utterly disgusted by the thought. King Raimund was older than Father, and fat, and not interested in anything except racing horses and his sons and drinking.

"King Raimund finds you desirable. You would be Queen, and all you need to do is one small thing I ask. Raimund is easily distracted, and easily led by a beautiful woman. You need only follow my instructions. Besides which, I am assured by the Court monitors that he has drunk and eaten himself into a weak heart. You may find yourself a widow very quickly. This would be very much to your advantage."

He said the words but he did not take care to shield the thoughts as deeply as he should. I had been careful that he never thought of me as a serious person. I saw him give me a small vial and ask me to drop one drop into the King's wine. One drop, every other night, not so much as anyone could taste, nothing that anyone would ever notice. I knew from his mind that it was poison.

He wanted me to help him murder the King. He has the Hastur Gift of persuasion and I could feel the power of it trying to slip into my mind. It felt like a wisp of smoke curling around my own clear beliefs, but it found no purchase. It appears that I am immune to this Gift of my bloodline.

"No. I will not."

His face grew brilliant red, fury mixed with shock. I am not sure anyone had ever defied him before. He raised his hand as if to slap me, but then lowered it. "Indeed. I only requested that you flirt and flatter an old man who is your King. Surely there is no harm in that. Any damisela *in the Domains would do as much." His voice was calm and smooth, as if his request had been entirely reasonable. For a moment I doubted what I had heard, the images I had seen coming from him.*

"Then ask your daughter," I said. "Melissa is far more beautiful than I in any case."

"And Melissa has too much laran *to waste in a barren bed," he answered.*

That was the first I knew of his plotting, but I learned more. And because my brother never thought much of me or paid attention, it was easy for me to follow him with him none the wiser. I saw him in the herb shed with the King's gloves, fine kid, dyed blue. He used a stick to spread paste from the tiny green pot in them. I knew what was in that pot, for Maralys the midwife had instructed me in the use of herbs and healing portions. She had cautioned me many times that small green pot held a potion dangerous for someone with a weak heart. I saw him give the gloves to the King when they went out to ride one morning and the King put them on.

They hunted that morning, they feasted that evening, they took to their beds after midnight, and the King never woke again.

Nor had there been a catman to kill Lorenz. "This is necessary. Lorenz is a danger. He will destroy us all." As he said those words I could feel the necessity of them, the pressure of the compulsion growing. And this Gift does not touch me! How must Petro the huntsman have felt, overwhelmed with Lewis-Gabriel's laran and his own naïve desire to save the Domains.

"You must cut Lorenz, as if catmen had come down from the hills." This time Lewis-Gabriel projected the need along with the image of a body ravaged by a catman far out near the Serrais caverns. Long curved slashes had torn the poor man across the chest and face, leaving him unrecognizable, and his throat torn out by savage teeth. The rest of his clothes and much of his skin had been reduced to ribbons.

Petro was almost in a trance as Lewis-Gabriel reinforced his instructions. "Lorenz will leave after dinner. Wait for him outside the lodge on the road to the tavern. Drag him well off the road. You may kill him first and then slash the body. Then you must wash and burn your clothes, and then you may go to the tavern and enjoy a girl as your reward."

The boy was barely conscious. Lewis-Gabriel's will animated him. "Yes, vai dom, as you command."

I felt the power of his desire, of his laran directed at his instrument. I left at first light for Hali, only to learn that Lorenz had been attacked by a catman in the night.

Why did he not kill Lorenz himself? I asked inside her mind.

Lewis-Gabriel enjoys the power, bending another's will against their nature. Petro is a good man and was loyal to Lorenz.

I felt the revulsion shake her so deeply that she was nearly sick. Then the rapport between us thinned and she and I were separate again.

The great bloody sun, which had barely risen over the horizon when we had walked the shore, now hung well above in the morning sky. The two honey cakes that had remained had crumbled in my hands and the crumbs trickled through my fingers. Strange lake creatures glided up from below to feast on the bounty. Suddenly I needed to be back in the solid walls of the Tower.

Lanil Storn had suggested that I make memories, and truthspell them, around King Lorenz's coronation. Now I thought I should make such a memory matrix about his death. I could put any memory into a yellow matrix, and if I could truthspell it as well, that would vouch for its veracity.

I did not broach the subject to Camilla until I saw her the next day. She had worked at making herself useful assisting Fiona in the organization of the kitchens and the laundry. Indeed, I had to seek her out at Fiona's small office near the front gate. I waited while Camilla drove a hard bargain with the dried fruit seller.

"That was fun," she said. I could not imagine bargaining with merchants as anything approaching fun, but I appreciated the pleasure of victory in my *breda*'s eyes.

"I thought you should make a memory," I started hesitantly, and then explained my project. "If you are willing, with my stones the truth will not be forgotten."

Some of the pleasure left Camilla's face as the fear reasserted itself. And then she shook her head quickly. "Maybe. It might help. I cannot hurt, if it is sealed against being opened. No one else must know, or Lewis-Gabriel...."

"We will lock the stone," I suggested. I needed to try the experiment anyway. "We will make two of them so that I can do the work, to experiment, you understand. We will lock the final version to the life of Prince Mikhail and the Regent, so that if either of them dies, the memory will unlock of its own accord. But if they live then it will remain sealed. Does that sound safe enough?"

Camilla considered and nodded. "It is possible that

Mikhail will die of threshold sickness, but his brothers have survived. He is not frail. Our father is not a young man."

"But he is in good health," I countered. "Anyway, I cannot think of better. There is no way the stone would know how they died. I cannot lock it otherwise."

We made a plan for her to come to my workshop on the next day. I would have preferred that very moment, but she had to oversee storing the fruit and looking over a contract with the carpenter to repair the stair rail in the living quarters. "Fiona thinks I drive a harder bargain than she does," Camilla confided. "But it is the work I was trained to do."

I never thought Comynara did anything except sew and breed.

That night I met Felix of Neskaya in the relays. I had missed him for a full tenday and we had much to discuss. I told him of my sister, of some of her revelation to me, though not the whole of it, and how she had agreed to embed it in my memory matrices.

"You can use this to stop Lewis-Gabriel," he said, his thought so soft that I was not certain at first that it came from him.

I froze. "You mean, to threaten him? I—could not do such a thing. It is wrong."

I could barely feel Felix in the screens. His mind closed down and he had drawn within himself to some stillness. Time hung, silent. "What Lewis-Gabriel has done is wrong, and more than wrong. What he might do in the future is evil. Which is worse, that you threaten to expose him, or that you possibly keep his evil secret?"

I wanted to run. I wanted—I wanted everything to be the way it had before when King Raimund was alive. I could feel Felix's sadness and warmth around me. "We all want that. We can only do the best we can, and sometimes in the world we must choose." He remained silent for what seemed like no time and forever. "But if Camilla needs a place of refuge, remember that you have yet to give us the Comyn matches for the breeding program. And one of the young Comyn is the Heir to Serrais, and so would be a worthy match for her. She would be protected there."

I nodded though he could not see me, but my heart broke. This would be a perfect solution for Camilla, but I couldn't bear the thought. I would be utterly alone.

It was the only way for her to be safe.

And so it was decided. I decided. I vowed that Camilla would never know the true purpose of the memory stones.

The next night she came to my workroom and we made the two memory stones. One I linked to the life forces of the Crown Prince and Regent of the Domains. The work was new and while I had the theory of how to imprint them from the memory into a release mechanism, I had never done it before. So first I tried with the memory of the day my mother had taken me to Hali, and found that while I could key my memory of her *laran* into a lock, the recollection in the crystal itself seemed less vivid than I thought it had been.

But the lock appeared to work well, and I made a second one on my memory of my first good Festival gown. And that memory, too, seemed just a bit faded from the stone I had made weeks before. The brilliant yellow butterflies embroidered around the neckline seemed a softer butter color than the striking brilliant creatures I had recalled and thought I had embedded into the amber stone.

The faded memories, I was sure, were the result of my own fear.

Camilla sat in the chair at my desk, where the two amber pebbles lay nestled in sky blue spidersilk. She could not tear her eyes from the crystals as I explained the rest of the plan. Her marriage to the Heir of Serrais would put her beyond the reach of Lewis-Gabriel, and I had checked that he was at least young and of good character. The fear, while not gone, had abated enough that she made her decision.

"Distance does not put me beyond my brother's reach," she said softly. "These do. The one that is locked to our father and Prince Mikhail, that one I shall hide in the Council chambers where Louis-Gabriel will never find it.

And this other one, the one that is mine? I shall count it my wedding gift."

Her sly smile confused me. The Camilla I knew did not have a trace of Lewis-Gabriel's cunning and deceit.

Then the shadow passed and her smile turned all sunlight and open pleasure. "Do not worry, *breda*, you have made us all safe. I will happily marry the Heir to Serrais, it is an excellent match. You may inform Neskaya the sooner the better."

"But Lewis-Gabriel? And Father? And Prince Mikhail?" I did not understand why suddenly Camilla seemed to have forgotten her mission, though I would be happy enough to see her simply safe.

"Father and Prince Mikhail will be safe," she assured me. "With your invention, Lewis-Gabriel will do no harm."

Then I understood. "What you are doing is blackmail."

"We are Hastur, sister. What I am doing is politics."

On my previous visits to Comyn Castle I had been an awkward *nedestra*. This time I arrived as the sister-friend to the bride-to-be, as well as a *leronis* of Hali in my own right. Servants treated me, the laundress' girl, with deference. I was assigned a room in Camilla's suite, furnished in elegantly carved silverwood with blue and silver bedcovers of the finest spidersilk, two armchairs, and a fireplace decorated with painted tiles. Two trunks of dresses had been furnished by the family, as Camilla had argued I could hardly attend all the functions in my Tower robes. A servant rubbed perfumed ointment into my skin after my bath, and another dressed my hair and braided it with blue flowers that matched the intricate embroidery at the hem.

I entered Camilla's sitting room.

"Carla, you are beautiful, *breda*." she beamed with approval. "Won't our brother be surprised? And we shall go to meet him now. I have a little surprise for him. A gift. And then tonight *Dom* Javier arrives and I meet my bridegroom!"

I trailed after Camilla with dread. I had barely met Lewis-Gabriel but had no desire to see him angered. I had less desire to see Camilla best him by his own methods, though blackmail was not murder.

She smiled as his door was opened to us. He sat relaxed behind his desk, his long legs crossed on a footstool He was handsome in the way that all Hasturs are, elegant, long-limbed, with an expressive, noble face.

"So you are to be married at last, little sister," he greeted her. He ignored me as if I were her serving maid. "We might have done better for you if you'd had any ambition." He let the statement hang in the air.

"I have a gift for you, brother," Camilla said, and held out the spidersilk bag that contained the memory stone. Lewis-Gabriel took it, shook out the stone, held it for a moment and shrugged. "A pretty thing but..."

"Open it with your *laran*," Camilla prompted him. "It is full of memories of you."

My shields were as strong as I could hold them, thick as the fortifications of Comyn Castle, wide as a fire breech in the forest, solid as the Hellers themselves. And yet I could feel his anger, horror and some emotion new to him as the memories held in the golden matrix washed through him. Fear. Lewis-Gabriel had never felt it before. He had never considered the possibility that anyone could know what he had done.

Anger threatened to lash out but fear reined it back. Another new emotion arose—amazement. He had been outflanked. He was confused.

Camilla smiled gently. "There is another stone, brother, with all the same memories, hidden in the Council Chamber. You will not find it. We have blinded it to your *laran* and locked it to the life signature of both Father and Prince Mikhail. If either of them dies in the next ten years, the stone will broadcast these memories. There is nothing you, or I, can do about it."

"How can it?" he demanded.

"It is quite simple really," I explained. "We have the

signatures in the memories themselves. Since both the Prince and the Regent attend Council meetings, their presence will relock the memory stone at regular intervals. When it relocks, it draws power for the next interval. If they fail to arrive in the Council Chamber every Summer and Winter, then the stone will broadcast. The mechanism is quite easy to set, but impossible to reverse"

Then and only then did Lewis-Gabriel deign to notice my existence. "You," he said, and there was more hatred in that single word than I had ever heard in my life. He was going to kill me. Even in Hali I would not be safe. Hastur owns Hali and we all knew it.

"No, brother," Camilla said. Her tone was so sweet and conciliatory that I could barely credit her words. "You shall not harm Carla, for if you do then any of us shall set off the Council Chamber stone, and if you harm me, or both of us, or my intended husband, the effect will be the same. Father and Prince Mikhail are not the only people life locked to the stone. Believe me, I respect you enough to take those necessary precautions."

Then she turned and I trailed in her wake, leaving Lewis-Gabriel off balance and utterly immobilized for what I assumed was the first time in his life. But he was also highly intelligent, entirely without scruples and ambitious beyond my imagination, and I knew that he would find some way to retaliate.

"We are safe, truly, Carla," Camilla said when we returned to her quarters. "If the Council learns what he has done, he will never be confirmed as the Heir of Hastur, let alone hold any other position in the Domains. He will be lucky to live, given the evidence we have provided and he knows it. Oh, he will try to do something in the future, but we will be prepared. It will be fine, I promise you. Father is still very strong, and Prince Mikhail shows every promise of becoming a strong King."

"But there is no life lock like that, and no one can set off the stones at a distance," I protested.

Camilla smiled that hard, frightening smile. "He does

not need to know that detail."

Camilla might be safe, but I had to return to Hali. Alone. Lewis-Gabriel could possibly get one of the servants to poison me. They already resented what they considered my jumped up position, and I would return to a world with no real friends. My contact with Felix of Neskaya would sustain me—perhaps I could transfer to Neskaya. No one there would remember me as the unschooled girl in the rough brown dress. In Neskaya I would just be a *leronis*. I would disappear from Lewis-Gabriel's sight.

I thought these things as Camilla fluttered around her chambers, waiting for the trumpets to announce her bridegroom's aircar. The presentation took place in the formal chamber of the Hastur quarters, with *Dom* Coryn presiding. *Dom* Javier arrived with *Domna* Michela on his arm and Camilla was introduced to them first. They appeared decent people and immediately embraced her and said how pleased they were to have such a talented, capable, lovely young woman join the family. Camilla, being a proper Comyn daughter, spent some time in conversation with them before turning her eyes to the very appealing young man who waited politely just inside the doorway. He had dark red hair, steady serious gray eyes, and the most sensuous mouth I had ever seen on a man.

"My son, *Dom* Felix of Serrais, lately of Neskaya Tower," *Dom* Javier said.

This was Felix of Neskaya? This was the matrix technician who had been my friend? *He* was the heir to Serrais?

I tried to leave the room but my sister caught me by the arm. "What trouble, *breda*?" she asked. "Do you fear you will be forgotten? Here, let me introduce you. My betrothed husband, please meet my sister, Carla of Hali Tower."

"Carla of Hali?" His face went as white as the stone walls. He reached out a hand and then it dropped to his side.

"Felix of Neskaya?"

He nodded and had the grace to look miserable.

Camilla looked back and forth between us. I do not think she could read Felix, but she surely read me. Until that moment I had not known, truly I had not. How can one fall in love through the relay screens over such a distance? Or had I built a story in my head that had shattered in light of reality?

The Heir of Serrais had to marry according the breeding program, as did my sister. By the strictures of the same program I was not permitted to breed.

Bereft, I stared at the floor. It took all the discipline I had not to break into tears and run out of the banquet hall until the meal had been brought.

When I left the feasting I had no desire to remain in the Hastur apartments, inside the confining walls, so I walked into the gardens and prayed to Avarra, though for what I don't know. Perhaps to die, for life held no hope for me, anymore.

Softly, gently, I felt a loving presence around me. Avarra? The Dark Lady was hardly known for her soft generosity, though I would count her taking my soul in answer to my prayers a great gift indeed. Laughter like a brook in springtime surrounded me.

Breda?

No!

But they came, both of them together, Camilla and Felix, and surrounded me with their bodies and their *laran*. And I, I was so lonely I could not resist and I drank in their presence and their love. No barriers existed between the three of us and so I knew the truth in them and accepted their love freely and knew them to the depth of their beings, as they knew me.

And so they knew how I felt at Hali, how isolated I was.

"I hadn't any idea," Camilla murmured when we had reestablished ourselves in our own bodies again. "I thought we could never ask you to leave there, that it was your haven. I am so glad."

She hugged us both very hard and then we were all

hugging and laughing, although I had no idea why, or why she was glad. "Come, we must return to the feast. It is our betrothal, after all."

The wedding followed three days later. Lewis-Gabriel suddenly was taken to his chambers, unwell. And me, well, I was heady and joyful, for I was not returning to Hali. Camilla and Felix had given me a wedding present of their own. The night before they had announced at their parents' contract dinner that they required me to come with them to become the house *leronis* at Serrais.

On our first anniversary in Serrais I took out the memory matrix I had made of my mother. I was happier than I had imagined possible with Camilla and Felix and hoped only that she realized that as I grasped the stone and sought for her beloved face. But the memories I had embedded into the crystal structure had faded to almost nothing. The stone hadn't held them. These yellow matrix stones were useless.

I almost panicked, but as long as Lewis-Gabriel *believed* the stone in the Comyn Council Chamber was powerful, that was all that was needed.

It was simply politics. And, after all, I was Hastur.

A PROBLEM OF PUNISHMENT

by Barb Caffrey

Sometimes, writers (and their readers) find certain characters so fascinating, they want to know more about the history. Of "A Problem of Punishment," Barb Caffrey writes, "I've been thinking about how Fiona [Fiona n'ha Gorsali, the Renunciate judge from "At the Crossroads," Stars of Darkover] started her studies with her father, and I'd like to explore that next. Surely Domenic, her father, had to be a most unusual man by Darkovan standards." I'm delighted she decided to follow her curiosity into this tale.

Barb Caffrey is the author of "A Problem of Punishment." She's also written three novels, An Elfy On The Loose, A Little Elfy in Big Trouble *(April 2015), and* Changing Faces *(also 2015), and is the co-writer of the* Adventures of Joey Maverick *series (with late husband Michael B. Caffrey) Previous stories and poems have appeared in* Stars Of Darkover, First Contact Café, How Beer Saved The World, Bearing North, *and* Bedlam's Edge *(with Michael B. Caffrey). Find her at* Elfyverse *for discussions of all and sundry, or at* Shiny Book Review. *(She promises she won't bite. Much.)*

Circuit Judge Dominic MacAnndra rode alone through the darkening woods, a loaded crossbow at his side. He hoped he looked like any traveling hunter—meek, inoffensive, skilled. He had put aside his judicial robes because he needed to find the murderous vermin who'd done the unthinkable. They'd broken the Compact.

His skin crawled just thinking about it. But too many people had come into his courtroom during his regular Nevarsin stop who'd said that a band of five, perhaps six toughs had done exactly that. They'd used weapons that left the hand, in order to rob people—badly injuring one old woman who'd offered no resistance, according to witnesses—in violation of their sacred laws.

But because none of the Comyn had been robbed, they didn't care about the problem. Or at least Rodolfo Aldaran, who'd been in court because of a minor agricultural matter, surely hadn't. He had all but told Dominic that the witnesses must be "making up stories."

Thinking about that made his teeth grind. Breaking the Compact was a fearsome thing; the Aldarans *should* care about that.

And not being able to do very much for the injured parties bothered him, even though he'd ruled *in absentia* on behalf of all who seemed to have reasonable claims against the unknown assailants. But he could not punish people who wouldn't come near his courtroom—nor would they attack him if they knew he was a seated judge.

Even the most hardened criminal knew that was a quick ticket to Zandru's coldest Hell.

Which is why Dominic was out here in the woods just south of Nevarsin, even though twilight was nigh. Ostensibly, he was looking for game—but in actuality he was doing his best to find the miscreants. In his youth, he'd been a good tracker of animals, and he was sure he could find the band of thugs.

He was hot on their trail. Once he found them, he'd go back to Nevarsin, round up some men (including his ailing bailiff, Rafael) and bring them to his courtroom.

Then he'd be able to give them exactly what they deserved—justice.

Dominic was bait in a trap. But he intended to spring that trap himself. Just give him time and...

As he rounded the next bend, he heard voices ahead on the trail. Someone sounded...angry? Frightened? He wasn't sure, but either way he knew he had to check it out.

He urged Midnight into a trot, hoping she'd not pick up a stone or worse, and saw two hooded figures struggling in the dirt alongside the trail just out of reasonable arrow-shot (not that he'd ever try to shoot a fellow person!) Only one chervine stood wearily at the side of the road. Had another fled?

Something definitely was wrong. This didn't look like a fight over the chervine, or like any rough-and-tumble hand-to-hand contest he'd ever seen. Instead, the smaller figure in the rich, rust-colored cloak seemed to be grabbing the taller figure in gray homespun to prevent the taller one from leaving. And Rustcloak wasn't wrestling, wasn't hitting, wasn't doing anything except trying to restrain the wriggling Graycloak. But Graycloak was kicking, punching, even biting, and using all his possible strength to get away...but oddly did not look like a trained fighter.

"Do you require assistance?" he called.

Graycloak said in a contralto, "Yes! He pulled me off my chervine—"

Rustcloak snarled in a deep baritone, "Go away, little man! This is not your fight!"

"I know that," Dominic said levelly. "Still, I asked—and the lady answered. What's going on here?"

"A minor...family matter," Rustcloak wheezed. "Leave us!"

"Sorry, I never leave a lady in distress," Dominic said easily. "Against my code and all..." But he was thinking furiously. *One's male and the other's female. The man said it's a "family matter," which might explain why he wasn't trying to hurt the woman. I don't believe him, somehow; could this be a ransom grab instead?*

But she's not dressed like a fine lady, and she's giving a good accounting of herself, too...what a day for Rafael to be down with the ague! He could really use his bailiff's help right now.

Of course, if he pointed out that he was a judge, that might put an end to whatever was going on. No one in his right mind wanted to harm a judge; the penalties were too steep. But that would halt any possibility of him finding the thugs he'd come out here to find in the first place.

Perhaps he could solve this another way?

Rustcloak stopped trying to restrain Graycloak, which allowed the woman to get up. Her hood fell back to show short, cropped brown hair and a lively, intelligent face. Rather than answer Dominic, she yelled at Rustcloak, "I am not your meat, Rumal. Nor am I any part of your family. Not any longer. I'm a Renunciate, damn your eyes! Don't you know what a Renunciate *is*?" And she tried to hit him again, but somehow ended up tangled in Rustcloak's— Rumal's?—cloak.

Odd tactics, Dominic noted as he urged Midnight a bit closer to the fray. *She doesn't seem to be able to land many blows. Why not?*

In the ensuing tussle, Dominic saw a serviceable sword with a jeweled sheath on the man's back, but Rumal didn't draw it. He didn't even try to hit Graycloak over the head with it, which lent credence to Graycloak's story.

Someone's come from money—or he's a very good thief, Dominic thought. He urged Midnight ahead so he might do his best to snatch up the woman and make a run for it. But the chervine refused to move forward.

No matter. He was now close enough that if the woman could get free, he should be able to scoop her up, ride off with her, and get the full story once they were safely away. Because something was definitely wrong—

The woman wiggled free again. But instead of running toward him, she started off in the opposite direction.

Why must we do this the hard way? Dominic thought.

Before Dominic could move, Rumal jumped toward Graycloak and tackled her soundly, then forced her back up again. This time, Rumal held her close to his body—one hand around her waist, the other around her shoulders.

Dominic studied Rumal's face. He looked like a typical arrogant Comyn lord. But Dominic knew all of those, so that meant Rumal was dressing above his station. And his blond hair and blue eyes certainly gave him no hints...even the fact the man had six fingers on his left hand meant nothing, because *chieri* blood was to be found all over the Hellers. *He's never been in my courtroom,* Dominic thought slowly. *Not in all eight years of riding this circuit. So he's either law-abiding, or he's a* particularly *good thief.* He thought harder. *The only Rumal I've heard about who might do something like this is one of the younger sons of Sain Scarp...but whether he is or not, I don't like this. If I told them I'm a judge, he'd probably stop—but I can't. Not when the Compact's been broken. Not yet.* So he watched, observed, and awaited his chance instead.

"You are my sister, and you will be wed as I say," Rumal said, a hint of steel in his voice. "Now, come away with me."

"Or what?" she asked defiantly. "You need me, or you'd have hurt me like you hurt my sisters—"

Could that have been what Midnight had sensed? Blood? Dominic quickly assessed the area; it was possible a larger fight had already occurred. Meaning Rumal was either a very good fighter...or he had allies. Where were they?

And...sisters? Blood, or otherwise? What were they doing here, anyway?

No matter what the answers were to those questions, his duty was clear. "Rumal, let her go," Dominic said, already feeling tired. "If you believe you have a case, the circuit court judge will hear your petition back at Nevarsin. We can all ride up there together, in fact..." *Take the deal,* he inwardly urged Rumal, even though he knew it wasn't likely to be that simple.

"This is not a matter for anyone's court," Rumal told him. "Nor is it your affair. Just leave us be, and no harm will come to you."

Dominic patted his crossbow. "Oh, you can't harm me. But I can harm you—unless you let the woman go." He did his best to put conviction into every word, but inwardly he quailed—*I cannot break the Compact!*

"I haven't seen you use that bow yet," Rumal snarled. "I'm betting you won't."

Dominic, nettled, shot the bow near to Rumal's head— knocking a particularly fat grouse to the ground. "Don't try me," he growled. "Now. Let the woman go."

"No," Rumal answered. "I need her."

"Why?"

"Marriage." Graycloak spat. "He wants to marry me to—"

Rumal yelled over Graycloak's words, "I was trying to do this nicely, but—" and he made a circular hand-signal.

Dominic heard rustling in the woods, then *felt*, rather than saw, several slung stones, which narrowly missed him. *So the rumors are true,* he thought grimly. But he let none of this show on his face; it wasn't likely a simple huntsman would care about the Compact, at least not enough to say anything about it when he was obviously outnumbered.

He was meant to flee, he knew. But Dominic would be damned if he'd leave an unarmed, struggling woman alone in the woods under these circumstances. So he held his ground.

"Why are you being so stubborn?" Rumal asked, sounding despairing. "I have no quarrel with you...Judge MacAnndra."

Damn. He knows who I am! That explained why Rumal's band hadn't dared hurt or kill him—he knew the penalties, all right.

Five brutish thugs carrying crude, wooden bludgeons along with their handy slings emerged from the woods and placed themselves between Dominic and the two combatants. Some were limping, while at least one seemed to be cupping his midsection—perhaps Graycloak had offered some resistance?

Dominic recognized the leader, Shane, as the man had appeared before him many times, mostly for public drunkenness and petty theft. Maybe divide and conquer tactics would work?

"So, Rumal must not have paid you yet, Shane?" Dominic purred. "That must be why you're not in the nearest tavern pinching the barmaids. Surely you'd not stay, else..."

Shane looked pained, but only said, "We don't want to hurt you, Judge. But we will, unless you leave."

Then, oddly enough, the woman yelled, "This is between

you and me, Rumal. Keep Judge MacAnndra out of it."
Then she gave Dominic a look that clearly said, *Go, now.
But do come back...*

He gave her an ironic nod, then trotted Midnight away.

As derisive laughter faded into the background, Dominic
knew he needed to get to the bottom of this. Why were
these men flagrantly violating the Compact, apparently
over and over again, but were unwilling to harm him? Was
it just because of his judicial status, or was it something
more?

And why had Rumal brought Shane and his four
roughnecks along to abduct one lone Renunciate?
Especially considering the fact that a Renunciate, Rumal's
blood sister or not, could *not* be forced into marriage?

He rode for a few minutes, then decided to turn back.
Even though he wasn't normally a man of action, he could
not leave any woman to the devices of men who willingly
and flagrantly broke the Compact—because who knew what
else they might do, given time? Perhaps if he approached
them from the rear and watched for a while, he'd have an
opening and could snatch the woman and get her out of
there.

Besides, it stuck in his craw to leave that woman to her
fate.

It was now full night. Dominic had gone back to the
clearing he'd first found Rumal and the woman in the rust-
colored cloak, and was thoroughly searching the area. His
crossbow was slung across his back, and he held his staff at
the ready. He used the low light of the moons to see by in
case any of the band had been left behind as rear guard—
not likely, not with that bunch, but he could not take
chances.

He knew it was likely there were more Renunciates
around—perhaps hurt, perhaps dead—as there was no way
that poor woman had been alone. Usually Renunciates
traveled in packs of three or more, for safety's sake.

The clearing had been deserted, as he'd expected, and

the tracks led straight downhill with no subterfuge... possibly to Sain Scarp, possibly to a number of other destinations. But a closer examination of the muffled hoof and boot prints revealed an oddity: two sets of boot prints, one thicker and fuller than the other, had gone into the bushes at his left. But only one—the thicker pair—had come back out again. That could mean anything.

But it was a lead. He followed it.

Once he got to the bushes, he went forward until the tracks ended, then turned around. There was a disturbance in the grass where a person had lain, but that person was gone now...or was she?

On instinct, he called, "Is anyone here? Do you need assistance?"

Suddenly, a woman dressed in a dull brown hooded cloak stepped out from behind a tree. She was favoring her right leg, but walked proudly and with assurance toward him. Where had he seen her before?

"Justice Dominic MacAnndra, at your service." He gave her a courtly half-bow, as this one was a power—no question about it. "How can I help, *mestra*?"

"Guild Mother Kestra n'ha Piedra," she responded. "Very happy to see you, Judge."

She shook her hood back, and he immediately recognized the head of the Nevarsin Renunciate Guild House—a woman noted for her honesty throughout the Hellers. What was *she* doing there? Shouldn't she have had at least six guards around her?

When asked, she told him, "I was on my way back to Nevarsin with two of my guild sisters—Gorsali n'ha Ygritte and Cassilde n'ha Elorie. Cassilde's a good fighter, so I hoped that would be enough to get us back to the Guild House in one piece."

"Sensible, in context," he agreed. "What went wrong?"

"I wasn't expecting six men," she said shortly. "Certainly not men with slings, firing rocks at us. We tried to dodge them and get into the trees. I didn't see what happened to Cassilde, but I know they took Gorsali and our chervines."

Her eyes promised retribution for the insult.

"No one should be throwing rocks at anyone else, as it's a violation of the Compact," he agreed. "That's why I'm up here; I'd had word of this in my court." Then, delicately, "Do you have any idea why the men grabbed...Gorsali, you said?" He turned the missing woman's name over and over again in his mind. Gorsali. An unusual name, and a musical one—it suited her, he decided.

"I'm not sure," she admitted. "But I'm sure you don't care about that—"

"Actually, I do," he interrupted. "As a man, it bothers me when an innocent young woman is abducted in front of her companions. And as a judge, I will not allow such an event to occur on my watch."

"Others wouldn't care. Why do you?"

"I'm not them." But he noticed what she hadn't said. "Have you found your sister, Cassilde?"

"Not yet. I just came to a few minutes ago, and I heard someone—you—ride in. I wasn't about to be hurt again, so I was laying low."

"That makes sense," he muttered. "Let's find Cassilde, then." *And pray we won't find her body.*

The Guild Mother went deeper into the woods, calling out Cassilde's name, while Dominic decided to go back toward Midnight. Perhaps he'd get a lead there...and he needed to check on her anyway.

Once there, he was surprised to see a raw-boned blonde-haired woman stroking Midnight's head and trying to mount. But *trying* was the operative word; if Mother Kestra was favoring her leg, this one—Cassilde?—was dragging it. And now that the moons were higher and brighter, he saw that there was blood on the ground...which would bring predators, and quickly, without intervention.

"Are you Cassilde?" he asked.

The woman jumped, whirling toward him. "Who wants to know?"

"I'm Justice MacAnndra," he told her. "Guild Mother Kestra is looking for you, and I'm helping."

"Oh." After a long beat, she added, "Thanks."

"Don't mention it," he said dryly. "Why don't you stay here with my chervine, and I'll go get the Guild Mother?"

He went and told Mother Kestra that Cassilde had been found.

"Is she all right?" she asked.

"She's dragging her right leg," he told her. "And she doesn't seem to be the overly chatty sort, so I figured I'd come get you and you two could catch up."

"Lead me to her, then."

Once they were back in the clearing, the Guild Mother went right up to Cassilde and gave her a quick, yet very real hug.

Cassilde looked surprised, but hugged her back. "What's this for, Mother Kestra?"

"I'm glad you're alive," she breathed. "I was so worried—" Then the Guild Mother's voice broke off. After a long moment, she asked, "What happened to you, Cassilde?"

"Those—those vermin!" Cassilde looked like she wanted to spit. "They kept throwing rocks, and I ran for the trees, and—" She gave Dominic a sidelong look.

"He's a friend. Go on," the Guild Mother urged.

"Two stones got me—one in the leg, and the other in the back of the head," Cassilde confessed. "I woke up not too long ago, and saw the chervine. I knew I couldn't walk far, not like this, so I tried to mount—"

"To look for me?"

Definitely not to look for me, Dominic thought.

"Partly, but also to see if I could spot any tracks to tell me where those cretins took Gorsali," Cassilde told the Guild Mother.

"Admirable," Mother Kestra told her. "You did well, Cassilde."

"This is *well*?" She indicated her injured leg.

"No one fights well when rocks are being thrown at her head," Dominic put in. "Trust me; I wouldn't have been able to do any better, and may have done a damned sight worse."

Cassilde gave him a long, low-lidded look, but said nothing.

He decided to make a fire, partly to give them some privacy to continue their reunion without his undue interference, partly because it might keep the predators away long enough to do them some good. Then, once they were completely caught up and had eaten a bit of Dominic's shared trail rations, he convened a council of war.

"What do you know about this man, Rumal, who claimed to be Gorsali's brother?" he demanded.

"He *is* her brother," Cassilde said, sighing heavily. "He's a bandit, one of Sain Scarp—so is she, though she's no bandit."

"I know that already," he said, nettled. "What is her trade?"

Mother Kestra flicked him an unreadable look. "She's a beekeeper, and sometimes she cooks."

"When we're lucky. Her honeycakes—mm, mm!" Cassilde smacked her lips.

"Good to hear," he murmured. "Does Rumal have any other siblings?"

"Not as far as I know," Mother Kestra assured him. "Gorsali has told us about her cousins, the one brother, and a father. None of them have ever come to the Guild House to visit. So they're not close."

"Rumal's older, isn't he?" Dominic asked. He wasn't sure why he cared, exactly, but he needed to find out all he could about the missing Gorsali—maybe it would help, somehow. "And what's this about a marriage?"

"No, he's younger. He's nineteen, I think, while she just celebrated her twentieth birthday," Cassilde told him.

"Gorsali told me her family wanted her to marry an arrogant lordling, and she wasn't having any of it," Kestra put in. "But I'd always wondered—"

"She'd been beaten," Cassilde interrupted. "I was there in Caer Donn when she stumbled into the Guild House. She needed our help, so we fed her up and found her a trade.

Then she took the Oath, as was proper. She's a good woman—nothing like her brother." She spat to the side contemptuously.

"But how well does she fight?" he asked, exasperated. *What I saw earlier was not promising.*

"Why do you care?" Kestra countered.

"Because we're going to have to rescue her." He ran his hand through his thinning brown hair and scowled. "We *can't* leave her with Rumal. It's wrong!"

"Yes, it's against the law for him to abduct her," Cassilde said quietly. "But we're not exactly in fighting shape right now. How do you intend for us to aid her?"

Quickly, he outlined his plan...and they agreed.

He mounted Cassilde on Midnight, reassuring his chervine in gentle tones that their separation would be for just a little while. Then Cassilde trotted up into the mountains, aiming for the Nevarsin Guild House and help.

"Now it's up to us," he told Kestra. "How well can you walk?"

"I can do anything, if it gets me back my sister."

He nodded firmly. They set off again, this time using a little-used foot path that snaked down the mountainside at a steep angle. He told her, in hushed tones, that he believed they were at least a few hours behind Rumal and his band (as they didn't have many chervines and were using the main roads). Providing they didn't break an ankle on this path, they should be able to catch up by daybreak.

As they walked, Mother Kestra asked, "Why are you helping us?"

"I'm a judge," he spat out. "What Rumal and his men did is deeply offensive." *How can anyone trust someone who has broken the Compact?* he thought indignantly. *Isn't that enough of a reason right there?*

But Kestra's dark eyes demanded more of an answer.

Unwillingly, he added, "They abducted a blameless young woman. I'll be damned if I'll allow that on my watch!"

She nodded serenely. "I think it's more than that, but I'll

respect your privacy."

What does she mean by that? he thought.

Then Mother Kestra stumbled over a rock and started to fall. Fortunately, Dominic caught her before she could do more than lose her dignity.

"Thanks," she muttered.

"It's all right," he told her. "Are you sure you can continue?"

Her eyes blazed as she muttered an epithet he pretended not to hear.

"Good, then." Discreetly, he continued to aid her down the path. Her lame leg hobbled her, but she did not complain.

After a candlemark or so of hard travel, his tired mind woke up. Why was Rumal going straight to Sain Scarp? Was he trusting to their fortress, figuring that no one short of an army—or high-powered *laran*—would be able to get him out again? Or was that the place of the wedding?

And why would *anyone* want to ally with Sain Scarp?

Besides, Dominic hadn't heard of any impending marriages among the wealthiest men in the Hellers, much less the Comyn, and certainly not to anyone of Sain Scarp. They were notorious—everyone knew about them! Would any of the Comyn, even the least of the Aldarans like Rodolfo, be willing to marry a woman from Sain Scarp? Or would they just *say* they were marrying her and make of her a *barragana*?

Thinking of that lively, intelligent woman being forced into concubinage made Dominic furious, but he continued to hold to a measured pace on behalf of Mother Kestra. *No wonder Gorsali became a Renunciate, if this is how her brother treats her.*

As he and Kestra picked their way with care and continued to descend the winding path, Dominic thought harder. *Gorsali cannot become a* barragana, *cannot wed* di catenas. *Rumal, damn him, probably doesn't care.*

But he left unexamined the wistful, half-formed thought that someone like her should *not* have been kidnapped, should *never* have been taken...because that way lay madness.

The barest hints of rose-red dawn tinged the sky as Dominic and Mother Kestra left the steep, winding footpath for the more solid, better-traveled road. Their clothes were full of holes, they'd been scratched in multiple places, but they'd made it safely and that was all that counted.

"Why this place?" was Mother Kestra's only question.

"This is the last easily accessible place between here and Sain Scarp," he muttered. "There's concealment—" he noted the trees and scrub to the either side "—and we can hide for a few hours in the hopes that we'll be able to get Gorsali back unharmed." He left unspoken the fact that if Rumal and the others had already gotten past this point, they had no hope at all of recovery—not without an army they didn't have.

"Let's hope Cassilde has reached the Guild House, then," Kestra said briskly.

He nodded, surveyed the road—no dust, no riders, no nothing as far as the eye could see—and listened hard. Again, he heard nothing.

There was time, then, for him to do what needed to be done. He held out the longer of his two belt knives, still in its sheath, and said, "'I noticed that you don't have anything to fight with, Guild Mother. Would you accept this knife so we may recover Gorsali unharmed?"

"I'm not much of a knife fighter, Judge," Kestra said with real regret. "I'm like you—I use my wits instead of my fighting skills."

"What can you use, then?" He hated to press her like this, but they both needed to have weapons.

"I'm fairly decent with a staff, and I'm good with tactics," she told him.

Well, that makes sense, he thought. "Will you accept my staff then?"

"But you may need it yourself!"

"True enough, Mother Kestra, but you need to have something. And since you have refused my knife, I don't have much else to offer..."

She smiled wryly. "Oh, I beg to differ. But I won't refuse you twice, especially as you asked nicely."

He handed over his staff and took up his station on the left hand side of the road. The Guild Mother took the right, as it was a bit better protected by trees.

Now, they needed to wait—and watch for an opening.

Three candlemarks later, Dominic's eyes were gritty and his body ached with tension. Surely someone would come down the mountain soon. The only question was, who would it be, and why?

Another half a candlemark brought a party of Aldarans— he recognized their mounts—thundering down the mountainside. They seemed somewhat preoccupied as they looked neither to the right nor the left—an extremely unwise thing to do in the mountains.

But since they didn't have Gorsali with them, he let them go by.

A few minutes later, Shane and his four brothers rode by—alone. If Dominic had a team with him, he'd have tried to stop them and bring them to Nevarsin for their crimes— but under the circumstances, as they also did not have Gorsali, he let them alone.

Finally, Rumal rode into the clearing on a dappled chervine. Gorsali was bound and gagged behind him.

Dominic knew he only had a matter of seconds to act. He darted out and tried to grab the reins, while Mother Kestra jumped in from the other side and hit Rumal with Dominic's staff. The chervine reared, dumping Rumal and Gorsali to the ground. Rumal was thrown clear, but Gorsali landed directly underneath the mare's hooves.

Fortunately, she'd landed on some leaf litter. But bound and gagged, she couldn't get away from the mare. She could be trampled!

He made cooing sounds to the mare, and it stopped to

stare at him. That was a good sign.

But first things first. "Where's Rumal?" he called to Kestra. "Do you have him?"

"I've got him," she replied. "Worry about Gorsali, not me."

He glanced her way, and saw her using the staff capably, keeping Rumal's sword away without too much effort. Rumal did not glance in his direction.

He put their fight out of his mind and concentrated on the mare. Projecting stability, serenity, and peace would be the easiest way to get the mare to trust him. "Whoa, girl," he told the chervine. "We're not here to hurt you." Slowly, he ambled toward the animal, pretending all the while that he was back at home checking on Midnight. "That's it, Dapple. I'm a friend." He reached out, petted the chervine's damp neck, and allowed Dapple to nuzzle him a moment. "Isn't this better?"

Once the mare's breathing had calmed, he grabbed the reins and gently led her to a nearby oak tree. "I'll come back soon, girl," he told Dapple as he tied up her reins.

He looked toward where Mother Kestra had last been, and saw nothing. Had Rumal gone free? If he had—

Someone cleared her throat behind him. He whirled, only to see the Guild Mother capably cutting Gorsali's bonds, Rumal out cold at her feet. *Damn, I'd wanted to do that,* he thought, then cursed himself. Who cared who did it so long as Gorsali was safe?

He walked up to where Gorsali still lay, eyes closed. Even though her gag was now off, she wasn't speaking or moving. What was wrong?

"How are you at first aid, Judge?" the Guild Mother asked him.

"Tolerable," he replied. "You've checked her arms and legs, I trust?"

"Yes. No breaks that I saw. Possible sprains, and she'll have some spectacular bruises. Her reflexes seem sound. But she's not talking, and Gorsali normally never shuts up. Why isn't she talking?"

He knelt and quickly assessed Gorsali. He looked first for injuries that the Guild Mother might have missed, but found none.

So far, so good.

Next, he gently felt Gorsali's scalp. While he didn't feel any bumps, his hand came back bloody. He looked closer, and saw a long scratch at the base of her neck.

"Flesh wound, I think," he reported. "We need to see if she'll come around."

"There's no time to waste, so—" The Guild Mother reached out and slapped Gorsali on the face.

Before Dominic could protest, Gorsali abruptly sat up and opened her eyes. "Where am I?"

"You're in the woods between Nevarsin and Sain Scarp," Dominic told her.

"Do you know who you are?" the Guild Mother asked.

"Gorsali n'ha Ygritte," she said. "Beekeeper, sometime baker...why do you want to know?"

"Who am I?" the Guild Mother persisted.

"Guild Mother Kendra n'ha Piedra," Gorsali snapped. "And he's Judge Dominic MacAnndra, before you ask."

He felt absurdly happy that she'd remembered his name, even though he didn't know why.

As the Guild Mother continued to ask questions, Gorsali answered them. All of her answers were right.

After a few more minutes of this, Kestra told him, "I'm going to watch the road, Judge, just in case there's any other trouble nearby."

"Good thinking, Mother Kestra," he told her.

"After all we've been through, call me Kestra," she told him. "At least in private."

He felt greatly honored. "I will...Kestra. And you must call me Dominic." Then he turned back to Gorsali and continued with the concussion assessment. "How many fingers do you see?"

"Five," Gorsali said.

"Any blurred vision or spots?"

"No, but I have a horrible headache—" She attempted to

push herself up, but couldn't quite do it. "And I feel dizzy. Why?"

"I think you were hit on the head when the chervine threw you," Dominic told her. "You're lucky you didn't get killed."

"Not just then," Gorsali said cryptically.

He couldn't help it. He had to know what she was talking about. So he asked.

"Rumal was going to take me to Sain Scarp and string me up. Because I'd refused the Aldaran lordling's offer— Zandru's Hell, he didn't even offer marriage!"

"Not that you could've accepted it anyway," Dominic muttered. "Against the Renunciate Oath to marry, except as a freemate—"

"And I'd never have married someone like that, thank you," she put in with asperity.

"I'm relieved to hear that," he said with a smile. "Will you allow me to help you up?"

After she stood on wobbly legs, she asked, "What happened to Rumal?"

"I knocked him out and tied him up." Mother Kestra grinned in triumph. "He thought he could take me, old as I am. But he was wrong."

"Tell me," Gorsali muttered. "I've seen you fight. He never stood a chance."

"I'd never bet against you, Mother Kestra," Dominic agreed politely.

"What did I just say, Dominic?"

"All right...Kestra."

"You're on a first-name basis with the Guild Mother?" Gorsali asked, scandalized.

"You get to know someone fast when you're going to rescue someone," Dominic told her. "She's an excellent trail companion."

"Actually, I think of him as a friend," Kestra put in.

As Dominic started to stammer, Gorsali's eyes brightened. "I hope you'll be my friend, too...or must I call you Judge MacAnndra like everyone else?"

"Certainly we can be friends," Dominic told her. "And you may call me Dominic any time you like, providing we're not in court."

"I know how to mind my manners," Gorsali said with a sidelong look. "Still, I've never been rescued before. I'm not sure how to act. I might need...help."

Was she flirting with him?

Then he shook himself into sense. "Kestra, do you see any signs of Cassilde and the others? Because if they don't come soon, others from Sain Scarp might—"

"They won't," Gorsali interrupted. "From what Rumal said, this was a last-ditch ploy on his part to get the Old Man—our father, mind you, though he never had any time for me—to allow him to inherit."

"What would he do with it, though?" Dominic asked, allowing his annoyance to show through. "Sain Scarp has nothing but bandits...and a few good women," he added, considering the company. "Does he want to sell the jewels the bandits of Sain Scarp have stolen for legitimacy, then?"

"I don't know, and I don't care," she replied. "I'm more worried about you, Dominic—"

"Me?" he squeaked.

"Yes, you. I now owe you a debt. Renunciates are not supposed to turn to men for any reason—"

"But rescues are different," Kestra said before Dominic could point it out. "And he offered. I did not ask. He's a kind man, Gorsali."

"I can tell," she said, looking him up and down in a way he'd only once seen before: when his mother had greeted his father after a long stint in Lord Ardais' forest rangers.

Now he knew she was flirting with him, even though he wasn't sure why.

"I knew you couldn't ask," he mumbled. "It's against your code."

"It's just...well, we're supposed to do the rescuing, not be rescued," Gorsali told him.

"Next time, I promise. It's your turn."

"I'll hold you to that." Gorsali smiled like a promise.

His heart turned over and started thumping wildly. How could he make her smile like that again?

A far-off thunder of hooves sounded in the distance. Many people—perhaps as many as twenty—were coming down the mountain at great speed. He knew this must be the rescue party...

But they were no longer needed. He and Kestra had rescued Gorsali all on their own.

"Once we get back to Nevarsin, I will arraign Rumal in court," he told them. "We need to find a proper punishment for him—because while he's ordered others to break the Compact, I'm not sure it can be proven that he broke it himself." He wished he didn't have to point this out, because he'd rather hang Rumal from the highest branch. "But it definitely can be proven that he's ordered others to break the Compact, so he will be punished."

"What do you have in mind?" Kestra asked.

"Hanging's too good for him," Gorsali muttered.

"Depending on what can be proven, at minimum I believe he can be sentenced to five years of hard labor up at the monastery," Dominic told them after a bit of thought. "Between working for them and listening to their sermons, that should straighten him right out. But if Rumal refuses such a punishment, we'll hang him high and be done with it."

Gorsali gave him a bloodthirsty grin.

"What about the other men?" Mother Kestra asked.

"Oh, Shane and his brothers are always in my courtroom for one reason or another," he told her. "They're too stupid to realize the consequences of breaking the Compact—so I'll just have to inform them, while giving them a few years of hard labor up at the monastery as well."

"I'm glad you have it all figured out," Kestra said, the very personification of gracious calm.

"It's my job," he said. "Besides, I can't wait to punish them. I just wish I could give them the punishment they deserve. How dare they hurt Gorsali? How dare they break the Compact? How—"

Then he realized what he'd said, and felt his face heat up. *Somehow, I've come to care for this woman. Already. But what if she doesn't...*

"Still," Gorsali pressed, giving him a big, inviting smile. "Isn't there something I, personally, can do for you? Let me buy you dinner, at least. I'm sure we could find... something...to talk about." Then she gave him a huge wink.

What else could he do but agree?

HIDDEN GIFTS

by Margaret L. Carter

Of the psychic Gifts specific to the Seven Domains, perhaps none has generated more stories than the Alton Gift of forced rapport, the ability to dominate another's mind. From its description in The Spell Sword *(Marion Zimmer Bradley, 1974) to the short story "The Alton Gift" (Elisabeth Waters,* The Keeper's Price, *1980) and novel* The Alton Gift, *(Marion Zimmer Bradley and Deborah J. Ross, 2007), writers and their readers have been fascinated by the potential for good or for ill that comes with such great power. Here Margaret L. Carter offers a tale of the awakening of that Gift in a most unlikely heroine.*

Margaret L. Carter holds degrees in English literature and worked for many years as a legislative editor for the Maryland General Assembly. She specializes in vampires, even having included chapters on Carmilla and Dracula in her PhD dissertation. In addition to vampire-related lit-crit such as Different Blood: The Vampire As Alien, *she's had horror, fantasy, and paranormal romance published. Her latest novels are* Sealing the Dark Portal, *a paranormal romance with Lovecraftian elements, and* Legacy of Magic, *a sword-and-sorcery fantasy in collaboration with her husband, Leslie Roy Carter (prequel to their "Wild Sorceress" trilogy). Margaret and Les, a retired Navy Captain, have four sons, two cats, a St. Bernard, eight grandchildren, and now a great-granddaughter.*

Surely no threat could be stalking the streets of Adereis on a sunny afternoon in the middle of the market square, yet Dorys sensed the pressure of a hostile gaze. She glanced at the spot the feeling seemed to emanate from, a fruit stand across the way. For a second she caught sight of a lanky, bearded man who made her chest tighten with anxiety. The next instant, he was gone.

Dorys considered mentioning her uneasiness to *Domna* Gavriela but immediately shrugged off the thought. The crawling sensation on the back of her neck had already disappeared as completely as the unpleasant-looking man she had glimpsed. *Domna* Gavriela would either make light of Dorys's nervous reaction or become alarmed for nothing. Shifting baby Elisa in her arms, Dorys trailed silently a few paces behind her mistress. She resisted the temptation to clutch at the starstone hidden in a silken pouch on a cord under her bodice. Nobody was supposed to know *Dom* Cyril and *Domna* Gavriela's son, Errol, had given it to her. The lady was probably aware of her son's secret gift, but Dorys was sure nobody else had noticed. *Dom* Cyril, a man of old-fashioned attitudes, would have made his disapproval plain. A lady's maid, even one who was kin in a sense, had no right to possess such a gem, even a small one.

Elisa giggled and tugged at a lock of hair that had worked loose from Dorys's braid. Dorys tickled her under the chin and shifted her weight once more. At six months, the baby was getting heavy. *Domna* Gavriela had decided to bring Elisa along while calling on the wife of the newly-appointed council chief, and as the lady's attendant, Dorys had the task of carrying the child. Upon arriving at the council elder's home, her mistress had dismissed the litter they had arrived in and announced her intention of walking back to *Dom* Cyril's manor after the visit. Given the mild weather and the short distance between the town center and the manor, the servants had no grounds for objection. While a grander lady might consider foot travel beneath her, as wife to the head of a minor branch of the Alton line, *Domna* Gavriela enjoyed casual strolls among her neighbors. Dorys had never seen any sign that the townspeople lacked respect and even affection for their lord and lady. Her momentary prickle of fear must have been a random, nervous flutter.

Errol, if he were here, would take it seriously. He had recognized a trace of *laran* in her when she had fallen sick with headaches and stomach upsets two summers previously. That was why he had given her the starstone and taught her the rudiments of its use. At two years older than her own fifteen, he treated her more like a younger sister than a servant. His parents' flat refusal to have her tested for *laran* hadn't stopped Errol from offering her the help he thought she needed.

As *Domna* Gavriela circled the fountain in the center of the square, the sense of danger flared anew like a flash of lightning. Dorys convulsively tightened her arms around the baby. A second later, a shaggy brown dog charged out of an alley straight toward her. Its head came up to her waist, and it bayed like a hound on the trail of a rabbit-horn. Lady Gavriela cried out, while Dorys yelled at the beast to scare it away.

Growling, the dog lunged between the lady and Dorys. To her terrified eyes, the animal's mouthful of fangs looked wide enough to swallow her in two bites. The dog shoved her sideways. Taking a firmer grip on Elisa, Dorys stumbled toward the gap between the two nearest shops. The beast veered away from her to charge at the lady.

A red mist swirled before Dorys's eyes. She tried to shout again, but no sound came from her lips. Only her thoughts reached out. She felt as if she grabbed the dog in a phantom grip and squeezed. The growling stopped abruptly. The fog melted away, and she saw the dog lying motionless on the cobblestones.

Did I do that? Impossible.

A hard hand closed on her arm and pulled her into the alley. Before she could draw air to scream, another hand clapped a rag over her mouth. She gulped a breath of foul-smelling fumes that made her head spin. Her knees wobbled. Someone snatched the baby from her suddenly limp arms. Her vision went gray, then black.

She woke to a baby's crying. As far as she could tell, she lay flat on a pallet of blankets over a hard surface. When she tried to sit up, her head whirled and her stomach lurched. She clamped her jaws against a wave of nausea. When it faded, she pushed herself upright more carefully and opened her eyes.

She was sitting on the stone floor of a cellar room. Through one high, narrow window came the crimson glow of the late afternoon sun. The wailing came from a basket where Elisa lay on her back, waving her arms. A pitcher, basin, mug, and folded cloths sat nearby. Other than a chamber pot in the far corner, the room held nothing else. Her head pounding, Dorys poured herself a drink of water from the pitcher. She dismissed the fleeting suspicion of poison. If their captor wanted them dead, he wouldn't have bothered to lock them up.

Dorys picked up Elisa, whose sobs quieted as she rocked and hummed. "Hush, *chiya*, I'm here." A smell of sour milk pervaded the air. Dorys filled the basin, soaked a rag, and cleaned as much as she could of what the baby had spat up in her screaming fit. Dorys breathed slowly and deeply, trying to calm her racing pulse. She didn't want to transmit her fear to the baby. What did the kidnapper want with them? Most likely he intended to demand a ransom for Elisa. Why bother dragging a lady's maid along, though?

After a minute's thought, she answered her own question—to save himself the trouble of caring for an infant. Had anyone seen them being spirited away? Probably not, or surely bystanders would have chased the kidnapper and rescued them already. Maybe the man had carried them out the back of the alley and whisked them away in a closed carriage.

Before she could brood over her plight long enough to goad herself into a panic, the door of the makeshift dungeon opened. The tall, rangy man with black hair and beard she had noticed in the town square stepped inside. With him came another man, shorter and stockier with straw-colored hair and a bushier beard. Both of them wore daggers at their belts. The second man carried a small box.

After a dismissive glance at Dorys, he echoed her own thoughts. "Why did we lumber ourselves with this wench, anyway?"

"Patience, Tomas. This test should clear that up." The darker man took the box from his companion, tipped it sideways on the floor, and opened it.

A gray rat the size of a half-grown kitten darted out, straight toward Dorys. A shriek escaped her as she sprang to her feet. Elisa started crying again. The same scarlet mist as before pooled in front of Dorys's eyes, and in a spasm of revulsion she mentally struck at the rat. The illusory fog dissolved instantly this time. Like the dog, the rat lay inert on its side.

The dark man scooped the animal into the box. "It's dead."

Tomas's eyes widened. Dorys sensed a trickle of fear emanating from him. "She killed it? With her mind?"

The other man said with a grim smile, "The same way she killed our dog. It's as I suspected. She has the Alton Gift."

Dorys found her voice. "What are you talking about? I'm not an Alton, only *Domna* Gavriela's personal maid." Although that claim wasn't completely true, she had no desire to reveal personal information to these brutes.

"Maybe not an Alton by name, but you share their blood. The copper in your hair makes that plain enough."

Granted, it was no secret that Dorys was the *nedestra* daughter of *Dom* Cyril's unmarried younger brother. When her mother died, *Dom* Cyril and *Domna* Gavriela had taken her in. People seldom mentioned her bastard status, but the family had always treated her well, and Errol had accepted her as a cousin from the beginning. That did not mean she had any more than a trace of *laran*, certainly nothing compared to the great leroni of the noble houses. *Dom* Cyril would definitely see it that way, and even *Domna* Gavriela would doubtless laugh indulgently at the notion of Dorys's having the Alton Gift.

"What does that mean?" Tomas asked. "She can kill things?"

"The traditional Alton Gift is forced rapport. I've heard of a rare variation that grants the power of killing with a thought. Seems it's true."

At the idea of having such a power, Dorys shivered and choked down a fresh surge of nausea. "What do you want with us? Ransom for Elisa?"

"Not exactly. It's like this." The dark man leaned against the door frame and folded his arms. "My name is Rumal. Your master slaughtered my brother and the rest of our band a year ago. Only Tomas and I escaped. I've been planning and waiting for a chance to strike back ever since."

"I remember." *Dom* Cyril and his retainers had wiped out a nest of highwaymen in the Kilghard Hills who had been raiding farms and robbing travelers. "So your brother was chief of the bandits?"

Rumal glowered for a second, then relaxed. "Call us that if you wish. I intended to use the baby to settle the score, but not by demanding gold. A threat to her life would have forced *Dom* Cyril to meet me alone at a place of my choosing, where I could slay him. But now I have a better idea."

Her heart racing, Dorys clasped the baby closer to her breast. "What's that?" She glanced at the narrow window, wishing she could see where they'd been taken.

Rumal's gaze followed the direction of hers. "Don't even think of screaming for help. If you try that, the babe dies."

"Monster!"

His ironic smile reappeared. "So says the girl who kills with her mind. Thanks to the lucky accident of finding you, I've decided on a safer way to destroy the Alton lordling, a way that won't require me to risk my own life. You're going to do it for me. He'll drop dead, with nobody suspecting the cause."

"I will not!" Aside from horror at the idea of murdering anybody, *Dom* Cyril had always been kind to her in his distant way, and *Domna* Gavriela treated her with outright fondness.

"Again, if you balk at this, the babe dies. And don't imagine you can use your power against us. If you strike down Tomas or me, the other one will live long enough to— well, you get the idea. We're not stupid enough to come near you one at a time."

She slumped onto the pallet of blankets. Rage welled up in her chest. She felt the power struggling to burst out. She swallowed it, sharply aware of what would happen to the baby if she unleashed her gift against Rumal. It felt more like a curse to her. "When do you expect me to commit this murder?"

"Tomorrow at noon, when *Dom* Cyril presides over the installation of the new council chief. They're having a public ceremony in the town square. We'll be watching, hidden in the shadows of an alley. You do your job, I'll hand over the child, and we'll make our escape."

So she had less than a day to discover some way out of this trap. "How can I trust you to release the baby if I obey you?"

"You have my word."

She sniffed. "The word of a bandit."

"You can trust me to slay the child if you don't obey," he said. "But think logically, girl. Why would we put ourselves in even greater danger by killing her after we've got what we want?"

"Do you imagine I won't tell everybody who you are and what you made me do?"

"Do you really want the surviving family to have you executed as an assassin? Anyway, whether you identify me or not, we'll be long gone."

Dorys struggled to keep her voice from quavering. "Meanwhile, are you going to let Elisa starve?"

He shrugged. "I'll take care of that." He and Tomas left, with an audible thump of a bolt falling into place on the outside of the door. Several minutes later, the two men returned with a pitcher of milk, a bowl of porridge, and a plate of bread and fruit. Clearly, as Rumal had warned, he didn't intend to let her catch either one of them alone.

Once her captors left her in peace, she dribbled milk into Elisa's mouth, a sloppy procedure with a baby who had never drunk from anything but a nipple before. Dorys mixed milk into the porridge and offered it from a spoon. Elisa grimaced, for she had only started tasting solid foods at home and took a dim view of this strange method of nourishment. Still, Dorys managed to coax a portion of it into her. After cleaning her as much as possible, Dorys stripped off her wet breechclout and replaced it with one of the cloths piled next to the water jug. Then Dorys laid the baby in the basket and forced herself to eat some of the bread and fruit.

While Elisa napped, the men came back for the dishes. "I hope you're carefully considering what we want of you," Rumal said. "After all, you can't expect to rein in that gift of yours forever. You're bound to kill somebody sometime, so why fight it? Do you owe the Alton lordling so much you'd throw away the child's life, not to mention your own, to save his?"

She turned her head away in silence.

"Have it your way," he said. "We'll see how you feel after a night to think it over."

After they left, she collapsed onto the pallet. Sobs racked her until her throat and chest ached. Her crying upset the baby. Dorys picked her up, wiped away her own tears, and sang and played with Elisa until the child grew sleepy. When Elisa dozed off, Dorys paced the cell and stared up at the narrow window. The cool mountain breeze that wafted through the gap brought some relief from the chamber's stale, foul-smelling air, but the window did her no other good. It was too high for her to reach, with nothing to stand on to boost herself up. Brief glimpses of legs walking by gave her no hint of where she was. She settled on the blankets again, groping for her starstone and clasping the silk pouch for comfort. Her head spun with hopeless fantasies of striking down both bandits at once the next time they opened the door. Even if she could act fast enough before one of them could stab the baby, though, could she bring herself to kill a man, even a kidnapper and murderer? The sun set, and twilight darkened to night. Liriel rose, as she could tell from the faint violet glow that tinted what little she could see of the outside world.

By now she felt sure Rumal had meant his reference to morning literally. He would have no reason to intrude before then. She could use her starstone without getting caught. She was lucky Rumal hadn't considered her enough of a threat to search her. If she could contact Errol, at least she could let the family know Elisa hadn't been harmed.

Seated with her back braced against the clammy stone wall, Dorys took the blue stone from the pouch and cupped it in her palm. She breathed slowly and relaxed her muscles one by one, as Errol had taught her. She conjured up the memory of sitting with him on a bench in the walled garden of his parents' manor, practicing *laran* exercises. She visualized his head with its untidy shock of golden red hair bent over his own starstone while he guided her to trace the currents of life force flowing through a fir tree in the corner of the courtyard and the fish in the pond. She imagined gazing into his gentle eyes, the same color as the stone.

He had explained to her about the Overworld, a space where spirits drifted free of their bodies, a realm of energy shaped by the minds of all who traveled through it. Could she speak to Errol if she could free her mind from her body and enter the Overworld? He had barely started to teach her that skill, though. Did she dare to cast herself into the void? Suppose she couldn't find her way back?

She had to try. She couldn't wait here and do nothing if she had any chance to save herself and the baby.

She stared into the gem, breathing deeper. She blocked out the shadows thickening around her, the chill of the walls and floor, the sour odors, the murmur of sound from the street above. The gem came alive with an azure glow. Its aura expanded to fill her sight. Shedding all consciousness of her flesh, she visualized herself floating out of her body. The blue glow swirled around her and enveloped her.

She found herself surrounded by a featureless landscape of mist that stretched as far as she could see. Glancing down, she saw her body, though she couldn't feel it, draped in the same clothes her material form had been wearing, but fresh and unstained. A glittering cord emerged from her midriff and coiled into the distance until the other end vanished in the mist. Now she remembered Errol's description of that cord, which connected her spirit to her body. As long as it stayed intact, she couldn't lose her way back.

How could she find him? Which way was home in all this emptiness? She struggled to calm herself, although here she had no breath or heartbeat to get agitated. What had he taught her about moving in the Overworld? Without muscles and nerves, everything depended on will. She simply had to focus on where she wanted to go. She summoned up an image of the house, its courtyard, the garden with its flowers, trees, and fish pond. More important, she recalled the feel of Errol's mind when their thoughts had touched during those lessons.

Errol, where are you? Can you hear me? Show me where to go. Her insubstantial body started to glide as if it knew its destination. Her speed increased as she mentally stretched toward her goal.

An astonished voice spoke in her mind: *Dorys, is that you?*

A wordless affirmation of joy burst from her.

Come to me! Errol's psychic voice called.

An instant later, she saw him standing a few paces away from her. *Breda, are you really here? I hardly dared to hope. I've been trying to reach you for hours.*

Arms open, she rushed toward him. Their fingertips met with sparks like miniature lightning. Somehow she realized trying a real handclasp or embrace here would be a waste of effort. *Thank Evanda I found you.*

Where are you? What about Elisa?

She's not hurt. Dorys told Errol about Rumal and how he had captured them. The next thing Errol wanted to know, of course, was the location of her prison. Her shoulders sagged as if despair pressed with tangible weight on her astral body. *I don't know. He brought me here unconscious, and I can't see enough through the window to pick up any clues.* A hopeful idea occurred to her. *Now that our minds have touched, can't you track me down?*

Errol's somber expression didn't lighten. *Locations in the Overworld have no direct connection to places on the physical plane of existence. If it were that easy, you could use your own* laran *to survey the outside of the building where you're locked up.*

A chill crept over her, even though she had no flesh to experience cold. *After this, I may be afraid to use my* laran *at all. Rumal wants to force me to kill your father.* She revealed what she had learned about her "gift." Trembling inwardly, she cast down her gaze, expecting Errol to recoil from her in horror.

Instead, his fingers grazed hers. Warmth radiated from them up her arms and spread throughout her astral form. Looking up, she saw his eyes shadowed with sadness but no sign of revulsion. *That is exactly why you need better teaching than my amateur attempts. When you get home, I'll insist that Father and Mother place you under the training of a skilled leronis.*

No! They'll think I'm a monster. She would lose the shelter of the only home she'd had since her mother's death. *I can't let them know.*

Errol sighed. *I hardly see how we could keep them from knowing. Your* laran *is clearly too strong to hide.* Again he gave her a comforting touch that she felt as a spark and a rush of warmth. *We'll discuss that later, though. Meanwhile, I'll tell my parents that you and Elisa are alive and well for now. We'll do our best to unearth Rumal's hideout by ordinary investigation.*

What if you can't find us before noon tomorrow? She

suppressed another fear, that if *Dom* Cyril and his guards did find the house and raid it, Rumal would kill Elisa before they could capture him.

We'll fly that hawk when its pinions are grown. She sensed hesitation before Errol continued, *But consider that you may have to risk casting your* laran *outside the cell to strike down both of the bandits before they get close enough to threaten the baby.*

A shudder convulsed her. Kill men in cold blood? Granted, she would choose Elisa's life over theirs anytime, but would she be able to force herself to the act?

Errol's "voice" turned gentle. *You don't have to think of it now. Rest, and I'll be prepared to hear from you again at dawn.*

Do we have to leave this place? It's so peaceful.

Aside from the danger of losing our links to our bodies and being stranded in the Overworld forever, you must go back to care for Elisa. Not to mention that you can't let Rumal realize you have the power to reach beyond your prison.

She nodded. Of course, she couldn't deny the importance of either of those factors. After a murmured farewell and a final brushing of fingertips, Errol vanished. Dorys willed herself to retrace the glittering cord that bound her to her flesh, like rolling up a coil of rope. Returning held none of the uncertainty of the outward flight. She glided through the pale blue mist at such speed that only seconds seemed to pass before she landed in the cellar.

She slammed into her body as if falling onto the floor with a thud. Gasping, she opened her eyes It was still night, and Elisa slept undisturbed. Dorys restored the starstone to its pouch, which she hid in its usual place inside her bodice. After stretching her cramped limbs and taking a drink of water, she lay flat on the pallet. Rest? How could she sleep in the same house with a pair of murderous brigands? Exhaustion overwhelmed her, though, and she sank into oblivion.

She woke again to faint daylight from the window and Elisa's whimpering. About the time Dorys finished cleaning herself and the baby, their two captors showed up with milk, porridge, fruit, and a pitcher of fresh water. Tomas even replaced the used chamber pot with a clean one. Dorys tried to reassure herself that the amenities proved Rumal meant to keep his word about freeing them if she obeyed him, but the thought gave scant comfort.

"We'll leave for the ceremony shortly before noon. Get prepared." The scowl he cast at her before leaving did nothing for her confidence.

She fed Elisa as fast as she could persuade the baby to eat, satisfied her own suddenly ravenous hunger, and waited impatiently for the men to fetch the dishes. As soon as she felt sure of being undisturbed, she gazed into her starstone and launched herself into the Overworld again. Floating out of her body came easier this time. Within seconds, she found Errol waiting for her as he'd promised. She told him the little that had happened to her since the night before and asked whether *Dom* Cyril had made any progress at finding her prison.

His mental voice sounded heavy with reluctance to pass on bad news. *Not yet. We've traced some rumors of Rumal's having been seen in Adereis, but we haven't found anyone who knows where he might be hiding.*

Then your father should cancel the ceremony.

What reason would he give? Errol asked. *Besides, in that case Rumal would only hold you until he found another opportunity to strike. Father can't hide behind walls forever. One thing he can do is post guards in the guise of ordinary townsfolk to watch for you and the bandits in the crowd. There's a chance they could rescue you and Elisa.*

Dorys kept silent about her fear of how remote that chance was. As long as one of the kidnappers was holding the baby, any attack would pose a terrible risk.

Errol's fingers brushed her cheek in a comforting

gesture. *Thanks to you, we have warning of their plot, and they don't know that we know. Contact me when they take you out of the cellar. If Rumal said he would return for you shortly before noon, the house can't be far from the center of town.*

I can't go into a trance and leave my body with them watching!

Errol explained that since Dorys had gotten in touch with him, they didn't need to move into the Overworld for future telepathic communication. *Remember how our thoughts meshed while we practiced your* laran *exercises? When you want to speak mind to mind, simply call me. I'll be waiting.*

Too quickly, he receded away from her into the mist. She sank back into her body, exhausted.

The morning dragged on with no measure of time except the snail-like creep of a narrow sunbeam across the floor. Dorys tried to keep the baby entertained and resisted the desire to contact Errol for reassurance. The family had to concentrate on searching for the kidnappers' hideout. When the slant of the light warned her that noon was drawing near, she held Elisa on her lap and clasped the starstone in her hand. At this point, drawing strength from it mattered more than concealing it from her captors.

She was bouncing Elisa on her knees, trying to keep her from squirming, when the tramp of feet sounded in the corridor outside the locked door. Dorys reached out to Errol. To her relief, she felt the answering touch of his mind.

They're coming now, she told him.

He replied, *When they take you out of the house, you can describe the streets and maybe we can send the guards to intercept you.*

At that moment, Rumal shoved the door open and saw her holding the gem. "What are you doing?" He glowered at her from the doorway, with Tomas hovering at his shoulder.

"Should I take the stone from her?" the other man

asked.

"No, you fool. Seizing it by force would stun her. She'd be useless to us. Anyway, she knows better than to try anything if she wants the child to survive." He turned to Dorys. "Hand her over."

"What—no!" She leaped up, hugging Elisa to her chest, and mentally cried to Errol, *They're not waiting until we get outside. They want to take her from me now.*

Errol's voice reverberated in her head: *Kill them before they get close enough! This is your only chance.*

Kill? Her stomach churned at the thought. Slaying a man wasn't like lashing out at a vicious dog or rat. But Rumal was striding toward her, reaching for the baby.

Squeezing the stone, she gathered her power and flung it at him—not at his heart, but his legs. They crumpled under him. He collapsed to the floor. She struck the same blow at Tomas, who fell in a heap on top of Rumal.

She still couldn't escape, though. They blocked the door, and she couldn't guess how soon they might recover. Elisa wailed in protest at her tight grip. Dorys closed her eyes and reached for Errol again. She felt a response like a psychic clasp of a hand.

A shuffling noise mingled with Elisa's cries. Maintaining her link with Errol, Dorys opened her eyes and found Rumal hauling himself upright. He started to shamble toward her.

The urge to escape flooded her whole being. *Errol, help me!* Still clasping the baby to her chest, she launched herself toward her cousin.

I have you, breda. I won't let go. She felt him pulling as if to draw her out of a bottomless lake where she was drowning. A gale-force wind rushed over her. Blue fog enveloped her and faded to black.

Shrieking, she fought to hold onto Elisa while the wind swept them through the void.

Silence fell. A hard surface pressed against Dorys's back. The baby screamed, struggling in her arms. Dorys opened her eyes, expecting either azure mist or total darkness.

Instead, she lay on the floor of *Domna* Gavriela's sitting room. The lady and Errol, brandishing their starstones, loomed over her.

Errol helped Dorys sit up while *Domna* Gavriela took the baby and wept, kissing her hair and face over and over. "Thank the gods it worked," he said, cradling Dorys's head on his shoulder.

"What happened? How did we get here?"

The lady wiped her tears away and said in a tremulous voice, "Teleportation without a matrix screen. I never thought it was possible."

"I tried to tell you she had strong *laran*," Errol said.

Stumbling to a chair with his help, Dorys gazed at her lap, afraid to meet *Domna* Gavriela's eyes. "What will you do with me now? I'm too dangerous to live among you."

"Nonsense, *chiya*, nobody will punish you for something that isn't your fault." The lady threw Errol a dubious glance, though.

He said, "You must do better than that, Mother. The world is changing. Why, the Aldarans claim people from a distant star have appeared in the Hellers. Should we be surprised if *laran* gifts can spring up in people who don't have pure Comyn blood? We must cultivate these gifts to the fullest, not pretend they don't exist. We all know the danger of that." He rested a hand on Dorys's shoulder. "After this, you must admit her *laran* is as powerful as ours, if not more. You have to grant her the same teaching any child of our bloodline deserves."

Domna Gavriela gave Dorys a long, steady stare before answering, "You are right, son, and we should have listened to you from the beginning. Her gift must be cherished."

Warmth flowed through Dorys. She would learn, and she would win mastery over her power to protect herself and her kin.

CLIMBING TO THE MOONS

by Ty Nolan

Whenever talented writers tackle a world created by someone else, they inevitably make it their own, and this has certainly been the case with the Darkover anthologies I have been privileged to edit. Some stories fit neatly into "established canon," the descriptions and timelines from the stories of Marion Zimmer Bradley. Others fill in the gaps or take place in places or eras never explored by Bradley herself. On rare, breathtaking occasions, a story will be so true to the original spirit that the details of consistency fade into irrelevance. Ty Nolan's "Climbing to the Moons" fits into the category of "alternate but faithful" Darkover stories. As far as I know, Marion never imagined intelligent bear-mammoths, bred during the Ages of Chaos as instruments of war and now destined for something finer. Classical Darkovan or not, I fell in love with them. I believe Marion would have, too.

Trained as a traditional Native American Storyteller, Ty Nolan had his first short story published by Marion Zimmer Bradley in Sword of Chaos. *His book,* Coyote Still Going: Native American Legends and Contemporary Stories, *received the 2014 BP Readers Choice Award for Short Story Collections and Anthologies. He is a New York Times and USA Today best-selling author. He currently splits his time between Arizona and Washington State.*

Brin watched the younger man carefully. He didn't trust him, but Brin really didn't trust anyone. Darkover was a dangerous place and the inhabitants were worse. He comforted himself by knowing he was a force of nature that happened to other people. The man in front of him was still wearing his hood up, his face half-hidden. To Brin he felt off. These were the times he wished he were a telepath like his Alton in-laws. Well, he had his own talents.

"And you promise these things are not the products of the Terrans?" He watched a grin form on the handsome face beneath the hood.

"Ask me no questions and I'll tell you no lies." His voice was deep and teasingly smooth. "But I can assure you these *products* as you call them, are as Darkovan as your sainted granny. Now pay heed as I show you how to set them—I must be leaving to attend to business in Thendara."

"What the hell are those?" Roman leaned over the railing and looked down at the enormous herd of animals below. "They look like the love child between an elephant and a bear."

"They're closer to a Wooly Mammoth than to an elephant," Fiona Aldaran said. "There was an older time called the Ages of Chaos when genetic manipulation was all the rage. If you think about it, a Mammoth has a much better chance of survival on Darkover than an elephant."

"And the bear DNA?" He looked back at the Darkovan woman beside him. She was taller than he, and her hair was an odd strawberry blonde that was almost white.

"As I recall, the genomic intervention went further back than the bears you might have read about. The decision was made to create an omnivore so they wouldn't be completely dependent on foliage. As you might imagine, they need to consume a lot. They're also related to the *Lormus*, one of the largest native mammals. They were on the edge of extinction, and at this point we mainly know about them because of the *Starrfhiacails* you're admiring." Fiona leaned forward as one of the animals noticed them. There was a definite gleam of intelligence and interest in those crinkled eyes staring out of the dark and hairy head. The large trunk of the creature seemed to wave at Fiona and Roman.

"The tusks looked like they don't belong without the big floppy ears." Roman critically examined what she had called the *Starrfhiacails*. They reminded him of Fiona—unusual in size and appearance. Hardly beautiful in a classical sense, but still oddly attractive. After the months he had spent on Darkover, the Terran had become used to a certain look among the population that differed from the diversity of the humans he knew from his own colony and the others he served with. Fiona wouldn't elicit a second look at most spaceports. Here she seemed overgrown and mannish, her clothing ill-fitting compared to the other Darkovan women he had met.

"Big floppy ears are a great adaptation to a very hot environment to dissipate body heat," she said, looking down at the *Starrfhiacail* below them. "But they'd be dangerous here. You probably can't see them from this height, but the small ears help her maintain her core temperature when it starts getting cold."

Roman laughed to himself, wondering when this ice bucket of a planet wasn't cold. "You seem to have a lot of knowledge about Terran biology."

"I earned one of the first undergraduate degrees from the college at the Spaceport. I majored in Biology with a minor in Genomic Medicine. My senior thesis was on the genetic engineering of the *Starrfhiacail*." She smiled as she looked down at the herd. "I'm considered the foremost authority on my friends down there." Fiona looked at Roman. "It's not hard to be the top of your field when it's a small field. Of course, I had a head start. I grew up around them. My family has worked with *Starrfhiacails* for generations."

"Is this one your favorite?" Fiona was showing far more interest in what appeared to be the largest animal of the herd than she had shown about anything since they had been introduced a few days ago after he had arrived at the compound.

"Aye," she smiled, and she was suddenly pretty. "Her name is *Mo Chride*—it means My Heart." Roman was used to women (and some men) paying that sort of attention to him. By Terran standards he was a strong and handsome man. He was the tallest male on this icy rock of a planet, if the Darkovans he had met were typical. Fiona was obviously Darkover's version of an Amazon from Terran mythology. He vaguely wondered if she was also an unexpected consequence of genetic manipulation or just an example of Nature's personal sense of humor. He was a bit put off from the lack of attraction she seemed to feel towards him. He was used to being fawned over.

Maybe she just prefers taller men, he ironically thought to himself, *or maybe she prefers women.*

He looked back at the animal that was still staring up at them. As near as he could tell, the planet's culture didn't seem to celebrate diversity of any kind, including sexualities and genders.

Not that he cared, one way or the other. Maybe at one point he'd walked past the equivalent of a gay bar, but he certainly hadn't noticed at this point. He fit into the Darkover worship of *machismo*. Roman thought how much his youngest brother and his husband would have hated it here. In the relatively brief time he had been on the planet he had heard both the men and women insult others for violating their rigid gender roles. He assumed the word he had heard most often—*emmasca*—was their general term for someone who "wasn't enough"—whether female or male. It was one of the many words not programmed into the language chip he had downloaded. He had just dismissed their unsophisticated attitude as yet another example of how really primitive the planet was.

The chip gave him a rudimentary grasp of the Darkovan language but he had found it useless when it came to a lot of cultural terms. He wondered how much of its shortcomings was the result of a poorly programmed chip and how much was there not being exact translations between Terran Standard and what the Darkovans were speaking.

Drop off a few shiny electronic toys in ancient Northern Europe and you'd pretty much have a recipe for Darkover. He had heard tales of some psychic strains in the culture, but he figured superstition was just part of the overall primitive standards. Looking at the *Starrfhiacails*, he shook his head and felt a sense of pity when he saw how much these people had devolved after their colony ship had crashed. Based on his recent experiences, he doubted anyone would be able to achieve any sort of meaningful genetic engineering these days. Fiona was the first local he had met who claimed a Terran Empire degree. After his many travels he had come to the conclusion that formal education was really a type of indoctrination in terms of the inherent superiority of Old Terra. Why else would most people with Terran training be taught about elephants and bears that had never existed on the planets they had colonized, let alone Woolly Mammoths?

The other locals seem to be divided over salivating as soon as they saw Terran technology or being too terrified by what it represented to do more than condemn it. That push/pull dynamic was something he had found in each of the communities he had visited so far. Fiona was the exception that proved the rule of finding some sort of viable balance. He walked away from the railing, feeling as cold as he normally did when outside. The wind was starting to pick up and swirled across the observation deck where they were standing.

Fiona looked at him. *He seems so big and strong*, she thought, *but he's like a little girl the moment the wind changes.*

She nodded to *Mo Chride*, her favorite of the herd. Her grandfather used to say they were twins. Fiona and *Mo* were born the same year and just a day apart. When she had returned from her studies, *Mo* had been one of the first of her family she sought out—and she considered the powerful ones a true part of her family. *Mo* had come to her and wrapped her trunk around Fiona, pulling her into a tender embrace. There was an almost magical connection between them. Nothing had changed. Her head filled with memories as she walked over to join Roman. She found herself uncomfortably attracted to him—an unusual complex of feelings she had never really felt for a man before. On the two occasions she had spent time with him, she kept internally pointing out his failings to convince herself as to why she should not get personally involved with him. Better they keep things strictly business. They were from two different worlds—literally. Terrans didn't belong on Darkover.

She led him back inside and they ended up in a library—with actual books. To Roman it seemed more like a museum than a library. He was just grateful for the warmth from the fireplace. Above the wide mantel was an enormous carving. It was obvious to him the artwork depicted the *Starrfhiacails* involved in various tasks, using their trunks to hold and manipulate what appeared to be logs.

"So—they're work animals," he said. He reached up and felt the carving. Even though it was above the fireplace, the carving remained cool to his touch.

"They have far more endurance than horses and are much stronger. Their trunks have an almost human level of manipulation—it's like they have an arm and a hand—if a human hand could pick up nearly a thousand kilograms. Their trunks have over 60,000 muscles inside—more than you have in your entire body. At the tip of the trunk are two prehensile fingers that can pick up a single seed."

"What are they doing over in this corner?" He pointed to the lower left part of the carving.

"Building a bridge. It seems to be something they're born knowing how to do. They have what appears to be an instinctive way of knowing how to press their logs together to form a bridge that uses no binding materials but will hold their weight as the herd crosses."

"Without instruction from human masters?"

"Oh, it's more like cooperation instead of master and servant—at least that's true now. A handler is called a *cabhróir,* our word that better translates as helper. We show them where we need something moved or done." She ladled out boiling water from a metal pot that hung above

243

the fire and poured it into a teapot she had taken down from the mantel. "When I came back with my brand new degree, one of the Aillards came with elaborate blueprints for a fancy bridge he wanted built. He assumed if I had a Terran education it meant I could do anything. I looked at all those beautiful drawings and pushed them back to him. I told him that wouldn't work way out here. I told him what he needed me to make was a *Starrfhiacail* bridge. I explained what it was—these extremely simple structures are logs pulled together very close to one another by the *Starrfhiacails* who could not only pull down the logs from the woods, but they could act like cranes. The *Starrfhiacails* could lift them up. Then once they knew where the bridge needed to go, they went ahead and built it. They didn't need to be shown how to do it. They were able to—so amazing—one by one—squeeze the logs one against the other to form a bridge."

She poured some tea into two cups she had taken from a rack on the mantel. "Rhymer Aillard said, 'I need a bridge that will enable two-way traffic. Can they do that?' and I told him a *Starrfhiacail* bridge could not. But I explained I could just make two *Starrfhiacail* bridges that were side-by-side. That would do the same thing. He approved." The Terran sipped the tea—it was naturally sweet and minty.

"No offense," Roman said, sitting with her at the table where she had placed the tea pot, "but you've given me more Darkovan history than I've heard from anyone else. I was offered a contract to come here. I'm still not exactly sure what I'm hired to do. Mr. Aldaran—your uncle?—told me when we arrived I'd need to wait a few days before I got to work. Am I supposed to help you in some way? Xenobiology isn't my specialty. I've never seen or heard of Darkovan elephants—sorry—Starr-somethings—until just now."

"Alister Aldaran is my great-uncle." She took a long sip of her tea and watched the steam form patterns. She seemed to be carefully considering what her answer should be. Frowning, she set her cup down and looked directly at

Roman. In the light of the fireplace her eyes were an unusually light gray. From where he was sitting they almost seemed silver. He assumed it was a trick of the light. "The Aldarans have a—history that differs in a lot of ways from the Comyn." She stopped for a moment and asked, "You know who the Comyn are, do you not?"

"The aristocracy of Darkover?"

"Well, they function in that way. Our lineage has the same roots, but we refused to sign the original Compact so we were never technically part of the Comyn. That isn't important now. My interest isn't in giving you the boring details of our genealogy. What concerns you is the fact if it weren't for my family, the Terrans would have been denied a place in our world. It was my grandfather who saw to it the Spaceport was built at Thendara. It was the primary reason I was one of the first Darkovans to go there for training. We were reared to see the Terrans not as a danger to our kind but as a resource." She picked up her cup and breathed in the sweet scent.

Seeing Roman's cup was empty she filled it again. "Unfortunately, there are many of the Comyn who are," she hesitated a moment, "very conservative. If you offered them assistance they would refuse. They still haven't figured out how to integrate Terran technology into the Compact." She sighed, seeing the lack of comprehension in the Terran's face. "Varzil's Compact was a major turning point in Darkover's history. It bans all weapons that can be used at a distance—making it a matter of honor that one who seeks to kill another must him or herself face an equal risk of death." Fiona looked at her still steaming cup. "One of the uses of the *Starrfhiacail* was as a beast of war." She seemed ashamed of this admission.

"That just seems logical," Roman said. *Why would I care about some animals on a battlefield?* he thought. *Hell, if I didn't have access to drones and war machines, of course I'd saddle up the Starr-beasts and ride them over my enemies.*

He held his cup in both hands, enjoying the warmth.

"Why does that part of your history appear to upset you?"

"There's been an increasing number of conflicts with an Alliance that wants a renunciation of Terran influences. As you might imagine, my family is hardly held in high regard by them. If they had their way they'd be salting the land with bonedust where the Spaceport used to be. They also have long memories of how we used to use the *Starrfhiacails* and fear we'd use them that way again after they had a chance to burn the Spaceport down." She looked down at her hands. He was struck by how long and thin they looked. "We have a great shame over how we once used our friends. Many of the *Starrfhiacails* were slaughtered even as they won their battles. This was before the time of Varzil the Good, so no one was restrained by the Compact. A Tower used *laran* weapons." A single tear fell down her cheek. "So many of the *Starrfhiacails* were lost. So many of our own people, as well. We swore our own Oath—recognizing that our friends were inherently peace-loving and that we would never use the *Starrfhiacails* as weapons of war again. Ever since that time they simply help us with the forest. We've lived simple lives."

"And now?"

"Everyone on Darkover has their history drummed into them before they can walk. Everyone remembers the role my family played in the shaping of how things are. The Alliance continues to grow and they've sworn to kill every last one of our friends. A neighboring ally has agreed to let us take the herd there, where they should be safe. The *cabhróirs* have been bringing our friends from all around to entrust them in my hands. They risked their own lives to do so, but they also love those shaggy giants." She looked up at him, her eyes appearing silver again. "You were hired because you have experience in logistics and you have an impressive war record. You were in the military until you fulfilled your contract and started hiring out as a consultant. I will never lie to you. If you help me relocate the herd, you will be placing yourself into great danger if the Alliance finds us along the way. We needed someone we could trust and someone we knew would not break under the pressure of a deadly enemy on his trail. You were also willing to comply with the Compact."

"Not happily."

Fiona laughed. "Do you think we happily accept it? The one real advantage is that it takes the *laran* weapons off the table. There are some things that should never be used." She was now coldly serious. "You're not here to serve as my bodyguard with your Terran weapons blazing. But the truth is—we haven't done anything of this scale for many generations. These days, that part of our history seems like a legend. I've personally supervised groups as large as twenty *Starrfhiacails*." She glanced at the carving. "We need to move nearly a thousand of our friends. We need to move quickly and unnoticed. The Alliance will arrive and find our friends gone—but frankly, it doesn't take a skilled tracker to discover the trail of a thousand *Starrfhiacails*. I can't afford to risk betraying our friends because we encounter something I hadn't planned on that delays us before we can reach sanctuary."

She looked at the sculpture on the table of a calf nursing as it walked beneath its mother. "I wanted someone I could trust—because then my friends would also offer their trust. I wanted someone who could think outside of the box—and who better to do that than a Terran who served in battles on three different worlds?"

Roman sipped his tea thoughtfully. "Do you know the area well? Will they be able to forage for themselves along the way so we don't have to also carry food and water for them? We will need to travel as lightly as possible."

"I know these woods like you know the back of your hand. Where we're going we have a treaty and before I left to study in Thendara I would take our friends to do logging there. One of the reasons the herd is here is because there are enough resources—including rivers—to sustain them. I can hunt to provide for the two of us, so we can travel as lightly as you desire." She looked at him intensely. He could *feel* her mind working even if he couldn't tell specifically what she was thinking. "I also wanted you because I know you've served under female commanders. Not all men of Darkover would accept my being in charge of this operation. I need to know you will not question or defy me. I need to know you will accept me as your commanding officer."

"I have no problem serving under a woman," he smiled. "But I want to be upfront with you that as a consultant I will not hesitate to let you know if I feel you should reconsider your decisions."

"I have no ego to invest. My sole concern is the safety of my friends. You're hired to advise me. I will welcome your observations and suggestions. But do remember this world is like nothing you've experienced before. You served on a desert planet and two water ones. Some decisions I may have to make will be based on things you can't possibly know about, like the Ghost Winds. Pray to whatever deities you honor our journey will be easy and uneventful. I've been trying to plan for any eventuality, but we have a saying—*Draw up your plans and then throw them away, because Darkover won't bother to read them.*"

She topped off her tea. "I suspect you have questions."

"Many." And he did.

"How much longer?" Brin asked, slamming down his empty wine glass in front of the two men before him. One was tied to a sentry bird and looked nearly as bright. The other was fleshy and sullen—the hazard of involving relatives. These were the times he wondered if the criticism that the Comyn suffered from in-breeding might be true.

"The scouts left at dawn as you ordered," the doughy one said. "We but await a second sentry bird wielder, who should be arriving soon."

"I want the last of the Tuskers dead and no danger to our plans." He scowled at a servant who rushed over to refill his wine glass.

Roman and Fiona set out early under the light of four

differently colored moons that looked like precious jewels in the sky. Darkover had more moons than any other planet Roman had known. They rode on the back of *Mo Chride*. Fiona had a sedan chair attached and its canopy offered them some protection from the icy rain that had been falling since they left.

"I can't believe animals this large can move so silently," Roman remarked after the red sun was clear of the horizon.

"The soles of their feet are basically a spongy cartilage. It not only cushions them while bearing the great weight of their bodies, but it muffles anything they step on, like a snapping branch. The soles are also rippled, which gives them better traction on snow and ice." She pointed to an animal on their left. "A male's movement is significantly different than that of a female. *Mo* will perfectly match the steps of her front legs to her back ones, so she leaves only two sets of footprints. As you can see with the male on your side, the front and back legs don't match up in the same way, so he leaves four footprints."

The *Starrfhiacails* appeared to have worked out a coordinated system of stripping off leaves as they walked and they efficiently kept moving forward. The large herd seemed to march in patterns so they could make maximum use of the available trees and no individual tree was left bare. There seemed to be ponds, lakes, and rivers around them, providing all the water they needed.

Fiona pulled some travel bread out of a bag by her feet and shared it with Roman. "I can't believe just one person can ride herd on almost a thousand of these beasties," he said. The travel bread was dense and had a slight tang. He wondered if he could export it. If so, his retirement fund would be set.

"They aren't really following my orders," she said, putting the rest of the loaf back into its sack. "They just need to follow *Mo* and *Mo* knows where to go." She chewed thoughtfully on her breakfast and added, "It's said in the long ago we used to put a chained band around the ankle of a *Starrfhiacail* calf a few days after it was born. It grew up believing that the chain could hold it. Even as an adult, when no chain could withstand the strength of our friends, they could still be restrained by the ankle chain." She looked at Roman. "What really restrained them was only the belief that the chain could still hold them. When I was a little girl my grandfather used to tell me that story and warn me to never be trapped by my own beliefs."

"So your first bridge for one of the Comyn was a success?"

"Oh, absolutely. As soon as others saw a *Starrfhiacails* bridge seem to magically appear in the space of a few breaths and that they were so functional, everyone was wanting one." Fiona sat silently for a moment. "I told you I would never lie to you. All the ones who happily ordered bridges were also convinced I would never make it to sanctuary with my charges. They told me they'd rather stay where they were and starve in the war zone of the Alliance than come with me." She looked up at the sky, relieved it had stopped raining. "I had no choice. I knew if I were to stay behind, my friends would all be killed."

The days passed without incident. The weather was clearing and the nights were noticeably warmer. Then just as Roman had decided their troop couldn't be any larger and still function, they were met by a group of refugees. They spoke with such a thick accent Roman could barely understand them.

As Fiona talked with them, Roman was busy counting. He also questioned if he could complete their mission, since having to bring 37 women and children would dangerously slow them down. Almost ten percent of the *Starrfhiacails* had calves, but the little ones were nimble and quick—far more so than the refugees. Fortunately, some of the women and older children were able to hunt and gather to feed themselves, but they were still greatly dragging down the herd's progress. In addition to counting the new additions, Roman was also counting the kilometers they were facing. Their path took them over too many mountain ranges to their sanctuary. He worried that every kilometer would be a form of hell. He remembered Darkovan conceptualized nine levels of hell, each one colder than the next. He could believe that. He had drawn a straight line on the map Fiona had provided. It was the fastest way.

After two weeks, the vegetation grew denser. When Roman endured yet another stop to accommodate the refugees, he saw something in the sky he first assumed was a drone. When he pointed it out to Fiona she grimaced and said, "It's a sentry bird. A nasty thing someone from the Alliance is riding—borrowing its eyes to scout the territory." She spoke so rapidly to *Mo* that Roman was unable to follow her. *Mo* felt around with her trunk and discovered a stone the size of Roman's fist. She stopped and took careful aim. She threw the stone with great force and knocked the bird from the sky.

"Isn't that in violation of the Compact?" Roman asked. "That whole *can't leave the hand* thing?"

"And what hand was involved?" Fiona laughed. "And in what world does a bird get an equal opportunity to kill us? The Compact was drawn up to control humans—not our friends or a sentry bird."

"Back up for a moment," he said. "What do you mean someone from the Alliance was *borrowing* the bird's eyes?"

"It's a *laran* gift. Not everyone has it. A lot depends on the skill of the handler. There's a chance the one riding the bird was unable to get clear images or may have been distracted with other things and missed us."

"That's the best case scenario," he said, still looking up where the bird had been. "It's better we act as if we were spotted." He turned to Fiona. "I had thought psychic abilities were just a superstition. You're telling me they're real? Can you do things like that?"

Fiona stayed silent for a moment. "When I told you about the *Starrfhiacails* being genetically engineered, I was talking about what we call matrix technology. What you're calling psychic abilities we call *laran*. It's a real force that has shaped our history and survival. These days most of those who really know how to use it are sealed away in the Towers so the majority of people don't see it being used."

She looked out at the rag-tag group of refugees that stayed within eyesight of them. "If you were to ask the majority of our guests, they would treat it not only like a superstition, but they would also be afraid of it. They have good reason. Our history is full of stories of how the *laran* weapons were misused. There are still areas that remain barren from the bonedust the Towers created, along with clingfire that will burn through anything. There's a Lake that has no water but contains heavier than air clouds."

Brin watched one of the sentry bird wielders as he cried out and fell off his horse. He cursed and called to the other one, who was finishing his meal. "Get him up and find out where the bastards are. There are a limited number of ways they can take in their cowardly flight. I want to be there before them and test out the special packages we're carrying." Frightened, the new arrival nodded and jumped up to attend his brother.

Fiona was quiet for a few more moments, apparently lost in thought. "During the Ages of Chaos there was a eugenics program that forced the most gifted to breed as if they were animals in order to lock in those special abilities. Even now among the Comyn, one may not hold office unless they can demonstrate their control of *laran*. But it's our dirty secret that the Comyn have become badly inbred and political marriages have left some with relatively little power when it comes to wielding *laran*. Some are barely able to pass their qualifying tests. Ironically, the ones with the greatest gifts were locked away in the Towers in the belief only virgins could work the matrices. That removed their contribution to the gene pool while the gifts of the Comyn continue to dwindle away."

She looked out once more at the refugees. "I own no

starstone. Maybe I have a touch of a gift in terms of communicating with our friends." She turned and smiled at Roman. As she did, he noticed she seemed to have grown more slender. The rough travel would cause her to lose weight, but this didn't seem to be related to that. She seemed—more delicate. Her eye color seemed to have stabilized in the silver color he had seen briefly in the library. Her hair had also taken on a shine he had not noticed before.

"I'd say it was just as likely the *Starrfhiacails* are the gifted ones when it comes to inter-species communication—not me. But on a very serious level—if I did have *laran* gifts, I would never use them in front of our guests. It would terrify them. For the poor and powerless, other than healing, *laran* rarely did them any good. And if truth be told, *laran* healers have always given priority to the Comyn, no matter what their dedication might be to making healing available to all who have need of it."

Roman thought about this for a moment. "So your great-uncle Alister had to demonstrate his *laran* ability in order to claim his throne?"

"Aye—it's why my grandfather could not claim it, even though he was the eldest." They rode on in silence, Roman scanning the sky and wishing he could rush their passage in order to arrive before the Alliance forces could find them.

The next day, as the refugees slept, Fiona and Roman scouted ahead. They found a lush growth with a stream that would provide for the refugees and the *Starrfhiacails*. Fiona's skill with a bow and arrow provided yet another set of meals for them all. As she butchered and cleaned, he noticed she gave the discarded parts to *Mo*. The huge tusks were so prominent he hadn't noticed the sharp teeth that made short work of the animal bits. For at least a moment Roman allowed himself to relax and hope for the best.

Then they came to the face of a sheer cliff that was nearly 80 meters high. Roman's heart broke. The top might as well have been as far away as one of the jewel moons.

They would have to walk straight up a wall. Then they could just keep walking into the sky. Climbing to the moons seemed like it should belong in a children's collection of stories.

They investigated the south. Then they investigated the north, but the escarpment didn't seem to end. Fiona looked desperate. There was no possibility for them to go back. If the Alliance forces were anything like the enemies he had faced on other planets, they would be capable of torturing and raping the women.

His human charges could not go back to confront their enemy, and he didn't want the *Starrfhiacails* to confront them, either. In the time he had spent with them, they were so intelligent and gentle that he understood Fiona's shame that they had once been used for war. It was like what she had referred to as *laran* weapons—the fact you could do something didn't mean you should.

He kept thinking of the children placed in his responsibility. He had always loved children and looked forward to the day he'd have a family of his own. All of his siblings had made him an uncle many times over. One day he'd return the favor. He told himself he'd keep the refugees safe.

They returned to the stream and waited for the rest of them to catch up. They explained to the others what they had found. "What are we going to do?" one of the children asked, a question the adults wanted to ask but were too frightened to do so. It was a grim moment. They told the children they would camp where they were for the night and then in the morning they would pick the most able of the refugees to form a third group, who would join Roman and Fiona to scout out an end to the escarpment or any possible way over it.

They left once more, splitting into the three groups with some of the *Starrfhiacails* accompanying them out of curiosity and companionship. Fiona noticed a few of her special friends acting oddly, the way they did when encountering something new, but she saw no evidence of anything out of the ordinary. She had gone a kilometer or so away with *Mo* when she heard a loud noise. The only thing like it she had experienced was when they were doing some blasting while clearing land to expand the Spaceport. Without hesitation she ran in the direction of the explosion.

She began to hear screams and crying from both the refugees and the *Starrfhiacails,* and arrived nearly at the same time as Roman and two of the young male beasts that tended to follow him. Three of the *Starrfhiacails* were dead, their magnificent bodies ruined from the blast. When *Mo* and the others who had arrived saw what had happened, they let out high piercing screams that sent chills down Roman's spine. The child who had asked what they were going to do was also lying in a pool of blood in the shadow of the body of one of the older shaggy females. Roman counted five more of the refugees killed by the Alliance, giving him a morbid flashback of what war was truly like. Three of the surviving women and a toddler were looking stunned.

Then another keening *Starrfhiacail* came into the open space. There was another blast and its enormous body blew apart, splattering Fiona and Roman with its blood. A shard of its tusk hit the trunk of *Mo* and she began to bleed.

"No one move!" Roman shouted. "We don't know if there are more of the explosives planted here!"

"They must have smelled them earlier, but didn't recognize what they were," Fiona said numbly.

Roman reached into his pack and pulled out an instrument she had seen carried by some at the spaceport but she didn't know what it was for. He held it out and slowly turned in a circle while it began to make a high-pitched buzzing. As he pointed it to the left of the remaining refugees, its sound went up another octave. He finished his scan with just the one last device exposed. He pointed the equipment in the direction of where it had sounded and made an adjustment to it. In the distance was a muffled sound like a bag bursting.

"I've deactivated it. We're safe for now, but you'll need to follow me single file as I keep scanning for any other surprises. If they're following standard procedures there would have only been three buried in a pattern for maximum destruction."

"Are these from a Terran hell?" Fiona was unconsciously stroking *Mo's* wounded trunk while the beast trembled.

"I never make assumptions," he said hoarsely. "Is it still Terran if a local madman made one from Darkover resources using Terran plans? Or maybe these really are Darkover weapons that are close enough to a Terran design to respond to the Bromley." He hesitated for a moment. "The device was named after its creator. I've used it in all the campaigns I've been in. The most important thing now is to make sure the others are safe."

They all returned to their camp without incident and reported the terrible news to the rest of the refugees while several of the beasts surrounded and stroked *Mo* to comfort her. Fiona felt empty and could only think of escape. With wide eyes and an ever growing sense of fear, they all stared at the sheer cliff face.

Roman and Fiona both noticed at the same time a high up ledge they had missed. Below the ledge they could see some rocks cropping out. An insane thought went through Roman's mind. The cliff was made of a type of sandstone. It wouldn't be that hard for him to cut it with the tools he had brought with him. He could create additional footholds. He kept calculating. Would it be possible to burn out steps with his laser? Then he let out a deep breath. Even if he could make it work for the humans, what would they do with the *Starrfhiacails*? He looked again at the cliff. Would it be possible to create a stairway for the *Starrfhiacails*? And would it be possible that the ones Fiona called her "friends" might be able to climb it?

But even as he turned it over in his head, Roman thought how impossible it really was. Even if he could cut out the stairs—real stairs—he could count the number of dangerous places where the best he was likely to do was turning the porous stone into a sort of ladder.

"Can your friends climb a ladder?" he asked Fiona.

Fiona knew they couldn't, but she had spent her whole life trusting her friends and never being disappointed by them. But even she thought it was an impossibility. She couldn't begin to imagine how nearly a thousand *Starrfhiacails* could even be convinced to start. She shook her head silently, wondering what would happen if one of her huge friends were to look down, and lost his balance and fell. He would knock out all the ones beneath him. The image of so many of her friends falling and crushing other herd members and the refugees made her shudder. She already felt she had failed them. *Mo's* trunk was still bleeding.

Fiona looked back at her friends. When they would cross a river, it was always the decision of the *Starrfhiacails* as to which of them would lead. It would almost always be a female and the decision could take hours. They didn't have the luxury of taking that much time. She turned to Roman. "If it can be done—we have to trust *Mo* to do it." The others had been following *Mo* since they had left her home.

Roman had his doubts that this could work—but he didn't see there were any other options. He needed to modify the cliff before they were attacked by the Alliance forces directly this time. He had to make the cliff passable. He nodded and pulled out his laser cutter and began. It sliced easily through the rock.

It was an unspoken truth that the ones from the Alliance who had set the bombs might return at any moment and Roman drove himself to finish his work to save the ones who remained.

By the time the Bloody Sun was setting and he could see the first of the moons, he stepped back and felt he had worked a minor miracle. He admired the ragged and zigzagging structure that continued up the face of the cliff. He felt it was obviously too narrow in places and in others too vertical. He decided he needed a second day to see if he could significantly improve it to make it more passable.

257

Over the cooking fire he kept watching Fiona when she was interacting with her friends and the refugees. She was very good with the children. She had definitely changed in ways he couldn't really understand, but he found himself more and more attracted to her. It wasn't only that he admired her intelligence and dedication. No—this was something on a very primal level. She was becoming more and more ethereal as if she were starting to step away from her humanity in the way he hoped her large friends could step away from the land and just keep climbing to the moons. He looked back at his handiwork. He knew it was the only chance they had—even if he knew in his heart it couldn't work.

While Fiona inspected the herd and tried to reassure the refugees, she was always aware of Roman. She thought of him as she and the women attended to their dead. Maybe it was a minor type of *laran,* where she knew where he was without looking. It was as if he were a magnet and she were steel. He was always pulling at her, although he was not actively doing anything to make that happen. He was respectful but had given her no indication he thought of her as anything more than his current client. He'd finish his contract and be gone, just as he had left his colony. Just as he had left the last three planets before he retired from the military.

Chiding herself for being too self-centered, Fiona stroked *Mo's* trunk. The only thing she could do was hope her friends could succeed. She and Roman agreed she would go up the stairs first. *Mo* and Roman would follow her, then the other *Starrfhiacails.* The refugees would bring up the rear. She had been clear no talking would be allowed. They needed to concentrate totally on the ascent.

Roman was at the top of the ridge when another explosion went off and the *Starrfhiacails* screamed, blending with the cries of the refugees. Brin and two of his men emerged from the forest, attacking Fiona. She grabbed her bow, twisting it around the wrist of one of them while simultaneously turning and bending at the waist as she heard his wrist snap. *Mo's* great trunk wrapped itself around the waist of another of the Alliance and she squeezed, snapping his spine and tossing his broken body away.

By now Fiona had grabbed the sword from the man she had injured, and drove it deep into his stomach and pushed upward as he cried out. Around her, she was aware of the agitation of her friends who were responding to being attacked. They had spent generations in peace but deep within their DNA their true power was waking and they began attacking the troops of the Alliance. Brin struck at Fiona, his wide face contorted in anger. She blocked his blow and spun, the sharp edge of her stolen sword opening up his right arm, and his blood joined that of the dead *Starrfhiacail* that still covered her face and hair.

"You Aldaran bitch!" Brin screamed and tried to cut her down as if his sword was an ax. Gracefully she danced past his weapon but he managed to kick her so hard she fell forward and he lifted his sword to kill her.

Mo was frightening in her rage. She grabbed Brin with her trunk and smashed his head into her mouth and bit down, decapitating him, and Roman was suddenly beside Fiona watching the blood spill out of the great beast's mouth as she slowly crunched what was left of Brin. In the eerie sudden silence, Roman used the Bromley to seek other explosives the Alliance might have left. Three more of the *Starrfhiacails* had been silenced forever. Twenty-five of the enemy were being slowly consumed by the shaggy ones they had sought to slaughter. When he had deactivated another two of the explosives, he returned to Fiona.

"This would only have been the advance guard," she said. "The Alliance is much larger than this. I think our greatest protection has been their reliance on using the bombs to kill the *Starrfhiacails*. They're sadly effective, but not in taking down a large number." She touched *Mo* gently. "And they obviously did not count on our friends fighting back. I think they must have believed them under our command and if they were to take us out, the

Starrfhiacails would simply be dumb animals they could easily dispatch."

Roman wiped at the blood on his face. "If this was just the first wave, then we need to get to sanctuary before the rest of them arrive."

As the Bloody Sun rose to chase away the moons, Fiona began her climb. She told herself she and *Mo* were so close, when they touched it would be as if they were both contact *laran* masters. She believed they could read each other's minds. But she hesitated, fearing that *Mo* would pick up on Fiona's lack of confidence. She went ahead and climbed halfway up the stairs. She sat on an outcropping and pretended to be patient. She listened to the stream below.

She worried the rest of the Alliance forces were catching up to them. How awful it would be for them to be found now at their most vulnerable position. The battle would be catching up to them again and she promised herself she would not ask her friends to return to being the war-beasts of their shared past.

Below her the herd and the surviving refugees gathered at the foot of the cliff face. Roman accompanied *Mo* to the base and pointed to the first of the steps, the way Fiona had shown him. "*Tóg!*" he said firmly. She explained it meant "climb." Roman prayed that *Mo* deserved the faith Fiona had in her—that the beast's combination of courage and intelligence would let her know what was expected—no—what was needed of her.

On Roman's command, *Mo* put up her front feet without hesitation and then she placed her back feet on the first step. Then she stopped. For a full minute she just stood there. Then another minute passed. Then a third. Then eight minutes had gone by. The only sound was the stream and the breathing of the herd and refugees. He looked up at Fiona and caught his breath at her beauty. How could he have ever thought of her as mannish and overgrown? Roman was of Irish heritage and as she sat on the outcropping, she reminded him of the illustrations of a fairy princess in one of his favorite childhood tales.

He turned his attention once more towards *Mo*, knowing everything depended on what she was about to do. He wondered what she was thinking and if the alien animal was just too fundamentally different for Roman to even guess what was going through her mind. Was she weighing her choices? Everyone else was waiting for her. Would *Mo* do it or not?

Fiona had her eyes shut, listening from her position above to the sounds below. She had no idea what was happening. She didn't know if her twin had even started.

To Roman it was all too clear *Mo* was just glued to the first step. She was not moving forward or backwards. But he knew only too well from what Fiona had shared—if *Mo* would not, could not climb—the rest of the herd would not go. The huge beast seemed to give a light sigh. Then she moved upwards. And yes! Once she started climbing she simply kept going without hesitation.

Fiona was quietly sitting on her perch, nearly 40 meters up the cliff. To center herself she was looking out at the valley where they had come. Then all of a sudden—her view was blocked by the wonderful and enormous head of *Mo* and her tusks as she made it up. Fiona grew excited at the sight of her twin but kept her tongue still. As *Mo* continued, Fiona simply moved herself. Scrambling, she went ahead of *Mo*. She couldn't imagine what it was like for the ones below—what they were seeing.

Roman looked down—and saw the women and children were swallowing their hearts as they watched each of Fiona's special friends begin to climb after their leader. He shared their collective fear for every moment the amazing beasts used to keep moving. It took *Mo* and then each *Starrfhiacail* after her six hours to make it to the top. When *Mo* had made it and Fiona was waiting for her she could not express how she felt. The *Starrfhiacails* had not only achieved what Fiona thought had impossible, but because they had made it they would all live. They had earned the chance to escape the horror of the Alliance and to claim sanctuary.

Just so, for Fiona and the twin she loved so much—they shared that moment together, with her leading the way and bringing the rest of the herd to the top. Roman's heart was bursting with pride. He didn't feel he would ever be able to let others know exactly how brave the *Starrfhiacails*—how glorious—how bright. But they had proved to be that and more.

The next week passed quickly as they arrived at the refuge and got the refugees settled. Without the time pressure of an attack by the Alliance, Roman and Fiona studied the maps for a relatively easy return to Thendara. More than one of their hosts had remarked on how different Fiona was looking. This was a comfort to Roman, who felt validated, but the more time they spent together the less he needed other people's opinions of her. He had his own and they were all positive. But he wasn't sure how she felt about him. She was difficult to read and he chalked it up to the differences in Darkovan culture. While it was obvious she was grateful to him, she appeared to have no personal interest in him.

She probably just thinks of me as a foreign mercenary, he thought.

They traveled on horseback and for the first time that he could remember, Roman felt relaxed. There was no real schedule or deadline for them to observe and the weather was the mildest he had experienced since he had been under the Bloody Sun. But after a few days out, Fiona seemed to become worried and distant. He wondered if she was just thinking of *Mo* and her other special friends she had left back in the sanctuary. On the fifth day, while they were drinking tea around the campfire, he finally broke down and asked her what troubled her.

"It's the warm and rainless weather," she said so softly he almost didn't hear her.

"How is that possibly a problem? Isn't this the very best

time for travel?" It was all relative. For Roman, the local version of warmer weather was still some of the coldest he'd experienced. At her insistence he had "gone native" and tried Darkovan travel clothing that included what he saw as a silly cape. But after only a day he had to admit he was warmer than he had been in all of his high-tech gear he had brought with him from off-planet.

"There's a strong chance we're in for a Ghost Wind. Weather like this will often trigger a pollen blow off from the fields of *kireseth* flowers that grow in this area." She took another sip of her tea and he almost caught his breath in terms of how beautiful she had become. He would not have recognized her from the awkward appearing young woman he had met over a Terran month ago. She looked delicate. It made him want to protect her even more.

"Do you have medication for what—asthma? Are you severely allergic to the pollen?"

Fiona laughed but it was a faint and sad laugh. "No—you don't understand. When the Ghost Wind blows, you never know exactly what will happen. It releases much of what we strive to keep hidden. What we pretend keeps us civilized."

"Sound like a three day drunk," he smiled. *God*, he thought, *I could just sit here and watch her forever.*

"It's not exactly a concern over a hangover. Would that it were," and she made that sad little laugh again.

She refused to say more, other than telling him the weather might change at any moment and the conditions for the Ghost Wind would be buried under snow and ice. Then she'd feel safe again.

Another three days out and the Ghost Wind hit. They had bedded down for the night and when the four moons were sailing gracefully across the sky, his eyes flew open and he felt a slight dizziness. At first it reminded him of some of the mild intoxicants he could pick up in most spaceport bars. He was highly disciplined but would allow himself some celebration time when he had made it through another assignment. Like many soldiers, this was often combined with hiring a commercial sex worker. He stayed in his bedroll for a few more moments, just staring at the different colored moons. There was a very minor color shift in his vision.

He suddenly sat up, wondering if Fiona was all right and if this was the Ghost Wind she had been so worried about. He looked across the fire and saw her bedroll was empty. He rose, the brightness of the four moons making it easy for him to see her tracks. He followed her and saw her at the top of a hill. In the moonlight her hair looked like it was made of liquid silver. Then she turned and his mouth dropped open when he realized it wasn't Fiona. He froze. There were many similarities but whoever this was seemed freakishly tall and more waif-like—and inhumanly beautiful. He continued to watch her. The stranger was dressed in what seemed to be the sheerest of clothing. He didn't understand why she wasn't freezing to death.

He hesitated. Perhaps this was what Fiona had feared— the intoxication of the Ghost Wind leading one to shed their clothes and freeze to death. Then his eyes caught another movement and he saw Fiona. She barely came to the shoulder of the stranger. He tried to calculate how tall the first one must really be.

The beautiful stranger suddenly turned and looked directly at him. Then she turned and it was as if she had never been there at all. He began to run up the hill to see if Fiona was all right. When he made it to the summit, she was kneeling and tears were streaking her face.

"Did she hurt you?" He asked? He suddenly hugged her, terrified she had been harmed.

"Only my heart," she whispered.

"What did she do to you?"

"Made me realize how much I've been missing in my life. He cracked my soul with his beauty."

"He?" Roman pulled back, fearing she just might be drunk after all.

"We may not have a lot of time. We've only gotten the

slightest edge of the effect. If the wind begins to pick up we won't be able to talk."

"Who was that? I first thought it was you." In his arms her hair was definitely a magical white silver and her amazing eyes seem to be holding the moonlight. Next to her he felt coarse and brutish. How could anyone like her ever want someone like him?

"We call them *chieri*. They're the true indigenous race for Darkover."

"We've never heard about native races." He held on to her, the earlier giddy feeling was starting to increase and he was feeling as if he had just done a number of shots.

"It is forbidden for us to tell Terrans," she said, putting her head against his chest. He couldn't think of a better feeling. "It was always feared the Terrans would try to exploit them. They are rare. He was the first one I've ever seen. Sometimes in traveling we'll find traces of them."

"You keep saying *he*. How could she be male?" He began to lightly pat her back to soothe her.

"The *chieri* are—are—both. They change as a response to their partner." Then she began to sob and her tears terrified him.

"What's wrong? What's wrong?"

"Don't you see," she cried. "It was all they talked about at the sanctuary. Before, when I was with other women, my body changed to be more masculine. Since I've been close to you, all I can think about is being with you. The more feelings I have for you the more my body changes. I've never looked like this before. You're so masculine it's been tipping me over into being more feminine. I was always so afraid that if I were just like most women I'd lose my freedom—whatever authority I've earned and I'd just be seen as someone to marry off and start popping out children." She wiped her tears with her sleeve. "But I just keep feeling stronger."

"You're confusing me. Are you saying you're part Chi—Cherry?"

She nodded. "It's exactly because of times like this when

the Ghost Wind blows and people end up having orgies and unprotected sex. The pollen even hits the *chieri,* although not to the extent it does humans. Over the long years we've been under the Bloody Sun there have been many times like this. But you scared him off—well, that's not exactly right—you repelled him because he was in a male form and if he had stayed here you would have started forcing him into the female form." She looked at him and started to cry again. "If you were not with me then he would have partnered with me." Her eyes went wide. "I might have had his child."

"Is that what you want?" He was having trouble concentrating. The wind was starting to get stronger and an odd fragrance was in the air.

"I don't know. I don't think so. It would be hard to raise a child who would be so different. Not everyone is comfortable around a child who is obviously part *chieri.* I'm at an extreme end where I'm getting a lot of notice but I'm not frightening anyone. At least—not yet."

She pulled away from him and opened her left hand. In it was a small blue stone and it seemed to have a tiny bit of starlight trapped inside of it. As he watched, the light seemed to flicker. "He gave me a love gift of a starstone. It's what they use in the Towers to help focus their *laran.* As I've been changing, I've been able to hear the thoughts of *Mo* and the others. There have been times at night when you're asleep but I can follow your dreams. I always thought I was like my grandfather and that I was mind-deaf. But I'm not."

She pressed the stone against Roman's forehead and then put her own forehead on its opposite side. The light of the moons seemed to brighten and strange images began to fill his head. It was as if someone was whispering in the background. Then the wind began to blow and it felt as if he had fallen into the stone. In every direction he was aware of others who were also using starstones. Then that all fell away and all he could see was Fiona. She had shed her clothes and she was swaying, her slender body so wonderful. All he wanted to do was touch her.

I have been wanting you, he heard, no—he *felt* her say.

He could still feel the stone pressing against his forehead and it confused him because that wasn't the reality his other senses were feeding him.

"All my life I've worked so hard to be in control. The Ghost Wind takes all of that way." She pulled the stone away and it was if a bubble had burst and his awareness of being on top of the hill with the wind blowing flared up.

"I want you to stay," she whispered. "I want us to be together."

"I want you to be with me," he said, his voice rough and breathy. *To be your man,* he thought, and he blinked twice because he knew she had caught his thoughts. It was so easy—so obvious now. He remembered what the stone had felt like when it was touching his forehead and suddenly he was with her again where it wasn't cold and they had both lost their clothes.

What's happening? he thought to her.

I've never had laran *before,* she thought back to him. *My only reference comes from legends and children's stories. If you're mind-deaf they don't bother to teach you anything.*

She stopped and looked around. "It's coming. Promise me you'll stay. We'll conceive a child this night. I can see him. He has hair like yours but his eyes are like mine. I want him to know you as his father."

Roman breathed deeply and he could visualize the pollen filling his lungs and his consciousness was starting to bleed away, and he felt wonderful. "Can we teach him to grow up and protect the *Starrfhiacails?* Hell—I want to grow up and protect them. I want to have our son know *Mo.* I swear to you—whatever happens—I will never leave you." Then the Ghost Wind took them both away. But—true to his word—he never left her.

ABOUT THE EDITOR

Deborah J. Ross is an award-nominated author of fantasy and science fiction, who has written a dozen traditionally published novels and somewhere around five dozen pieces of short fiction. After her first sale in 1983 to Marion Zimmer Bradley's *Sword & Sorceress*, her short fiction has appeared in *F&SF, Asimov's, Star Wars: Tales From Jabba's Palace, Realms of Fantasy, MZB's Fantasy Magazine*, and many other anthologies and magazines. Her most recent books include the Darkover novel, *The Children of Kings* (with Marion Zimmer Bradley); *Collaborators*, a Lambda Literary Award Finalist (as Deborah Wheeler); and *The Seven-Petaled Shield*, an epic fantasy trilogy based on her "Azkhantian Tales" in the *Sword & Sorceress* series. As of the publication of *Gifts of Darkover*, she was hard at work on the next novel, *Thunderlord*. She's part of the secret cabal of former Science Fiction Fantasy Writers of America Secretaries and a member of the online writer's cooperative, Book View Café.

Deborah made her editorial debut in 2008 with *Lace and Blade*. Since then, she's worked with many fine writers of fantasy and science fiction, although she occasionally encounters resistance on the subject of author bios and resorts to threats that involve pink flamingos. To her delight, a number of contributors to this anthology have come up with their own flamingo references.

THE DARKOVER® ANTHOLOGIES

THE KEEPER'S PRICE, 1980
SWORD OF CHAOS, 1982
FREE AMAZONS OF DARKOVER, 1985
OTHER SIDE OF THE MIRROR, 1987
RED SUN OF DARKOVER, 1987
FOUR MOONS OF DARKOVER, 1988
DOMAINS OF DARKOVER, 1990
RENUNCIATES OF DARKOVER, 1991
LERONI OF DARKOVER, 1991
TOWERS OF DARKOVER, 1993
MARION ZIMMER BRADLEY'S DARKOVER, 1993
SNOWS OF DARKOVER, 1994
MUSIC OF DARKOVER, 2013
STARS OF DARKOVER, 2014
GIFTS OF DARKOVER, 2015